PHOENIX
RISING

PHOENIX RISING

William W. Johnstone
with J. A. Johnstone

PINNACLE BOOKS
Kensington Publishing Corp.
www.kensingtonbooks.com

PINNACLE BOOKS are published by

Kensington Publishing Corp.
119 West 40th Street
New York, NY 10018

PUBLISHER'S NOTE
Following the death of William W. Johnstone, the Johnstone family is working with a carefully selected writer to organize and complete Mr. Johnstone's outlines and many unfinished manuscripts to create additional novels in all of his series like The Last Gunfighter, Mountain Man, and Eagles, among others. This novel was inspired by Mr. Johnstone's superb storytelling.

All Kensington titles, imprints, and distributed lines are available at special quantity discounts for bulk purchases for sales promotions, premiums, fund-raising, educational, or institutional use. Special book excerpts or customized printings can also be created to fit specific needs. For details, write or phone the office of the Kensington special sales manager: Kensington Publishing Corp., 119 West 40th Street, New York, NY 10018, attn: Special Sales Department; phone 1-800-221-2647.

ISBN-13: 978-0-7860-2348-6
ISBN-10: 0-7860-2348-1

First printing: July 2011

10 9 8 7 6 5 4 3 2 1

Printed in the United States of America

I may be changed by war,
but I will not be defeated by it.
—AUDIE MURPHY

CHAPTER ONE

Major Jake Lantz was thirty-two years old. A helicopter pilot and flight instructor in the Army Aviation School at Fort Rucker, Alabama, he was in the peak of physical condition, recently scoring a perfect three hundred on his latest PT test, maxing out on the three required events: push-ups, sit-ups, and the two-mile run. A not-too-prominent scar on his right cheek, the result of shrapnel wound in Afghanistan, ran like a bolt of lightning from just below his eye to the corner of his mouth. He had blue eyes, and he wore his light brown hair closely cropped, in the way of a soldier.

Jake, who was a bachelor, lived alone in a three-bedroom ranch-style house on Baldwin Court in Ozark, Alabama, the town that proudly bills itself as the "Home of Fort Rucker." He had kept the heat down during the day to save on his gas bill. Now he shivered as he turned it up.

Stripping out of his flight suit, Jake pulled on a pair of sweatpants and a red sweatshirt, emblazoned with the word ALABAMA across the front. He had not gone to school at Alabama, but had become a big fan of University of Alabama football.

Checking the digital clock on his dresser, he saw that he had but one minute left until the program he wanted to watch came on, so he hurried into the living room, settled down on the couch, picked up the remote, and clicked it toward the TV.

The initials GG appeared on the screen, then the voice-over introduced the show.

From New York! It's the George Gregoire show! And now, here is your host, George Gregoire!

The GG monogram moved into the background, and George Gregoire, with his signature crew-cut blond hair, slightly chubby face, and toothy smile, greeted his television audience.

Hello, America!

You are not going to want to miss the show today. I have information that, if I had been able to verify it before the election last November, might have saved our country the anguish, turmoil, and trouble we are going to go through over the next four years under President-elect Mehdi Ohmshidi.

In fact, I will say it here and now, this could be grounds for impeachment. Can a president be impeached even before he assumes office? I don't

*know, but if the men and women in the House and
Senate would put our country ahead of party, they
might just want to think about this.*

*Here is a video, recently surfaced, of President-
elect Mehdi Ohmshidi giving an address to the OWG.
The OWG stands for One World Government.
Ohmshidi is—well, let's just let the video speak
for itself.*

The video was somewhat grainy, obviously taken
not by a camera for broadcast, but by a small, personal camera. Nevertheless, it was quite clearly
President-elect Mehdi Ohmshidi standing at a
podium addressing a rather sizeable crowd. Many in
the crowd were holding signs, saying such things as:

U.S. Is An Obsolete Concept

One People, One World, One Government

No More Flags, No More Wars

Patriotism Is Jingoistic

Ohmshidi began to speak and because the
sound wasn't of the best quality, his words were su-
perimposed in bright yellow, over the picture.

*I see a world united! A world at peace! A world
where there are no rich and there are no poor, a
world of universal equality and brotherhood.*

*Such a world will surely come, my friends, but
it will never be as long as we are divided by*

*such things as religion, patriotism, the greed of
capitalism, and the evil of so-called honorable
military service. There is nothing honorable
about fighting a war to advance one nation's
principles over another. One world, one people,
one government!*

Ohmshidi's closing shout was met by thunderous
applause and cheers from the audience.

The picture returned to George Gregoire on his
New York set.

*The question of Ohmshidi's membership in
the OWG was raised during the election, but
spokesmen for Ohmshidi said that it was merely a
flirtation he had entered into when he was in
college.*

Really?

*Ohmshidi graduated from UC Berkeley twenty-
one years ago. I'm going to bring the video up
again, in freeze-frame. I want you to look at the
sign on the curtain behind him.*

In freeze-frame, on the curtain behind the
speaker's stand were the words:

**WELCOME TO THE ONE WORLD
GOVERNMENT CONVENTION**

*Notice, that beneath the sign are the dates
of the convention, June 6 to June 10—TWO
YEARS AGO!*

"Jake, are you in here?" a woman's voice called from the front door.

Jake picked up the remote and muted the TV. "In here, Karin," he called back.

Karin Dawes was a captain, an Army nurse, who was still wearing her uniform. She had short black hair, brown eyes, an olive complexion, and the same body she had when she was a college cheerleader. She was also a world-class marathoner who had just missed qualifying to represent the U.S. in the last Olympics. Seeing George Gregoire on the silent TV screen, Karin chuckled.

"You're watching Gregoire. Of course, it's six o'clock. What else would you be watching?"

"You should watch him," Jake said. "Maybe you would learn something."

"I do watch him," Karin said. "As much time as I spend over here with you, how can I help but watch him?"

"Ha! Now I know why you spend so much time over here. Here, I thought it was my charm. Now I find out it's just so you can watch George Gregoire."

"I confess, you are right," she said. She leaned over to kiss him, the kiss quickly deepening.

"Damn," Jake said, when they separated. "That's what I call a greeting. Do I sense a possibility that this could go further?"

"How can it go any further?" Karin said. "It's at least half an hour before Gregoire is over, isn't it?"

Jake picked up the remote again, and turned the TV off.

"You're sure I'm not taking you away from George Gregoire?" Karin teased. "I certainly would not want to be accused of alienation of affection."

"Woman, you talk too damn much," Jake said, kissing her again. "Besides," he said, "I've got a TV in the bedroom, I can always watch him while . . ."

"You try that, Major, and you'll have George Gregoire in bed with you before I split the sheets with you again," Karin said, hitting him playfully on the shoulder. Jake laughed out loud, then put his arm around her as they went into the bedroom.

There was an ease in their coupling, the assurance of being comfortable lovers who knew each other well, and yet their relationship was not so stale that it couldn't still be fresh with new discovery. Outside, the wind was blowing hard, and Jake could hear the dry rattle of the leafless limbs of an ancient oak.

Afterward they lay together under the covers, her head on his shoulder, his arm around her, his hand resting on her naked thigh. It was, as always, a feeling of total contentment.

"Jake?"

"Yes, my love?"

"Will we always have this? I don't mean are we going to get married, or anything like that. I just mean, will we always have this sense of joie de vivre?"

"Is there any reason why we shouldn't?"

"I don't know," Karin admitted. "I know I tease you about watching George Gregoire all the time, and about listening to all the right-wing radio shows. But, what if they are right? What if the country has made a big mistake in electing Ohmshidi?"

"There is no what-if," Jake said. "We did make a big mistake. Well, *we* didn't. I'm not a part of the *we*, because I didn't vote for him."

"I didn't either."

Jake raised his head and looked down at her. "What? You, Miss Liberal Incarnate? You didn't vote for him?"

"I couldn't bring myself to vote for him," she said. "Not knowing the way you felt about it."

Jake kissed her on the forehead. "Maybe there is some hope for you yet," he said.

"But you didn't answer my question. Will we always have this?"

A sudden gust of wind caused the shutters to moan.

When there was an uncomfortable gap in the conversation that stretched so long that Karin knew Jake wasn't going to answer, she changed the subject.

"I wonder if it is going to snow."

"Don't be silly," he said. "It never snows in Ozark, Alabama."

There were three inches of snow on the ground the next morning as Jake drove the ten miles into Fort Rucker. Because snow was so rare here—it had been fifteen years since the last snow—neither Ozark nor Dale County had the equipment to clean the roads. As a result, Jake drove slowly through the ruts that had been cut in the snow by earlier cars. He returned the salute of the MP at the Ozark gate, then drove down Anderson Road, which, like the streets in Ozark, was still covered with snow.

As chief of Environmental Flight Tactics, Jake had his own marked parking slot, though the sign was covered with snow. He exchanged salutes with a couple of warrant officer pilots as he covered the distance between his car and the front door of the building which held not only the offices of the faculty, but also classrooms for the ground school.

"Major, I thought you told me that it never snowed in Southern Alabama," Clay Matthews said. Sergeant Major Matthews was Jake's right-hand man, the non-commissioned officer in charge of EFT

"It doesn't," Jake said. "Disabuse yourself of any idea that this white stuff you see on the ground is snow. It's just a little global warming, that's all."

"Right," Clay said with a little chuckle. "Oh, Lieutenant Patterson called from General von Cairns's office. The general wants you to drop by sometime this morning."

"What's my schedule?"

"You don't have anything until thirteen hundred."

"All right, maybe I'll drop by his office now. I'm not surprised he wants to see me. I told him, he wouldn't be able to run this post without my help."

"Yes, sir, that's what I tell everyone about Environmental, too," Clay said. "You couldn't run the place without me."

Jake chuckled. "Yeah, well, the difference is, I'm just shooting off my mouth when I say that about the general. But when you say that about me, you are right."

Like Ozark, Fort Rucker had no snowplow equipment. But it did have a ready supply of man power and there were several enlisted men, under the direction of a sergeant, clearing off the parking lot and shoveling the sidewalks at the post headquarters. Because of that, Jake was able to walk from his car to the building without getting his boots wet.

Lieutenant Phil Patterson was on the phone when Jake stepped into the outer office, but he hung up quickly, and stood.

"Good morning, Major," he said. "Just a moment and I'll tell the general you are here."

"Thanks."

First Lieutenant Phil Patterson was a West Point graduate who had recently completed flight school. Jake remembered him when he was a student going through the Environmental Flight Tactics phase of his training. He was a bright, eager, and well-coordinated young man. Patterson had wanted an overseas assignment out of flight school, and was disappointed when he was chosen to stay at Fort Rucker as the general's aide-de-camp. But, he was a first lieutenant in a captain's slot, so the assignment wasn't hurting his career any.

Patterson stepped back out of the general's office a moment later. "The general will see you, sir."

Jake nodded his thanks, and stepped into the general's office. Major General Clifton von Cairns was pouring two cups of coffee.

"Have a seat there on the sofa, Jake," the general said. Jake had served in Iraq with von Cairns when he had been a captain and von Cairns had been a colonel. That was von Cairns's second time in Iraq—he had also been there during Operation Desert Storm.

"As I recall, you like a little bit of coffee with your cream and sugar," von Cairns said as he prepared the coffee.

"Yes, sir, thank you."

Carrying the two cups with him, von Cairns handed the one that was liberally dosed with cream to Jake. "I'm sorry I don't have any root beer," von Cairns said. "That is your drink, isn't it?"

"I like a root beer now and then," Jake said.

"Yes, I remember your 'beer' run when we were in Iraq," von Cairns said.

Jake's preference for root beer was well known by everyone who had ever worked with him. What the general was referring to was the time Jake had made a run to Joint Base Balad for beer and soft drinks. Beer wasn't actually authorized due to cultural concerns and was officially banned by the military; however the civilian contractors were not constrained by such rules and they were a ready source of supply for the Army. But Jake had come back with only one case of beer and nineteen cases of root beer in the helicopter. He was never asked to make a beer run again.

"How many students do you have in your cycle right now?" the general asked.

"I have twelve."

"Can you expedite them through? Double up on the flight hours?"

"Yes, sir, I suppose I could. It would mean rescheduling some of the ground schooling."

"I want you to do that," von Cairns said. He took a swallow of his coffee before he spoke again.

"Jake, I'm not much for politics—I've always thought that as a professional soldier I should leave the politics to others. But I don't mind telling you, this new man we're about to swear in scares the hell out of me. I've heard some disturbing talk from some of my friends at DA. They are afraid he is going to start cutting our budget with a hatchet. If we don't get this cycle through quickly, we may not get them through at all."

"Surely he wouldn't halt flight training, would he?" Jake asked. "So much of the Army is now oriented around aviation."

"Did you watch George Gregoire last night?" von Cairns asked.

"I rarely miss it."

"You might remember when Gregoire showed Ohmshidi speaking to the OWG group, he said, and I quote, 'the evil of so-called honorable military service.' This man doesn't just distrust the military, he hates the military. And he is about to become our commander in chief."

"I understand, General," Jake said. "I'll get the schedules revamped as quickly as I can."

"You are a good officer, Jake. Would that I had a hundred just like you. It is a pleasure to have you in my command."

"And I am honored to serve under you, General."

General von Cairns stood up then, a signal that the meeting was over. Jake stood as well, and started to leave.

"Jake, are you still seeing that nurse? What is her name?"

"Karin Dawes, sir. Captain Karin Dawes."

"Yes, she is the one I pinned the Bronze Star on last month, isn't she? She's a good woman. You could do worse."

CHAPTER TWO

Wednesday, January 18

> *Hello, America.*
>
> *With just two days before we swear in our new president, I would like for us to take inventory of just where we are in this country.*
>
> *Four decades of social engineering have begun to accrue in such a way as to presage disaster for the U.S.*

Gregoire held his hands over his head and waved them as he rolled his eyes.

> *This is not just the ravings of—mad—George Gregoire. No, sir, and no, ma'am. Events over the last several years have borne me out.*
>
> *Consider this. Stringent environmental laws have inhibited drilling in new fields for domestic oil. Those same laws have also limited refining capacity and dictated exotic cocktail blends of fuel*

*for certain parts of the country. Even during times
of critical fuel shortages, these blends cannot be
transshipped from region to region.*

*Automobile companies are mandated CAFE
standards and unnecessary safety features that
add thousands of dollars to the base prices of cars.*

*Do you remember when we were young, how
eagerly we looked for the new cars each year?*

Gregoire changed the tone of his voice, mimicking the excitement.

*Have you seen the new Ford? Yes, but wait until
you see the new Chevy!*

He was silent for a moment, masterfully playing
his audience.

*Tell me, America, when is the last time you
greeted the new models with anything more than a
yawn?*

*And have you noticed that fewer and fewer
models are being introduced now? Proud names
such as Plymouth, Oldsmobile, and Pontiac Trans
Am—cars which we once lusted after, cars with
style and performance—are no more.*

He began to sing,

*What a thrill to take the wheel, of my brand-new
Oldsmobile.*

America, we have had a century-old deep and

*abiding love affair with cars, but now we find
them boring. We look back on the cars of the
fifties and sixties with a reverent nostalgia, and
like most nostalgia, this is an unrequited love—
we will never return to those days. Do you remember those yesterdays when we were young? Do
you remember the sweetness of life then, as rain
upon my tongue?*

He began singing Roy Clark's "Yesterday When I
Was Young."

*Oh, and how is this for intelligence? In Califor-
nia, federal courts, in order to preserve a two-inch
inedible fish, have restricted the flow of water into
some of the most productive agricultural areas in
the country. And since California produces nearly
fifty percent of the nation's fruits, nuts, and vegetables, this water restriction is already having a
drastic impact on the market price.*

*Government interference with bank lending has
caused the housing market to go bust, resulting in
the loss of billions of dollars in personal equities
across the country.*

Gregoire, who was standing now, stuck his hands
in his pockets and looked at the floor, silent for a
long moment before he spoke again. The camera
came in tight on his face so he could give the audience his most sincere look.

*My friends, this is the country that elected
Mehdi Ohmshidi, a naturalized American born*

*forty-seven years ago in Islamabad, Pakistan. I
can only pray that we survive this monumental
mistake.*

Thursday, January 19

"All right, Candidate Lewis," Jake told his flight
student. "We've just received word from previous
flights that the LZ is bracketed by small-arms fire
from your nine o'clock, and shoulder-launched
ground-to-air missiles from your three o'clock. How
are you going to avoid the ground fire?"

"Make the approach below their angle of fire,
sir," the warrant officer candidate replied.

"Make it so," Jake said, mimicking Captain
Picard of *Star Trek*.

As WOC Lewis started his descent, Jake saw a
flock of geese approaching from the right.

"Watch the geese on your three o'clock," Jake said.

"I see them," Lewis answered. Lewis pulled the
collective to try and go over them, but the geese
were making the same maneuver.

"Damn!" Lewis shouted as several of the geese
collided with the helicopter. Blood and feathers
from those that hit the main rotor suddenly appeared on the windshield. There was also a sudden
and severe vibration at the same time they could
hear the high-pitched whine of the tail rotor drive
shaft spinning without any resistance.

"I've got it!" Jake shouted, taking the controls.

There was a loud bang as the tail rotor and a part
of the tail fin separated from the aircraft. The

center of gravity pitched forward and, without the anti-torque action of the tail rotor, the helicopter began to spin to the right. Instinctively, Jake depressed the left anti-torque pedal to halt the spin, even as he knew that without the tail rotor, it would be ineffective.

The spin was much faster than anything Jake had ever experienced, and earth and sky blended into a whirling pattern that made it impossible to separate one from the other.

Out of the corner of his eye, Jake saw Candidate Lewis start to grab the cyclic.

"Hands off!" Jake screamed.

They were about seventy-five feet above ground and had already spun around at least fifteen times. Jake knew he needed to kill the engines in order to lessen the torque, but the engine controls were on the cockpit roof and he had to fight the centrifugal force in order to get his arm up. Finally he managed to kill both engines. The whirling main rotor blades continued to generate torque but, mercifully, without the engines, the spinning slowed.

Then, just before impact, Jake jerked back on the cyclic and the nose of the helicopter came up. Now, with the spin rate down to half what it had been, and with the helicopter level, the Blackhawk made a hard but somewhat controlled landing.

Jake sat in his seat with dust streaming up around the helicopter and the rotor blades still spinning. He waited until the spinning was slow enough that he knew they would not generate lift, then pulled the collective up, putting enough pitch in the blades to slow them until they finally stopped.

"Are you okay?" Jake asked.

"What the hell happened?" Candidate Lewis asked.

"You got hit by an RPG," Jake said.

"What?"

"A goose, or some geese, took out the tail rotor," Jake said. "It was the same effect as being hit by an RPG."

"Damn. I'm glad I wasn't flying solo," Lewis said.

"Funny you would say that," Jake said. "I was just thinking I wish the hell you had been flying solo."

Although neither pilot was hurt, they were required by SOP to report to the hospital for a physical evaluation. Jake was in the examining room, just zipping his flight suit closed when Karin came in with a worried look on her face.

"I heard you were in a crash!" she said, the tone of her voice reflecting her worry.

"I resent that. I made a controlled landing," Jake replied. "A hard landing, yes, but it was controlled."

Karin threw her arms around him. "Oh," she said. "When I heard you had been brought in I was scared to death."

"It's nice to be worried about," Jake said. "But really, it was no big thing."

"Hah, no big thing, my foot. I heard some of the other aviators talking about it. You lost your tail rotor but were able to land. Everyone is calling you a hero."

"A hero?" Jake said. He smiled. "Yeah, I'll accept that."

"Well, now, don't let it go to your head," Karin teased. "You are hard enough to be around as it is."

"Really? How do you manage to be around me so much?"

"Because I'm a saint. Didn't you know that?" Karin asked. She kissed him.

"Careful. What if one of the other nurses came in now and caught you cavorting with a patient?"

"I'd tell them to get their own patient," Karin replied with a broad smile.

"I'm off tomorrow," Jake said. "Because of the aircraft incident, I'm supposed to take a forty-eight-hour stand-down. What about you?"

"I'm not off until next Tuesday, but I can trade with one of the other nurses."

"Come over to the house, we'll watch our new president be sworn in."

Friday, January 20

The pictures on the TV screen, taken from cameras stationed all through the nation's capitol, showed throngs of people ecstatically cheering as the car bearing President-elect Mehdi Ohmshidi drove by, headed for the capitol steps.

> It is estimated that the crowd gathered in Washington for the inauguration of our nation's first ever foreign-born president numbers well over two million people.

The television reporter was speaking in breathless excitement.

> *The excitement is contagious and the atmosphere electric—enough to send a tingle running up this reporter's leg. History is being made here today. President-elect Ohmshidi is the first person ever to take advantage of the twenty-eighth amendment to the Constitution repealing Article Two, Section One and making any naturalized citizen eligible to be president of the United States. Think of it. America is now the world and the world is now America.*

Jake was in his living room, eating popcorn and drinking a root beer as he watched the inaugural proceedings.

Jake had not voted for Ohmshidi, but then he had not really been enthusiastic about the other candidate either. His vote, as he had explained it to Karin, had been more *against* Ohmshidi, than it had been *for* Admiral Benjamin Boutwell, the former chairman of the Joint Chiefs of Staff. Jake had often declared that if he had omnipotent power he would replace everyone in government, regardless of their party, with someone new.

Ohmshidi had risen to national prominence as the federal prosecutor who tried the case against Masud Izz Udeen. Izz Udeen was an Islamic terrorist who released sarin gas into the ventilation system of Madison Square Garden, killing over seven hundred Americans.

As Izz Udeen received his sentence of death, he pronounced a fatwa against Ohmshidi and implored Muslims of the world to martyr themselves if need be in order to kill Ohmshidi. The fatwa against him, along with his successful prosecution of Izz Udeen, propelled Ohmshidi to national prominence, resulting in his election to President of the United States.

Jakc watched as Ohmshidi stood on the steps of the nation's capitol building with his right hand raised, and his left hand very pointedly not on the Bible, but hanging by his side. The chief justice of the United States administered the oath of office, then concluded with, *So help me, God.*

Ohmshidi responded with, *And this I, Mehdi Ohmshidi, affirm.*

"Damn," Jake said aloud, speaking to himself. "What was that about?"

Ohmshidi moved to the microphone to present his inaugural address.

> *My fellow Americans. As your new president I make you this promise. It is not a campaign promise; it is not a mere statement of ambition. It is a promise that will be fulfilled. On this day we are embarking upon a world-altering journey that will bring about a new paradigm in American culture. This fundamental change will enable the poorest among us to share in the bounty of this, the wealthiest nation in the world. I will accomplish this goal*

*by requiring more from those who have greatly
profited by the opportunities offered them.*

*That means that the wealthiest among us will
have to do their fair share in order to make all our
citizens truly equal. But from their sacrifice will
emerge a new order. Think of it. No more will there
be people with no place to lay their heads, with no
food upon their tables, without adequate health
care, and with none of the finer things that make
life worthwhile.*

*Such a thing has long been the goal of compas-
sionate people, and in the past we have introduced
welfare programs, food stamps, aid to dependent
children, Medicaid, Medicare, and yes, even Social
Security, to move in that direction. But any econ-
omist will tell you that all those programs have
failed. I will not fail. We will have, before I complete my first four years, a universal program of
shared wealth.*

There was a light tap on the door, and when it
was pushed open Captain Karin Dawes stuck her
head in.

"It's me," she called.

"Come on in, Karin," Jake invited. "You're late.
I've eaten almost all the popcorn already."

Karin walked over to the refrigerator and
opened the door. "Don't you ever buy any kind of
soft drink except root beer?"

"There is no soft drink except root beer."

"What a deprived life you have lived," Karin said
as she grabbed one. "What have I missed?" She

settled on the sofa beside him, pulling her legs up and leaning against him.

"Not much. Ohmshidi just admitted that he was a communist."

Karin popped the tab, and the root beer can spewed a fine mist. "You're kidding me!"

"Well, he as much as did. He's talking about sharing the wealth."

"Oh, that's all. Now, tell me the truth, Jake. Wouldn't you like to have some of Bill Gates's money?" Karin asked as she took a swallow of her drink.

"Not unless I did something to earn it. I believe in a fair wage for honest work, but I certainly don't believe in taking money from the successful to give to the losers who voted for this bozo."

"Come on, give him a chance. He hasn't been president for more than an hour, and you are already picking on him."

"It took him less than fifteen minutes to show his true colors," Jake said. "And forget the people who were calling him a pinko during the election. He isn't pink; he is red through and through."

Karin laughed. "Jake, I can't believe you are such a troglodyte. Just calling you a right-wing wacko doesn't quite get it. You are to the right of Attila the Hun. Are all Amish that way?"

"If you mean do they want to do for themselves, the answer is yes. And I agree with them. I didn't abandon everything the Amish believe in when I left the Life," Jake said. "I'm still a strong believer in the idea of individual self-reliance, rather than depending on the government for everything."

"He can't be all that bad," Karin said as she turned her attention to the TV screen. Ohmshidi was still talking.

"I thought you told me you didn't vote for him."

"I didn't vote for him, but millions of Americans did."

"I know. That's what frightens me."

"You will share the wealth tonight though, won't you?"

"What do you mean?"

Karin laughed. "Pass the popcorn. Unless part of your self-reliance means I have to pop my own."

Jake passed the popcorn bowl over to her. "Just listen to him," he said. "Every time he opens his mouth, he sticks his foot in it."

> *During my campaign, I promised you a trans-parent presidency, and, in adhering to that promise, I will keep you informed of my every action. So I am issuing now, in this inaugural address, my first executive order.*

"Damn," Jake said. "An executive order in the inaugural address? I don't think that's ever been done before."

"You can't say he isn't up and running," Karin replied.

> *For too long the United States has been perceived by the rest of the world as a nation with an intrusive*

military presence. Since World War Two we have
maintained a significant and, for much of the
world, intimidating force in other countries. There-
fore on this day, as my first official action as presi-
dent, I am ordering all American troops, wherever
they may be, to return to the United States. From
this date forward, we will have no deployed forces
anywhere in the world.

"Whoa!" Jake said, leaning forward. "What did
he just say?"

"He said he is bringing all the troops back
home."

"And do what with them? Where are they going
to go?" Jake asked.

"I guess that means I won't ever make it to Germany," Karin said.

"That is pure insanity," Jake said. "If this is the
first thing he does, where do we go from here?"

Karin picked up the remote and turned off the TV.
"I am getting concerned about you. I'm afraid that
you are going to get so mad watching this guy that
you may well have an intracerebral hemorrhage."

"A what?"

"A stroke. It is my medical recommendation that
we forget about him and go out for dinner."

"You're right. Even if I don't have a stroke,
watching this commie bastard is going to make my
head explode," Jake said. "We'll go out, but I choose."

"What do you mean, you choose? I'm the one
who suggested we go out."

"That's just it. You suggested it," Jake replied.

"That's like being challenged to a duel; the one challenged gets to choose the weapons. In this case the one invited to go out gets to choose the restaurant."

"I've never heard that. Is that some Amish rule?"

"Don't be silly, I never ate in a restaurant in my life until I was an adult. It's just the rule of common sense. You made the suggestion we go out, I get to choose where we go."

"Don't tell me," Karin said. "You are going to choose Bubba's All-You-Can-Eat Catfish Heaven, aren't you?"

"It is a great place, isn't it?"

"Oh, yes, it's just wonderful," Karin said, rolling her eyes.

"I'm glad you like it too," Jake said, purposely disregarding her sarcasm as he reached for his car keys.

"Jake, have you ever thought of maybe going to a quieter, more traditional restaurant where they have real silverware, elegant crystal, fine china, good wine, and maybe a strolling musician? You know. Something romantic?"

"You know what is romantic?" Jake asked.

"What?"

"Catfish fried golden brown, steaming-hot hush-puppies, a plate full of French fries liberally doused with hot sauce, a side of sliced onion, a dill pickle spear, and an ice-cold root beer."

"How can you possibly say something like that is romantic?"

"Because it is beautiful," Jake said. "And isn't romance supposed to be beautiful?"

"You are incorrigible."

"Not really. I'm just hungry," Jake replied as held the door open for her.

She laughed. "All right, Bubba's All-You-Can-Eat Catfish Heaven it is, then."

The restaurant was noisy and filled with customers, many of whom were soldiers from Fort Rucker. Half a dozen waiters scurried among the tables carrying trays upon which there were platters piled high with fried fish. Over in one corner a group of soldiers were doing their rendition of "All Out of Love," the singing discordant and loud.

"You wanted music," Jake said, nodding toward the table of singing soldiers. "You've got music."

"Oh, that's lovely. You think of everything," Karin said.

"I try."

"Any aftereffects from your incident yesterday?" Karin asked.

Jake took a swallow of root beer before he answered. "He tried to kill me, you know."

"What? Who tried to kill you?"

"The flight student I had yesterday. Oh, he might pretend that those geese hit us, but I know better. He went out looking for them. Every student I have ever had has tried to kill me. Oh, yeah, they all say they are just making honest errors, but I know better. I sincerely believe that it is a conspiracy."

"I'm sure it is. A left-wing conspiracy, no doubt," Karin said. "Every flight student you have ever had has been a part of the left-wing conspiracy."

"That's true. But it isn't just the flight students. I mean, think about this. Ever since I got my wings, people have been trying to kill me. Did you know that in Iraq and Afghanistan, they were actually shooting at my helicopter?"

Karin laughed. "As I recall, you were flying an Apache while you were in Afghanistan, and doing quite a bit of shooting of your own. You didn't get your Distinguished Flying Cross for making sight-seeing trips."

"Still, you would think they would have more respect for a disparate collection of oscillating parts that, somehow, manage to levitate." Jake held up his right hand to call one of the harried waiters over, even as he was using his left to push another piece of fried catfish into his mouth.

"We'll need another platterful," he said when the waiter came over.

"We don't need another whole platter unless you are going to eat them all yourself. I'm absolutely stuffed," Karin said.

"No sweat, I'll eat them."

"Do you ever fill up?"

"Eventually," Jake answered.

CHAPTER THREE

Monday, January 23

Major General Clifton von Cairns, the commandant of Fort Rucker, used one of the larger classrooms to have an officers' call for all department, division, and section chiefs to talk about the troops that would be returning to the States. He admitted, during the meeting, that he had no idea what this would portend. The problem would be in finding billets for all of them.

"We don't have space for them, not in our CONUS TO and E units, and not in our training commands. Department of Army has asked every post commander to inventory their facilities with an eye toward absorbing the influx."

"General, will we be able to handle such an increase?" a colonel asked.

"Yes, of course. We had much larger numbers of troops in garrison during World War Two. Of course, we also had a lot more military posts then.

The problem now is that since BRAC, so many posts have been closed down in the last several years that it is going to make it difficult."

"How long has DA known about bringing all the troops back to CONUS?" another colonel asked. "What I mean is, why didn't they give us prior warning?"

General von Cairns looked at the colonel with an expression that mirrored his frustration. "Colonel Haney, from what I was told by the Army chief of staff this morning, Department of Defense learned about this at the same time we did: when the president announced it during his inaugural address."

Monday, February 27

> *Hello, America. George Gregoire here.*
> *In his inaugural address, Mehdi Ohmshidi stated his intention to bring back to the United States every uniformed American stationed overseas. Well, he has done that. So, let's take a look at what has happened.*
> *All military training in America has come to a complete halt. The bases are overcrowded. There is no place to put the returning military, not in any training capacity, nor in any operational unit. Morale has sunk to an all-time low as officers and men report to work daily, but with no real work to do.*
> *And what has happened overseas? With America's withdrawal from NATO, all NATO operations have come to a halt. Terrorism has increased in Europe, and in the Middle East.*

Since 1945, U.S. troops in Korea have helped support the South Korean military, providing the security needed to lift that country from the third world to one of the economic giants of the world. But with the withdrawal of American troops, North Korea has become much more adventurous, last week sinking two South Korean fishing vessels and, just yesterday, penetrating the buffer zone that separates the two countries and killing three South Korean border guards.

But it isn't just Ohmshidi's foreign policy that is failing. Let me ask you this. How is this universal program of shared wealth working out for you?

Let's do give Ohmshidi credit for establishing a degree of equality in the nation. He has not been able to improve the plight of the poor, but he has been quite successful in bringing down the living standards of the rest of us. And I'm not just talking about the wealthy; I'm talking about working Americans. In barely over one month, the value of the dollar has fallen by eighteen percent.

I don't mind telling you, friends, I don't see this situation getting any better. In fact, I see it getting worse, much worse. I will do my part. I will ask the bold questions and I will always tell you the truth.

Just over one month after Ohmshidi ordered all overseas military to return to the continental United States, Fort Rucker was filled to capacity with returning soldiers, and in order to accommodate the influx, all training activities were suspended. It would have been difficult to continue training activities anyway, because, in a cost-cutting measure, the Department of the Army was now regulating the total number of hours that could be flown in any week. Once Fort Rucker got their allocation, it would hold the hours in a pool and pilots who needed flight time for pay purposes would have to apply for that time. The problem was there were not enough hours allocated to the fort to enable all the pilots to make their minimums, and as additional rated officers arrived, the situation grew even more critical. General von Cairns had been correct in anticipating difficulty in completing the flight program and his recommendation to Jake to expedite the last cycle barely enabled the twelve students to complete their courses.

At the post hospital, Karin was having her own problems. Reductions in Medicare and Tricare denied civilian health care to military retirees and their families, so they were remanded to military base hospitals. As a result the case load at the hospital was greatly increased. VA facilities all across the country were closed, and those who were eligible for VA benefits were instructed to go to active-duty military hospitals on a space-available basis only.

This increased patient load meant that Karin was working longer, harder hours each day, and was often too tired to visit Jake. But tonight she came by, bringing hamburgers and French fries from a local drive-in.

"Do you have any idea how much two hamburgers and two orders of French fries cost?" she asked. Then, without waiting for a response, she answered her own question. "Eighteen dollars! Can you believe that?"

"Everything has gone up," Jake said. "In order to have enough to meet all the new projects, the government has begun printing money hand over fist. Gregoire says that the presses are running nonstop. Obviously the more money you have in circulation, the less value it has, so that things that have real value, like food, are seeing drastic increases in price. I bought two twelve-packs of root beer this afternoon on the way home from work. Forty-two dollars."

"You might want to think about giving up your root beer," Karin said.

"I'll give up my root beer when they pry the last can from my cold, dead fingers," Jake teased.

"Jake," Karin said, the smile on her face replaced by an expression of concern and even a hint of fear. "Where is all this going? What is going to happen to us?"

"I don't know, Karin. God help us, I don't know."

"That's not what I wanted to hear."

"What did you want to hear?"

"I wanted to hear you say that everything will be all right."

Jake was quiet for a moment; then he sighed. "Karin, for us—for you and me—everything will be alright. But there is no way the country is going to get through this without serious, serious consequences."

"How can you say then, that it will be alright for you and me?"

"Because I will make it alright for you and me," Jake said. "That is a promise."

"Get the drinks, let's eat," Karin said, wanting to change the subject.

"How about root beer?" Jake suggested as he started toward the refrigerator.

"Root beer? I don't know, let me think about it. Ummm, yes, I think I would like a root beer."

Jake brought the drinks into the living room and put the cold cans on coasters on the coffee table in front of the sofa.

"Did you fly today?" Karin asked as she handed a hamburger and fries to Jake.

"Nobody flew today," Jake answered as he unwrapped his burger. "I haven't flown in two weeks. We are limited to one thousand hours per month, and as of now there are only six hours remaining in this month's flight-hour pool. You know how many rated aviators we have on this post?"

"A lot," Karin replied.

"We had almost a thousand before the influx of troops from overseas, and that added at least two hundred more. That means there are twelve hundred pilots who are now in queue for six hours. That breaks down to eighteen seconds of flight time apiece."

Karin laughed, spewing root beer as she did so. She wiped her mouth with a napkin.

"It's not funny," Jake said. "If aviators can't keep up their minimums, aircraft are going to start falling out of the sky because the pilots aren't going to be safe."

"I know it's not really funny, Jake," Karin said. She laughed again. "But I'm just picturing someone getting into a helicopter for eighteen seconds." She hopped up from the couch. "I'm flying," she said. She plopped back down on the couch. "Oops, time is up." .

"It's not funny, damn it," Jake said, but despite himself, he laughed as well.

"I'm going to turn on TV," Karin said. "Kentucky is playing LSU tonight."

"What do you care? You're not running cross-country for Kentucky anymore," Jake said. "And as far as I know, you are no longer a cheerleader."

"You think I'm not?" Karin replied. Getting up from the couch and standing flat-footed on the floor, she did a backflip, tucking in her legs at the top of the flip because she went so high that her feet would have hit the ceiling. Landing on her feet, she thrust her pelvis forward and held her arms over her head.

"Now, imagine me in my cheerleader outfit," she said.

"You're making me blush. Be nice now," Jake said.

"Are you sure you want me to be nice?" Karin asked, seductively.

"Maybe not that nice," Jake answered, pulling her to him for an open-mouthed kiss.

Gulf Shores, Alabama—Thursday, March 1

Bob Varney, chief warrant officer–4, United States Army retired, got a cookie and a cup of coffee from the welcome counter at the bank, then had a seat until he could speak to one of the bank officers.

"Bob?" Joel Dempster called, sticking his head out of his office.

Having finished both his cookie and the coffee, Bob dropped the paper cup into a trash can, then went into Joel's office.

"I read *Summer Kill* and *Death Town*. They were great," Joel said. "When is your next book coming out?"

"Within a month. It's *Murder in Milwaukee.* I'll be signing at the Page and Canvas in Fairhope when it comes out."

"Don't know if I'll be able to get there, but I'll for sure buy it."

"Thanks."

"I think Hollywood should make a movie of one of your books."

"From your lips to God's ear," Bob said.

"Now, what can I do for you?" Joel asked.

"I was just wondering. I went online to check my account; I didn't see the deposit for my Army retirement."

"Yes, I thought that might be why you were here. If it is any consolation to you, it isn't just you, Bob.

There was no deposit for anyone. We got a notice from DFAS that all transactions are being halted while they undergo reorganization."

"Wow. Really? Everyone?"

"Everyone. You are lucky. With your writing you have another income, a good income, I might add. But as you know there are a lot of military retirees here. And many, if not most of them, depend entirely upon their military retirement and Social Security."

"I didn't even check for Social Security."

"Don't bother, there was no deposit for it, either."

"That's not good," Bob said.

"I'll tell you something else that isn't good. We have been ordered to submit a report to the federal government providing information on the amount of money every depositor has in all accounts."

"Are you going to do that? Do they have the authority to make you do it?"

"As long as we participate in the FDIC program, we have no choice but to comply."

"Maybe I should take out what I've got in there," Bob said.

"You can't."

"What do you mean, I can't?"

"You just deposited a royalty check earlier this week, didn't you? A rather substantial check?"

"Yes, it was for signing four contracts, and delivery and acceptance of a completed book. A little over forty thousand dollars."

"At this point any withdrawal, or check, in excess

of ten thousand dollars, must be approved by the federal government."

"Why?"

"I'm sure you have noticed that the economy is a little shaky now, and is getting worse almost by the day. I think this is to prevent a run on the banks."

"Is the money safe?"

"It is as safe as money is safe," Joel said. "The problem is, how secure is the American dollar? I've been hearing things through the grapevine that make me wonder."

"Now you are getting me scared," Bob said. "First you say there are no retirement or Social Security payments, then you say I can't get the money I do have out of the bank. Joel, what the hell is going on?"

"I wish I could tell you, Bob, I really do. I've talked to all the other bankers; we are very worried about this. Banks are only as good as the service they are able to provide to their depositors. When you start breaking that trust, then you are putting into jeopardy a bank's ability to function. If I were you, and I'm cutting my own throat by telling you this, but if I were you, I would withdraw nine thousand, nine hundred and ninety-nine dollars and ninety-nine cents. As long as you don't go to ten thousand dollars on any one transaction, you are safe."

"Thanks, Joel, I guess that's the route I'll take."

"Then come back tomorrow and do it again, keep doing it until your account has just a few cents in it."

"I appreciate you telling me that, Joel," Bob said. "I'll do that too."

"Just write the check here, I'll cash it. There's no sense in causing anyone to get curious. And, if you would, be careful about who you tell this to."

"I will," Bob promised. "And again, thanks."

Bob wrote the check and handed it to Joel. Joel left the office, and returned a moment later with the cash in a bank envelope.

"Are you going to rent your house this summer?" Joel asked as he handed the cash to Bob.

"I don't know if we are, or not," Bob replied. "By this time last year, we had eight weeks rented already. So far this year, we don't have so much as a single nibble."

"I guess folks are a little frightened of what's ahead," Joel said.

"Yeah, it sure looks that way."

Bob got up and stuck his hand out toward Joel. "I appreciate what you are doing for me, Joel."

"You're a good customer and an interesting guy," Joel said. "And, I wouldn't worry too much about things. I'm sure it's all going to work out."

"If not, we'll just whistle past the graveyard, eh, Joel?"

Joel laughed out loud. "Sounds like a good plan," he said.

Fort Rucker—Thursday, March 1

From the office of the Commanding General, Fort Rucker, Alabama

Subject: Flight Time
Suspense Date: With immediate effect

1. All facility aircraft are herewith grounded. No flight will be authorized unless it is an emergency flight.
   a. Emergency refers to national emergency only.
   b. Authorization for emergency must come from Department of Defense.
   c. Said authorization will require authenticator.

2. All aviators are hereby ordered to submit flight logbooks showing most recent flying time for analysis of flying patterns.

3. All aircraft maintenance logbooks will be surrendered to flight operations, and all aircraft will be rendered non-flyable by removing lines from fuel tank to fuel controls.

4. Flight school students who have less than 200 flying hours will be dismissed from the course and reassigned to non-flying billets.

5. Flight school students with more than 200 flying hours will be subject to flight instructor's evaluation for further disposition. If recommended by flight instructor, they will be awarded the wings of a rated aviator.

Distribution:
By Electronic Transfer

For the Commander MG Clifton von Cairns

Joseph A. Wrench
LTC

Avn
Adjutant

"What is this nonsense, Major?" Captain Greenly asked. Greenly was one of the instructor pilots in Environmental Flight Tactics. "All aircraft are grounded?"

"That's the way I read it," Jake replied.

"For how long?"

"That I can't tell you, Len," Jake replied. "But I can tell you, it doesn't look good."

"I've only got one student who meets the two hundred-hour requirement, but hell, that's because he's so uncoordinated he had to fly extra hours just to keep up. My two best students are still fifteen hours short. What am I going to tell them?"

"Tell them the truth," Jake said. "At this point it doesn't matter whether they have their wings or not. Nobody is flying."

"Have you thought about where that leaves us?" Greenly asked.

"What do you mean?

"I mean if nobody is flying, there isn't much need for flight instructors, is there?"

"I see your point."

Greenly sighed, and ran his hand through his hair. He was a veteran of two tours in Iraq and one in Afghanistan.

"Jake, I've got forty-five days of leave time accrued. If you have no objections to it, I think this might be a good time to take leave."

"Why burn your leave time?" Jake asked.

"What do you mean?"

"Why don't you just take off? Check in with me

every week or so and let me know how to get ahold of you if anything comes up."

"You think that would be all right? I mean, to just leave without leave papers?"

"I don't know where all this is going, Len, but I seriously doubt that the Army will even know you are gone. I'm certainly not going to tell them."

Greenly smiled. "All right," he said. "Maybe I'll just do that. Drop in on the folks back in Kansas, unannounced." Greenly started toward the door; then he stopped and looked back toward Jake. "Jake, what would you say if I told you I've been thinking about resigning my commission?"

"You're a good man, Len. You've been a fine officer and an asset to Environmental Flight. I hate to say it, but, with the way things are, I would say that I can understand why you might."

Greenly stepped back into the room, then reached out to shake Jake's hand. "Good-bye, Jake," he said.

"Good-bye, Len."

Greenly came to attention and snapped a sharp salute. Jake returned it, then Greenly did a crisp about-face and left the room.

Jake stared at the empty doorframe for a moment; then he sat down and looked up at the wall. It was filled with photographs of Army helicopters from the H-13s and H-19s of Korea, to the Hueys, Chinooks, and Cobras of Vietnam, to the Blackhawks and Apaches of Iraq and Afghanistan. There was also a picture of a CH-47 Chinook in Afghanistan, and under it was a caption:

Yes, the Chinook is still here.
Nothing can ground this bird.

"Nothing except a dumbass president," Jake said aloud.

CHAPTER FOUR

Raised in the Amish community, Jake had no reason to believe that he would not be a farmer like his father, grandfather, and great-grandfather. Like all Amish boys, he had learned the skills necessary to live in a world that shunned modern conveniences. He was a good carpenter, he knew farming, he understood nature and knew what wild plants could be eaten and what plants would have medicinal value.

But even as a child he used to watch airplanes pass overhead and wonder about them. One day an Army helicopter landed in a field nearby. The occupants got out, opened the engine cowl, and made few adjustments, then closed the cowl, got back in, and took off. Jake knew, on that day, that he wanted to fly a helicopter. He also knew that such an ambition was not for an Amish boy.

When he was eighteen years old, Jake, like all other eighteen-year-old Amish, went through *rumspringa*, a period of time in which they were exposed to the modern world. Once this coming-of-age experience was over, the Amish youth would face a stark dilemma: commit to the Amish church—or choose to leave, which meant severing all ties with their community and family forever. Jake made the gut-wrenching decision to sever those ties.

Because of that, he was excommunicated from the church. Being expelled meant being shunned by everyone, including his own family. When he went back home, in uniform, after graduating from Officer Candidate School, his mother and father turned their backs and refused to speak to him. His sister shunned him also, but he saw tears streaming down her face and he knew it was not something she wanted to do.

After OCS, Jake went to college on the Servicemen's Opportunity College program, getting his BA degree from the College of William and Mary in two and a half years. After that, Jake attended flight school, fulfilling his ambition to be a pilot. His love for flying was not diminished even though he had three combat tours: one to Iraq and two in Afghanistan. There he flew the Apache armed helicopter and was awarded the Distinguished Flying Cross as well as the Air Medal with "V" device for heroic action against the enemy. He also received a Purple Heart when a shoulder-launched missile burst just in front of the helicopter, killing his gunner/copilot and opening up gaping wounds in Jake's face, side, and leg. He managed to return to his base, but had lost so much blood that when he landed he passed out in the helicopter, not regaining consciousness until he was in the hospital. That was where he met the nurse, Karin Dawes, who was then a first lieutenant.

Jake had never married, partly because before he met Karin, he had never met anyone he wanted to marry. He had been giving a lot of thought to asking Karin to marry him, but with the nation in turmoil, he wasn't sure it was the right thing to do.

Lancaster, Pennsylvania—Wednesday, March 14

It was the first leave Jake had taken in almost two years and because of that he had well over fifty days of leave time accrued. He took fifteen days, convinced Karin to take leave with him, but told her that the first thing he wanted to do was look in on his family if they would receive him. They flew to Harrisburg, Pennsylvania, and there, Jake rented a car for the drive to Lancaster.

"How long since you have been home?" Karin asked as they drove east on I-78.

"Twelve years."

"Twelve years? That's a very long time," Karin said.

"Yes, it is. Even longer when you realize that the last time I was home my parents wouldn't even speak to me."

"Oh, that's awful," Karin said. "What makes you think they will have anything to do with you now, if they didn't before?"

"Over the last couple of years, my sister and I have exchanged a few letters," Jake said. "She said that my dad has mellowed some."

"What about your mother?"

"I'm my mother's son," Jake said. "I think she was as hurt by my father's shunning of me as I was. But she must do what he says, so she had no other choice. Otherwise she would have accepted me back the very first day."

"That brings up another question. Why are you going back now?"

Jake was silent for a long moment.

"Jake?" Karin repeated, not certain that he heard her.

"I don't know that I can answer that question," Jake said. "It is just something that I feel I must do. Especially now, with our nation on the brink of disaster."

"I can understand that," Karin said. "I hope things go well for you."

"Karin, you understand why I can't take you with me to meet them, don't you? It would be . . ."

"Very awkward, I know. You don't have to explain, Jake. I understand." Karin reached her hand toward him and Jake moved his left hand to the steering wheel, then took her hand in his and lifted it to his lips.

They checked into a motel in Lancaster, and Jake brought their suitcases into the room. From his suitcase he removed a pair of gray, drop-front trousers, work boots, a blue shirt, a pair of suspenders, and a flat-brim hat. He stepped into the bathroom, and when he came out a moment later, the difference in his appearance was startling.

"What are you wearing?"

"Plain clothes," Jake said.

"You look—very handsome," Karin said.

"This is going to be hard enough without you teasing me," Jake said.

"I'm not teasing," Karin insisted. "You look very masculine and, I don't know how to explain it, but, very sexy, in an earthy way." She stepped up to him, then put her arms around his neck and pulled his lips down to hers for a deep kiss.

"You've got me all hot and bothered," she said.

"Can you hold on to that feeling until I get back?"

"It'll be hard," Karin said.

"I promise you, it will be," Jake replied with a bawdy grin.

Karin laughed out loud. "That was a statement, not a question. But go on, do what you must do. I'll find something to watch on television while you are gone."

Jake held up his cell phone. "I've got my phone," he said. "I'll call you when I can."

"I'll be fine," Karin said. "Don't worry about me."

Leaving the motel, Jake drove east on Old Philadelphia Pike; then, crossing the railroad, he turned left on Beachdale Road. Just before he reached the farm of his parents, he saw a large gathering of buggies and wagons parked at the Yoder farm. At first he wondered what was going on; then he saw that they were building a barn.

Jake stopped his car, and walked over toward the

barn. They had just finished assembling the frame for one end and several were in position to lift it up.

"*Wir brauchen jemanden, hier heraufzukommen und eine Hand zu verleihen,*" someone called from the bare eaves of the barn.

It was the language of Jake's youth, a request that someone come up to lend a hand.

"*Ich komme,*" Jake answered, and he scurried up one of the ladders, then got into position. Half a dozen ropes were thrown to the men on top of the barn frame, and Jake grabbed one of them, and pulled with the others as the end frame was raised into position.

Soon the framework of the barn was all in place and now the only thing that remained was to fill in the siding and the roof. There were at least twenty men working, so the barn was erected with amazing speed. After all the siding and roofing was completed, everyone grabbed a paintbrush and bucket of paint and, within three hours after Jake arrived, the barn had been erected and painted, and all the scrap lumber around it picked up and thrown into the back of the wagons.

During the time the barn was being erected, the women were preparing a meal, and now one of the women began ringing a bell. It was still too cold to eat outside so everyone tromped into the house, where tables had been set up in the dining room, the living room, and in the big, central hall.

It had been more than fifteen years since Jake was last in this house, but it could have been yesterday. Every piece of furniture, every wall hanging, was exactly as it had been the last time Jake was here. He remembered that he had been here for the funeral of the elder Yoder.

Moses Yoder gave the blessing.

"*Unser himmlischer Vater*, I ask that you bless these wonderful people today for their generous hearts, helping hands, and loving souls. And we thank you for the women who prepared the meal that will sustain us through this day of toil. *Segnen Sie dieses Essen zu unserer Verwendung, und wir zu Ihrem Dienst.* Amen."

There had been very little conversation among the men during the work, except for that which was required to do the work. Nobody had called Jake by name, which meant they either didn't recognize him, or were continuing the shunning. As Jake passed the mashed potatoes to the man on his left, he saw his father sitting across the table at the far end. He had seen his father earlier while they were working, and he was sure that his father had seen him, but his father had made no sign of recognition. Now his father was looking directly at him. Jake nodded at his father, but his father didn't acknowledge the greeting.

After the meal, Moses Yoder stood at the front door and shook the hand of every man as he left, thanking each of them for helping him replace the barn that had been destroyed by fire.

"You have come from another order?" Yoder asked as Jake was leaving. "I thank you for your help." Yoder did not recognize him.

"It is the way of the Christian," Jake said, implying, though not saying, that he was from another order.

"Indeed it is, brother, indeed it is," Yoder said, putting his other hand on top of Jake's to add emphasis to his greeting.

When Jake stepped outside he saw his father standing under a tree, obviously waiting for him.

"Jacob," Solomon Lantz said. "Have you returned to the Life?"

"I have not, Father," Jake said. "Too many things have happened; I am too far removed to return to the Life now."

"But you are wearing plain clothes, and you helped with the labor."

"These are things you taught me, Father. I may have abandoned the Life, but I have not abandoned your teachings."

"*Das ist gut,*" Solomon said.

"Father, I have been writing to Martha, and she has written me back," Jake said, speaking of his sister. "Did she tell you that I wanted to come and visit?"

"*Ja.*"

"I do not wish to make you uncomfortable. If you want me to leave, tell me, and I will go away now."

"You come," Solomon said. "Your mother will want to see you. And your sister too."

Jake drove behind his father's carriage, following him very slowly for the two miles that separated the Yoder farm from his ancestral home. This was where he was born and where he grew up. As a child, the big white house, the barn, and the workshop had seemed quite normal to him. Now he viewed them with the eyes of an outsider, and recognized, for the first time, how beautiful they really were.

He parked under a big oak tree and got out of the car, waiting until his father went into the barn to unhitch the horse from the closed buggy. Solomon walked quickly from the barn to the house; then, after a couple of moments, his father stepped back out onto the wide front porch.

"Come, Jacob. Your mother waits," Solomon called.

As soon as Jake stepped in through the front door his mother greeted him with a great hug, pulling him as close to her as she could. Jake could smell cinnamon and flour during the embrace—aromas of his childhood—and it was almost as if he had never left.

"*Jacob, Jacob, mein Lieblingskind, willkommene Heimat, willkommene Heimat,*" she said, weeping with joy as she welcomed him home.

Looking up, Jake saw his sister, Martha, and when he finished his embrace with his mother, Martha came into his arms. There was a small boy standing in the doorway that led from the entry hall into the parlor.

"And who is this?" Jake asked.

Shyly, the boy stepped behind the wall, and peeked around the corner of the door.

"This is my son, Jacob," Martha said.

"I did not know that you were married and had a child," Jake said. "How wonderful for you."

"Jacob, this is your Uncle Jacob," Martha said.

"His name is just like mine," young Jacob said.

Martha laughed. "That is because you are named after him."

"Where is his father?" Jake asked. "I would like to meet him."

Tears came to Martha's eyes. "He took sick and died, last year," she said.

"Oh, Martha, I am so sorry. Who was the father?"

"It was Emile Zook."

"Emile!" Jake said. "Emile is dead?"

Emile had been Jake's best friend as he was growing up.

"Yes."

"But, Martha, in your letters to me you said nothing of this. You did not tell me you were married, you did not tell me that it was to Emile, or that Emile had died."

"I did not want to trouble you with tales of your old life," Martha said. "If you decided to come to see us, I wanted it to be because you wanted to, not because you felt that you should."

Jake put his arms around Martha again, and pulled her to him. "I am sorry for your loss, my sister," he said. "Emile was a very good man. I have missed him these many years, and I will miss him the more, now that I know he is gone."

Although Jake had eaten an enormous meal at the Yoder farm, his mother insisted that he have a piece of apple pie and a cup of coffee. She served the pie hot, with a slab of melted cheese on top.

"Father, you have spoken little," Jake said.

"There is a reason God gave us two ears and one mouth," Solomon said. "It is because we should listen twice and speak once."

"Yes," Jake said. "I remember this is one of the things you taught me."

"Why have you come home?" Solomon asked.

"To see you, and mother, and my sister," Jake said. Then, looking over toward young Jacob he added, "And my nephew."

"You come home, but you do not stay. *Sie sehen nicht, dass diese Mittel mehr Schmerz für Ihre Mutter?*"

"It was not my intention to bring more pain to my mother," Jake said, answering his father's charge.

"Are you still in the Army?" Solomon asked.

"Yes," Jake answered. "Such as it is. The way things are going in the country now, this new president we have is doing everything he can to destroy the Army."

"Who is the new president?" Solomon asked.

"Father, I can't believe . . ." Jake started, but he stopped in midsentence. There was no television in this house, no radio, and no electricity. There was no news beyond Lancaster that could possibly be of any importance to Solomon Lantz.

"His name is Ohmshidi," Jake said.

"Ohmshidi? What sort of name is that for an English?"

Jake knew that by the term English, Solomon was referring only to those people who are not Amish. It really had no bearing on nationality.

"He is Pakistani," Jake said. "He has an American mother, but he was born in Pakistan and is a naturalized American."

For the next half hour Jake explained the condition of the country to his parents, sharing his fears that the president was only making matters much worse.

"It is not our concern," Solomon said.

"I hope you are right, Father. Believe me; I have never envied the Life more strongly than I do now. How I wish I could live here like everyone else in total ignorance to the world outside."

"Have you been to war, Jacob?" Solomon asked.

"Yes."

"Have you killed?"

"Father, that's not a fair question. Wars are fought as a matter of executive decisions. The men who fight them, men such as I, have absolutely no input into the decisions."

"Have you killed?" Solomon asked again.

Jake was quiet for a long moment. "Yes," he finally said. "I have killed. It was not something I wanted to do, but it was something I had to do."

Solomon got up and walked over to a long table that sat under the window and stared outside, as if trying to come to terms with the fact that his son had killed. Jake looked at the table and remembered how, as a child, when it would rain outside, his mother would sometimes drape a quilt over the table and make a tent. That way Jake could camp in the rain without ever getting wet.

"You say that you are afraid the country will collapse," Solomon said. "What does that mean?"

"I think it will mean no law and order. It will also mean runaway inflation and if that happens, money will become worthless. We may see wide-spread electrical outages, fuel and food shortages," Jake said. "If all that comes to pass, there will be riots in the streets."

"Will you survive?" Solomon asked his son.

"I—yes, I think I will."

"You only think you will?"

"I will survive," Jake said. "I am worried about you."

"Worry not about me," Solomon said. "All the troubles of the English will not trouble us. For many generations we have lived our lives and the English have lived theirs."

"Father, I fear that things may be different now. This new president . . ."

"Is not of our concern," Solomon repeated.

"Hide your food, Father," Jake said.

"Hide the food? Why do you say such a thing?"

"If, as I fear, there is a total breakdown of civilization, the English know that Amish keep a lot of food stored. They may come try to take it."

"I will not turn away a starving man," Solomon said.

"They will be more than starving. They will be desperate, and they could bring much harm to you and to the others. Please, Father, heed my warning. Hide your food and tell your neighbors that they

must do so as well. For if you don't, I fear what may
happen to you."

"I will heed your advice," Solomon said.

"Thank you."

"Will you stay with us now?" Jake's mother asked.

"No, Mother, I wish I could," Jake said. "But I
cannot."

There was no real reason why he couldn't stay,
but it wasn't entirely a lie either, because he did
wish that he could. But he had Karin back in Lancaster, and he did not want to leave her alone. Also
he felt a very strong and totally unexpected attraction for the Life that he had abandoned so long
ago. It was an attraction that he could not succumb
to. He needed to get away now, while his resolve
was still strong.

Jake stood then, and walked over to retrieve his
hat from a hat rack that was on the wall just inside
the front door. The hat rack was a thirty-inch-long,
highly polished piece of walnut. Carved into the
hat rack were the words:

Die Lantz-Familie

Jake ran his hand over the smooth wood.

"It was a Christmas present you made for me,"
Jake's mother said.

"Yes, when I was twelve years old."

"If go you must, do it now," Solomon said.

Jake's mother embraced him again, and he
could feel her tears on his cheek. Martha embraced
him as well.

* * *

Jake waited until he was back on Old Philadelphia Pike before he dialed Karin's cell phone.

"How did it go?" Karin asked.

"All things considered, it went well," Jake said. "They accepted me without shunning."

"I'm glad."

"Do you need me to pick up something to eat?"

"No, I walked across the street to a place that serves Amish food. Or so the sign says."

Jake chuckled. "That's for the tourists," he said. "It's pretty close, but it isn't real."

"Real or not, it was very good," Karin said. "How much longer before you get here?"

"Fifteen minutes, more or less."

"Are you still wearing your plain clothes?" Karin's voice took on a deep seductive tone.

"Of course. What else would I be wearing?"

"You'll need to get out of them."

"Yes."

"I'll help," she said.

CHAPTER FIVE

Fort Rucker—Thursday, March 15

General Clifton von Cairns swiveled around in his chair and looked through the windows of his office out onto the parade ground. He was the commanding general of an Army base whose sole reason for existence was to train aviators and aircraft maintenance personnel—but, by order of the Department of the Army, all training had been suspended until further notice. In the meantime he had over twenty thousand soldiers wandering around on the base with no specific jobs.

Worse, he had aviators who weren't able to fly, not even to maintain their minimums. He drummed his fingers on the arm of his chair for a moment; then he reached for the telephone, and dialed the direct line to the deputy chief of staff, U.S. Army, G1, at the Pentagon.

"This is General von Cairns. I would like to speak

to General Roxbury," he said when the phone was answered.

"Yes, General, what can I do for you?" General Roxbury said when he came on the line.

"Tell me, Bill, just when in the hell do you think we will be able to resume training?" von Cairns asked.

"We've been through all that, Clifton. Training will be resumed as soon as we can get reorganized. We have brought three hundred thousand troops back from overseas, the largest part of that number being Army personnel. That has put quite a strain on our military infrastructure as I'm sure you can understand. And right now, our first priority is reorganization."

"Alright, I can see that, but why restrict our flying time? As you know, I am not only CG of Fort Rucker and the Army Aviation School; I am also chief of the Army Aviation Branch. These flight-time restrictions are Army-wide, and they are having a serious impact in allowing our aviators to maintain their minimums. And that, Bill, could have dire, and I mean dire, consequences."

"I wish I could help you with that, Clifton, I really do. But that is out of my hands. The restriction of flight time isn't just for the Army. It is for all branches of the service, and it comes direct from the secretary of defense."

"Yes, someone who has never served one day in the military, who has never held a private-sector job, and who has never been in charge of anything larger than an office staff. Can't you talk to him,

Bill? Can the chief of staff talk to him? Hell, how about the chairman of the Joint Chiefs? He's an Air Force man, a pilot; he ought to understand better than anyone what this is doing to training, to operational readiness, to say nothing of morale."

"Believe me, he does understand. And he has talked with the secretary of defense as well as the president. But the flight limitations remain in effect."

General von Cairns was quiet for a long moment. "You still there, Clifton?"

"Yeah," von Cairns said. "I'm here."

"Look, I know what you are going through," General Roxbury said. "And I'm doing—we are doing—all we can to get this situation resolved as quickly as we can. All I can say now is for you to just hang loose and keep your personnel ready to resume training at a moment's notice. This can't last forever."

"No, it sure as hell can't," von Cairns said. "Good-bye, Bill, and give Connie my best."

"Will do," General Roxbury said. "I'm going to stay on this, Clifton, I promise."

General von Cairns hung up the phone. Nearly one hundred soldiers were moving across the parade ground performing police call. But there was nothing left for them to pick up, because another group of one hundred had performed a police call earlier this morning. This useless waste of manpower was the result of junior officers and NCOs "making work," for the men and women soldiers on the base.

The lack of mission was having a serious impact on troop morale.

Von Cairns looked over at a shadow box on the wall. Inside the box was a Distinguished Service Cross, a medal of valor second only to the Medal of Honor.

The framed citation was right beside it.

Citation: Distinguished Service Cross
CLIFTON VON CAIRNS

The President of the United States takes great pride in presenting the Distinguished Service Cross to Clifton von Cairns, Major, U.S. Army, Avn, for his extraordinary heroism in military operations against an opposing armed force while serving as an Apache pilot with the Third Combat Aviation Brigade during Operation DESERT STORM on January 21, 1991. On that date, Major von Cairns was flying a search-and-destroy mission at a forward-operating location when he received tasking to look for another Apache crew that had been shot down the night before. For three hours of intensive searching deep inside enemy territory, he risked his life as he had to fly at absolute minimum altitude to pinpoint the survivors' location. When an enemy truck appeared to be heading toward the downed crew, Major von Cairns engaged and destroyed it, thus enabling a Blackhawk helicopter to secure the rescue. Once the crew recovery was effected, Major von Cairns flew cover for the rescue helicopter, taking out two more enemy gun positions on the return flight. It was his superior airmanship and

*his masterful techniques at orchestration that made this
rescue happen. Through his extraordinary heroism,
superb airmanship, and aggressiveness in the face of
the enemy, Major von Cairns reflects the highest
credit upon himself and the United States Army.*

The door to his office being open, Lieutenant
Phil Patterson stepped through it, then called out,
"General von Cairns?"

Von Cairns swiveled back around. "Yes, Lieutenant?"

"You wanted the 1352 forms? The Matériel
Readiness Reports?"

"Yes, what do we have?"

"Forty-two percent of our aircraft could be made
flyable by reconnecting the fuel control lines."

"What? Only forty-two percent? What's the problem? You would think with as little flying as we are
doing that we could at least keep our aircraft operational."

"Yes, sir, well, it isn't the fault of maintenance,
General. Fifty-one percent of the red-X aircraft are
grounded for parts."

"Fifty-one percent? What's the holdup? Are the
parts on order?"

"Yes, sir, and they are on AOG, which as you
know is the highest priority," Lieutenant Patterson
said. "Evidently there is a hold on all resupply."

"How much authority can AOG have now, anyway?" General von Cairns asked. "Hell, all aircraft
are on ground."

"That's true, General. But I suppose that is the best they can do."

"Yes, I suppose it is," von Cairns agreed. "Thank you, Lieutenant."

Patterson returned to his desk. He had welcomed the assignment to run down the 1352s. That had given him something to do other than sit at his desk and read paperback novels.

Opening the middle drawer on his desk, he picked up *Death Town* by Robert Varney. The other officers sometimes teased him about his "high literary tastes," but he didn't care. He enjoyed the thrillers, and the way things were going right now, he needed all the escape he could get.

JFK Airport, New York—Friday, March 16

Pan World America Flight 103, out of Frankfurt, Germany, was just entering New York airspace for landing at JFK. Rena Woodward, the chief flight attendant, took the mic from its holder.

"Ladies and gentlemen, the captain has just turned on the seat-belt sign. Please make certain that all trays are stowed, your seats are in the upright position, and your seat belts are fastened. We thank you for flying PWA."

Suddenly, from the aisle seat in row twenty-three, Abdullah Ibrahim Yamaninan stood up and, using a cigarette lighter, lit the hem of his shirt.

"Death to all infidels! Allah hu Akbar!"

The shirt flamed as suddenly and as brightly as a magnesium flare.

"He's got a bomb!" someone shouted.

Mike Stewart, a former linebacker for Penn State, was a passenger one row behind. He grabbed the blanket off the woman who was seated next to him, then leaped up and wrapped it around Yamaninan, knocking him down as he did so.

"Get a fire extinguisher!" Stewart shouted as he tried to smother the flames with the blanket.

Yamaninan was screaming in pain from the severe burns all over his body. Reena arrived then with a foam fire extinguisher and she emptied it on Yamaninan and Stewart, whose clothes were, by now, also burning.

One of the other flight attendants called the flight deck to inform the pilot of what had just happened, and the pilot called JFK to declare an emergency.

"Pan World, what is the nature of your emergency?"

"It appears we have a bomber on board."

"Say again, Pan World. You have a bomb on board?"

"A bomber. Or a would-be bomber. Apparently he tried, but it did not explode."

"Pan World America, you are cleared for immediate landing on runway 13R, winds north–northwest at twenty knots, altimeter two niner niner seven."

"Pan World, 13R, roger."

"All inbound aircraft to JFK, be advised there is an emergency in progress. Northwest on short final for 13R. Please expedite your landing, exit runway at first opportunity. All other aircraft in queue for 13R go around for reassignment."

"Northwest, roger, expediting approach."

"JFK, this is Pan World, we request emergency equipment on site."

"Roger, Pan World, we will meet you with emergency equipment."

Back in the cabin, the fire was out, and Rena was applying ointment to the burns on Mike Stewart's chest and arms. Yamaninan lay in the aisle, untreated and moaning quietly. He was naked because most of his clothes had burned off, and his chest, abdomen, arms, and face were charred black.

"Cabin crew, we're cleared for immediate landing. Prepare to deploy slide chutes," the pilot's voice said over the cabin loudspeakers.

The big 777 made a much steeper and faster landing approach than any of the passengers had ever experienced. The landing was hard, and immediately after touchdown the thrust reversers were engaged at full power, causing everyone to be thrown forward against their seat belts.

Once the plane turned off the active it proceeded but a short distance before coming to a stop. The cabin crew opened the doors fore and aft and deployed the sliding chutes. There was an orderly debarkation of all the passengers except Yamaninan, who was now being watched over by Mike Stewart and a male flight attendant.

Fire trucks, ambulances, and busses were already standing by.

Fort Rucker—Monday, March 19

Although Jake and Karin had each taken fifteen days' leave, they used only five days, spending most of it in Philadelphia, before returning to duty. Coming back from his leave, Jake found that, if anything, the conditions in the Army in general, and on the base in particular, had gotten even worse. Captain Greenly had not returned from his leave, and Jake didn't think he was going to. Captain Greenly and the three warrants who were assigned to EFT were all gone now, ostensibly on leave, though Jake had serious doubt that any of them would return. All four officers had completed their mandatory service and could leave the service simply by submitting their resignation papers, and Jake was reasonably certain they had either done so, or were going to.

That meant that Jake was not only chief of the environmental flight detachment, he was the only officer remaining. And now, in an effort to keep his men gainfully occupied, Jake was totally reorganizing Environmental Flight Tactics, the department he was responsible for. He was redoing the curriculum and rewriting all lesson plans, lesson objectives, and specific objectives, as well as reevaluating the course exams.

He went home late that night, planning to eat alone, primarily because Karin had night duty at the hospital.

After warming a can of chili, Jake took it and a

can of root beer into the living room, where he turned on TV to watch the news.

President Ohmshidi announced today that, effective immediately, all banks in the nation with assets greater than twenty million dollars would be nationalized. CEOs and members of the Board of Directors of the affected banks will be asked to step down without any terminating compensation. The Federal Reserve will appoint government officials to run the banks, and any profits derived therefrom will accrue to the United States Government.

As a part of this proposal, all banking, savings, bond, and stock accounts are being inventoried, and a fair tax is being applied. An absolute limit of ten million dollars is being put on private wealth, and any amount of privately held funds greater than ten million dollars will be confiscated by the government. Persons with a net worth of between five and ten million dollars will be assessed a tax of seventy-five percent. Those people with a net worth of between one million and five million dollars are being assessed at a rate of fifty percent. There will be a twenty-five percent tax on all accounts between half a million and a million.

Those with a net value of from two hundred fifty to five hundred thousand will be taxed at ten percent and there will be no tax for those who have a net worth of less than two hundred and fifty thousand dollars.

Anyone who has less than one hundred thousand dollars will come under the president's new program of equalization. To those people, the government will be sending out checks within the week, totaling up to one hundred thousand dollars per check, the amount calculated to provide a baseline of at least one hundred thousand dollars for every American.

This is being done, the president says, to provide, fully and equitably, for all our citizens.

Jake did not have two hundred fifty thousand dollars, so he would not be subjected to a tax this year. He imagined there would be many people in the country who would welcome this tax relief, and many more who would welcome a government contribution that would elevate their net worth to one hundred thousand dollars. But Jake didn't feel good about it at all. This could not bode well. Where would be the incentive of the more successful and entrepreneurial people to build businesses, which provided jobs?

Finishing his bowl of chili, Jake went into the kitchen and opened the refrigerator door, then took out a block of cheese and carved off a thick slice. He grabbed a handful of crackers and another can of root beer, then returned to the living room to watch George Gregoire.

Hello, America.

I wish I weren't doing this show today. I wish I did not have to say to you, what I am going to say.

But I told you when I started this program that I would always question with boldness and I will always tell you the truth.

Well, I'm going to tell you the truth now, and it is something that I never wanted to say, even though it is exactly what I have been suggesting for three months now—ever since Ohmshidi took office.

I believe, in all sincerity, that this nation is now on a path to utter destruction. We are on a luge course, sliding downhill at ninety miles per hour, with no brakes, and with no barriers to hold us back.

My advice to you is to dig in, and hold on. While there is still food available, and while money still has some value, though its value decreases each day, start stocking up. Buy packaged foods and canned foods, foods that have a long shelf life. Make a survival bunker in your basement; fill it with food, blankets, water, clothing, and yes, guns and ammunition.

We are going down. Prepare for a very rough landing.

Tuesday, March 20

When Jake went into his office the next morning, he saw a lot of smiles on the faces of the lower grades. Although no checks had yet been issued, they were already spending their money.

"I'm going to get a new Mustang," one specialist was saying.

"Mustang, hell! I'm going to get new Caddy," a sergeant replied.

"Not me. I'm investing my money," a sergeant first class said.

"What makes you think you will be able to buy a Cadillac with one hundred thousand dollars?" Sergeant Major Clay Matthews asked. "Or for that matter, even a Mustang?"

"Cadillacs don't cost no hundred thousand dollars," the sergeant said.

"And for sure, Mustangs don't cost that much," the specialist put in. "I'm gettin' me a red convertible with white leather seats."

"Yeah," the sergeant said. "You know what? That don't sound half bad. Maybe I'll get a Mustang my own self, and save the difference in the money between that and a Caddy. Only I want mine to be white, with black leather seats."

"You're both crazy spendin' money like that. You ought to be like me, and invest it," the sergeant first class insisted.

"No," Clay Matthews said. "The truth is they have a better idea than you do. They are right about spending it as soon as they get it, because the way things are going, if you invest your money now, within six months it will be worth about half. If it takes that long."

"What are you talking about? I don't plan to speculate. I'll probably buy mutual funds. They will spread it out, and be very conservative."

"Jenkins, if you double your money in six months—say you run it up to two hundred thousand, or a quarter of a million, it won't make any difference," Clay said. "Two hundred fifty thousand dollars, six months from now, will be worth what fifty thousand is now. And fifty thousand now is worth what five thousand dollars was three months ago. My advice is to spend it as soon as you get it."

"Yeah," the other two said. "Come with us, we'll all three buy new cars."

"When is the last time you priced a new car?" Clay asked.

"I don't know. I've never had enough money to buy a new car before."

"You don't have enough money now, either. I have looked; the cheapest new car on the market today is one hundred twenty-five thousand dollars."

"What? That ain't right."

"Go online, find your dream car, then tell me what it costs," Clay invited.

"I'll do it," Jenkins said, sitting down at a nearby computer. He did an Internet search, found a car that the other two agreed they liked, then asked for the price.

"Holy shit! Two hundred and twenty thousand dollars?" the sergeant who had wanted the Cadillac said. "What's going on here?"

"Inflation," Clay replied. "Inflation like we've never had in this country before."

"Sergeant Major Matthews," Jake called. "Would you step into my office for moment?"

"Yes, sir," Clay said.

"Look on there, see what the hell kind of car we can buy," one of the men asked Jenkins as Clay went into Jake's office.

"Close the door," Jake asked. "And have a seat."

Clay closed the door, then took the seat Jake offered him.

"How are the men holding up?" Jake asked.

"They're gettin' a little antsy, what with nothing real to do," Clay answered. "Truth is I'm beginnin' to get that way myself."

"I know what you mean," Jake said.

"Major, do you know something I don't?" Clay asked.

"Like what?"

"I know that none of the officers are getting any flight time. None of the enlisted personnel who are on flight status are getting any flight time either. Are things ever going to get back to normal? Is the school going to reopen?"

"I don't know the answer to either question," Jake replied. "But if I had to guess, I would say no, things are never going to get back to the way they were, and no, I don't believe we will be making any more new pilots."

"Pardon my language, sir, but just what in the hell is going on? Does this new president have his head up his ass and locked so tight that he is going to be the ruin of us all?"

"I'm afraid that might be the case," Jake answered.

It was obvious that Clay was not expecting that answer, and he blinked in surprise. "You're serious, aren't you?"

"I'm very serious," Jake replied. He opened the middle drawer to his desk and pulled out a manila envelope. "This envelope is filled with signed requisition forms, DD-1195," Jake said. "I want you to take as long as you need to get every requisition processed and filled."

Clay pulled out some of the forms. "Whoa, twenty cases of MREs? Five cases of nine millimeter and five cases of .223 ammunition. Are we going on a field maneuver, Major?"

"As far as anyone else is concerned, we are."

"Ten barrels of JP-four. Why do you want that? Doesn't that normally come through the school?"

"I don't want any of this to go through the school," Jake said. "I don't want anyone to know anything about this. And if you are unable to get anything on this list by requisition, then I want you to get it in any way you can. I seem to remember that you are an expert at scrounging."

"And a water desalination device. A water desalination device? Major, you want to tell me what's going on here?" Clay asked.

"All right," Jake answered. "Clay, did you know that during the night, last night, the dollar was disconnected from the international money exchange?"

"What does that mean?"

"It means that the dollar is no longer the monetary standard for the rest of the world. Instead of saying that one dollar is equal to one and a half euros, the rate is now free to float. It might cost ten dollars for one euro, or one hundred, or ten thousand."

"That's not good, is it?"

"No, it isn't. There is a possibility, and I think a strong possibility, that this republic is going to come crashing down around us. And if it does, it's pretty much going to be every man for himself. Unless small groups get together for mutual benefit."

"I see. Do you have a such a group in mind, Major?"

"Not yet," Jake replied. "But when the time comes, I want you to be a part of it. If you are willing."

Clay stood up, saluted, then stuck his hand across the desk. "I would be honored," he said.

"Clay, until the time comes, this is between us," Jake cautioned.

"Right, sir." Clay put the forms back in the envelope. "I guess that, in addition to rounding up these items, I should also find a secure place to store them."

"I think that would be a very good idea," Jake said.

"I'll get right on it," Clay said.

The telephone rang and Jake picked it up. "Environmental, Major Lantz."

"Jake, have you seen the news this morning?" Karin asked.

"No, what has happened now?"

"Ohmshidi has turned Yamaninan over to the Islamic Republic of Yazikistan."

"What?"

"You have a TV in your office?"

"Yes."

"Turn it on. Ohmshidi is speaking now."

"All right, thanks." Jake held his hand up to stop Clay from leaving.

"What's up?" Clay asked.

"Wait. Before you go, you might want to see this," Jake said. He picked up the remote and clicked on the TV that was mounted on a stand high in the corner of the room. The president was talking.

> *By extending our hand in peace, by proclaiming to the people and the leaders of the Islamic Republic of Yazikistan that we mean them no harm, I am taking the first step in building a bridge of understanding between our two cultures. It is a bridge that I am certain will pay incalculable dividends.*
>
> *While some of you might consider Abdullah Ibrahim Yamaninan a terrorist, to the people of Yazikistan, this brave man is a hero who was willing to give his own life for the cause that is so dear to his country. All of us cannot help but admire someone who has the courage and dedication to give that last full measure of devotion to his country and to his cause.*
>
> *It is my sincere belief that this incident, which resulted only in injury to Yamaninan, offers us the perfect opportunity to end the hostility between us. Therefore I am returning Yamaninan to his country, along with a note of admiration for his courage and dedication. For too long now, there has been enmity between us, an enmity created by conflicting religious views. Now is the time for religious mythology to be assigned to its proper place so that secular humanity can rule our activities.*
>
> *Thank you, and good night.*

Ohmshidi's picture left the screen to be replaced by Carl Wilson, an anchorman for World Cable News.

This is Carl Wilson. We have just heard the president announce that Abdullah Ibrahim Yamani-nan, the terrorist who tried to blow up an airliner over New York, will be returned to Yazikistan. In the studio with me now is Lawrence Prescott, former head of the Yazikistan office for the CIA. Mr. Prescott, your thoughts?

My thoughts? I will be honest with you, Carl. If I shared my sincere thoughts with you, we would be taken off the air. If someone were to write a manual on what not to do when dealing with these people, this would be principle number one.

The Middle Easterner on the street sees negotiation of any kind as a sign of weakness. And this? Turning over a suicide bomber—or rather a would-be suicide bomber to the country that launched the attack, without any concessions? This isn't negotiation. This is surrender.

And, where do you think this will lead?

It can only lead to catastrophe. Look, Yazikistan has let it be known that they want a nuclear weapon, and they are willing to pay any amount of money to get it. The country is wealthy in oil money, and unlike America, or any western nation, the oil money goes, not to private investors, but directly to the government. If it costs them ten billion dollars to acquire nuclear weapons, they would be willing to spend it.

But, where would they find someone willing to sell the weapons to them? Aren't all the nuclear weapons closely guarded?

Are they guarded, Carl? There are some estimates that as many as one hundred nuclear weapons that once belonged to the Soviet Union are unaccounted for. Do not think for a moment that one or more of these weapons could not be bought if the price is right.

That is a frightening thought.

Carl Wilson looked at the camera.

Again, for those of you just tuning in, President Ohmshidi has just announced that Abdullah Ibrahim Yamaninan, the man who attempted to bring down Pan World America flight one zero three over New York City, is being returned to the Islamic Republic of Yazikistan, without any conditions.
We will keep you updated on the latest developments as they occur. And now, we return you to "Focus," our regular morning show.

"Major, I know that man is our commander in chief, and I need to show the proper respect to him," Clay said. "But he is a raving maniac."

"You'd better get started, Sergeant Major. I don't know how much time we have remaining," Jake said.

"Yes, sir, I will get right on it," Clay promised.

CHAPTER SIX

Moscow, Russia

When the Soviet Union collapsed, the emerging nation of Russia inherited a military designed to fight an all-out global war. At the end of the Cold War the Russian military was left with an air force that could no longer afford to fly its airplanes, a naval fleet that sat rusting in harbors, and an army in shambles. With no more clear-cut enemies in central Europe or on the Chinese border, the military-technical considerations that played a dominant role in Soviet force development and deployment throughout the Cold War period became obsolete. An army that was once one of the two biggest super powers in the world struggled in its brief, but bloody war with Chechnya.

Colonel Andre Yassilov, the commanding officer of a missile battalion on an army base near Moscow, was a victim of the chain of events in Russia. Yassilov's grandfather had been a hero of the Soviet

Union who was personally decorated by Josef Stalin for bravery against the Germans during the Great Patriotic War. Colonel Yassilov's father was killed in Afghanistan and given a hero's funeral. Colonel Yassilov, who had served with honor and distinction in the war in Chechnya, had been a member of the army for twenty-six years.

But now things had changed. There was no pay for the military. Worse, there was very little food. The desertion rate of Yassilov's soldiers was higher than fifty percent and Yassilov couldn't blame them. At one time being an officer in the Russian armed forces meant having a position that not only commanded great respect, but also paid very well. Now, however, Yassilov, whose missile battery was equipped with SS-25 nuclear warheads, was forced to wait tables. The irony of it was extremely bitter. He had more firepower under his command than the total amount of explosives used in all of World War I and World War II combined—but he was waiting tables, groveling before diners for their measly tips.

Yassilov had swallowed his pride to work at the Gostiny Dvor restaurant, which was situated deep within a decorated garden on Volkova Street. The restaurant had a large dining hall that could seat eighty persons, a VIP hall, and a summer terrace. The interior of the restaurant was vintage Russian with timbered walls, massive dark-brown furniture, decorative windows with shutters, and handmade carpets. In the yard in front of the restaurant there was a fountain and a small waterfall. It was a favorite dining place for tourists, and had especially been so for Americans before recent events had almost completely stopped American travel.

It was here that Yassilov was first approached. One year earlier Yassilov would have never even considered discussing business with someone who made an offer to buy nuclear warheads. Had he been approached even three months ago he would have reported the contact to the proper authorities. But his personal situation had so deteriorated, and the amount of money the man offered was so large that it staggered the senses. It was sufficient money for Yassilov to return his own family to the economic level they had once enjoyed, and there would even be enough leftover to buy food and supplies for his men.

What Yassilov was being asked to do was a terrible violation of the oath he once swore, but, he reasoned, that oath should go both ways. If he owed allegiance to his country, then didn't his country owe allegiance to him?

The SS-25 missiles under his command had been destined for destruction under terms of the SALT treaty, which meant it would be fairly easy for Yassilov to comply with the request.

Yassilov dismantled the weapons as ordered, but he adjusted the inventory so that all were accounted for, though in fact he held back ten of the warheads. He sold the three warheads for a total of one million five hundred thousand Rubles. That was a small outlay for the man who bought the warheads. He had a buyer in Germany who would pay ten million euros for them.

The buyer in Germany contacted a Venezuelan arms dealer who agreed to pay one hundred million euros for the ten warheads. The Venezuelan paid the money without haggling because he had a customer in Yazikistan who would pay him five billion Venezuelan bolivars. The weapons never left Russia until the final deal was completed; then they were transported quickly and easily from Russia to Yazikistan in containers marked MEDICAL RADIOLOGY.

Tuesday, April 17

> *Hello, America.*
>
> *Last month Mr. Ohmshidi made world headlines, incurring the wrath of most Americans and the incredulity of all the Western nations by returning the Muslim terrorist Yamaninan to Yazikistan. Even though he was still suffering from the burns of an unsuccessful attempt to detonate the PETN— not suffering enough, if you ask me—Yamaninan was placed in the backseat of President Rafeek Syed's personal open-top car and given a hero's parade through the streets of Kabrahn.*
>
> *The open hand of peace Ohmshidi said he was extending to Yazikistan was met, not by an open hand, nor even by a fist, but by a swinging scimitar. As many as one million Yazikistanis lined the streets of Kabrahn, cheering loudly for their hero, and shouting such things as "Death to America!" "America the Satan!" and "Ohmshidi will go to hell!"*
>
> *American interests all over the world are being*

*attacked now. United Technomics in Paris was
firebombed. In addition, every American news service in Europe has been attacked. Our embassies
are under siege, and we have no means of protecting them, or American businesses overseas.*

This is only the beginning.

That night Karin came to Jake's house, bringing
dinner with her, and because she was expected, she
let herself into the house. "Jake?" she called.

"I'm in the kitchen," Jake replied. "I saw you drive
up, so I'm getting the root beers."

"Are you ready to see the Reds beat the Cardinals?"

"Ha!" Jake replied returning to the living room
carrying the two soft drinks. "In your dreams. The
Cardinals have the Reds' number, and always have."

"What time does the game start?"

"At seven," Jake said, putting the drinks on the
coffee table. "I've got it on the right channel. The
clicker is on the lamp table right beside you. Just
turn it on."

*This is Carl Wilson with World Cable News. We
are waiting for an address from the President of
the United States. In the eighty-eight days since
President Ohmshidi took office, he has given
seventy-three televised speeches. He will be speaking
from the Oval Office shortly, and we are told that
the address will be only three minutes long.*

"Damn, has that man ever seen a television camera that he wasn't in love with?" Jake asked. "What did you get?"

"Hot wings and potato logs. I was in the grocery store and walked by the deli. It smelled good, so that's what I got. Hope you approve."

"Oh, yeah, it looks and smells great. Now, if we could just get this idiot to stop going on TV every day."

"Supposedly he is only going to talk for three minutes. We may as well hear what he has to say," Karin said.

"Why? Whatever he says, it is just going to make matters worse."

We at World Cable News, along with all other television networks, have been given a transcript of the president's speech, but were told that we cannot say anything about it prior to his address. I can tell you this, however. It will be, to say the least, a stunning announcement. Afterward, we will discuss the address with our distinguished panel of news analysts.

"That's what we need," Jake said. "Another stunning announcement." Jake picked up a hot wing, separated it, and began eating.

The picture on the screen showed the president sitting behind his desk in the oval office. Behind him were two flags, the flag of the United States and a white flag, bearing what had been his campaign logo but had since replaced the flag bearing the presidential seal as the image of the Ohmshidi administration. It was a green circle enclosing wavy blue lines that represented clean water, over which was imposed a stylized green plant.

"I know you aren't supposed to hate," Jake said, "but every time I look at that man, I come as close to hating as you can get."

"Remember," Karin said, "that's our commander in chief you are talking about."

"How can I forget?" Jake asked with a growl.

"Shhh," Karin said. "He's about to speak."

"Whoop-de-doo," Jake replied.

Ladies and gentleman, the President of the United States, an off-camera voice said.

My fellow Americans. For too many years now, we have been dependent upon fossil fuels to meet our energy needs. This dependency has been the cause of nearly every problem we have faced, beginning in the late twentieth, and continuing into this, the twenty-first century. It has poisoned our environment, caused cancer and countless other health problems. It has destroyed our ozone layer, leading us toward irreversible global warming. It has created severe economic problems, and it has been the cause of international hatred and war.

For the last fifty years, there have been discussions of moving to a green economy with alternative, clean, and renewable energy as our nation's engine. And while other presidents before me have announced that as their goal, they have all failed.

I will not fail because I am taking a bold, and admittedly very difficult, step. It is, however, a step that I must take. I am, today, ordering an immediate cessation to all drilling and refining of domestic fossil fuels. In addition, we, as a nation, will no longer import fuels. We will have only that fuel currently extracted, refined, and in our inventory. When that is gone there will be no more. My analysts tell me that with strict rationing of the kind used during World War Two, our fuel supply should last about six months.

Now, while this may seem like a draconian step to many of you, it is, I believe, a way of spurring our scientists and engineers into committing to a twenty-four-hour-per-day, seven-days-per-week effort to find a sustainable alternative energy program. Will it be hydrogen? Will it be cold fusion? Will it be some scientific breakthrough that we have not yet imagined?

We of course have no idea as yet what this new source will be, but our future is exciting because I have absolute faith in our scientists to find a solution. Until then, all Americans will have to tighten their belts as we embark upon this great adventure together.

Thank you, and good night.

"He can't be serious!" Jake shouted. "He has lost his mind! He has finally lost his mind!"

"You have won me over, Jake," Karin said in a quiet, hesitant voice. "I think he has lost his mind."

"Do you know how much jet fuel we use in just one week at Fort Rucker?" Jake asked.

"I know it is a lot."

"We use three hundred thousand gallons per week. That is, we were using that when we were operational. Now if just we were using that much, how much fuel do you think our whole country uses? Everything, and I mean everything, is going to come crashing to a halt."

"How long do you think before that happens?" Karin asked.

"The last time you filled up, what did you pay for gasoline?" Jake asked.

"I don't know, around three twenty-five I think. Or something like that."

"You mark my words, tomorrow gasoline will be ten dollars a gallon, and that's only the beginning."

"I don't mind telling you, Jake; I'm getting a little frightened, now."

"Only idiots aren't frightened now," Jake said.

Thursday, May 17

In the weeks following the president's announcement that he was halting all acquisition of fossil fuel, either by domestic drilling, or importation, the price of gasoline began to increase, jumping at the rate of at least two dollars per day. The cost of fuel was beginning to be a problem for Jake and he was making a good salary. He couldn't help but wonder how others were dealing with it.

It was ten miles from Ozark to Fort Rucker and Jake drove it every day. This was Friday morning and, as he did every Friday morning, he stopped his two-year-old Volvo at the Busy Bee Quick Stop service station to fill his tank. Though this was normally a "fast in, fast out" stop, this morning he saw several cars waiting at each fuel island. This had become routine in the last few weeks, and Jake was prepared for it. He was in no particular hurry and he sat listening to Vivaldi's "Four Seasons" on the satellite radio as he waited.

"You son of a bitch! You pulled in front of me!" someone yelled to the driver of a car in the next line over. The shout was followed by the incessant honking of a horn that did not cease until a couple of policemen arrived.

"That asshole pulled in front of me!" the driver yelled to the police.

"Both of you," the police ordered, "out of line."

Grumbling, both the aggrieved, and the aggrieving driver were ordered to leave.

"Find somewhere else to get your gas," the policeman said. "And don't both of you go to the same station!"

Jake watched the two cars drive away. There was a time when he might have been amused by the little drama, but he had been seeing television reports of similar incidents all over the country. People were afraid, and the more frightened they got, the more uneasy the situation was becoming.

After a wait of about fifteen minutes, Jake pulled up to the pump and saw the price of gasoline, then gasped. It was thirty-six dollars per gallon.

"What?" he shouted. Thinking it might be a mistake, he checked some of the other fuel pumps.

"It's no mistake, sir," said a sergeant on the next island over, when he saw Jake checking the prices. "I stopped here yesterday and it was thirty-four dollars a gallon. I thought that was too much, but if we aren't going to get any new oil, this is just going to get worse. I should have bought gas yesterday."

"You had better fill your tank, Sergeant," Jake said. "At this rate, it could be fifty dollars a gallon or more by this time next week."

It cost Jake four hundred and thirty-two dollars to fill his tank. He was still frustrated when he reached his office. There were now more soldiers at Fort Rucker than there had been at any time since the Vietnam War, but because all training operations had stopped, except for normal housekeeping duties there was not one soldier who was gainfully employed. Jake knew that it could not last like this.

When Jake reached his office, Sergeant Major Matthews was waiting for him.

"Good morning, sir," Clay said.

"Sergeant Major. How are you coming on your requisitions?"

"I've added something to the list. I hope you don't mind."

"No, not at all. If you can think of something else we might need, by all means, acquire it if you can."

"I already have," Clay said. "I have twenty barrels of Mogas."

"You have twenty drums of gasoline?" Jake asked in surprise.

"No, sir, barrels, not drums. Drums hold only fifty gallons, a barrel holds fifty-five gallons. I figured it might be good to have."

"You figured correctly," Jake said.

"I know gas is expensive now, but I don't think we should use this until we have to," Clay suggested.

"I agree," Jake said. "We need to put it somewhere safe."

"I thought I would hide it in a hangar out at Hanchey Field."

"No, too many people out there. We need a more remote place than that."

"How about one of the stagefields?"

"Yes, excellent idea," Jake said. "And I know where to go with it. TAC-X. It's thirteen miles away, has four buildings, and is totally abandoned."

"All right, I'll get a truck from the motor pool."

"No," Jake said. "You would have to get a trip ticket for TAC-X and since it is no longer being used, that might arouse some suspicion. I think you would be better off renting a truck."

Jake wrote a check for two thousand dollars and handed it to him. "I hope this covers your expenses," he said. "But I would cash it immediately. And use it up as quickly as you can. The way the value of the dollar is plummeting, it may be worth only half as much this afternoon."

"I hear you," Clay said. "By the way, Captain Gooding is the POL Officer. If you would happen to get a telephone call from him, maybe you could cover my ass with a bit of a runaround.

"I'll do it," Jake said.

"Thanks."

"I'll leave it in your capable hands, Sergeant Major."

"I'd better go find a truck."

CHAPTER SEVEN

Dale County Truck Rental, Ozark,
Alabama—Thursday, May 17

"You do realize that all I want to do is rent this truck, don't you? I'm not trying to buy it," Clay said to the proprietor. "And it is a local move, I'm not going anywhere with it."

"You'll have it back today?"

"I'll have it back by six tonight."

"Fifteen hundred dollars. And the gas tank had better be topped off."

"All right. You're robbing me blind, but I have to have a truck today."

"You got a beef, Sergeant Major, take it up with President Ohmshidi. It's his dumbass policies that have gotten us into this mess."

"Yeah, well, I can't argue with you there," Clay said. "That sonofabitch has been a disaster."

"Well, why didn't you tell me you hated Ohmshidi as much as I do? Tell you what. I'll take two hundred fifty dollars off. You can have the truck for twelve hundred and fifty."

"Thank you," Clay said.

When Clay drove through the Ozark Gate he was stopped by the MP.

"You'll have to get a visitor's pass for that truck," the MP said. "And I'll need to put down where you are going."

"I'm moving out of my quarters," Clay replied.

The MP entered the destination into his log, then handed Clay a visitor's pass with instructions to put it on the dash so it could be seen through the windshield. From there he drove to the POL center.

"I don't know, Sergeant Major," a specialist said. "I don't feel right about loading military fuel into the back of a civilian truck."

"What difference does it make what kind of truck you load it in?" Clay asked. "I have an authorized and approved requisition document."

"Maybe I should call Captain Gooding and ask him what I should do."

"Go ahead and call him if you want to. His name is right here on the requisition form," Clay said.

"I just don't feel right about putting the fuel onto a civilian truck," the specialist said.

"What would make you feel right about it?"

"Well, I mean, when you figure how much gasoline costs right now . . . I've got a leave coming up, but I can't go home because I can't afford the gas."

"How many gallons would it take you to get home?"

"About forty gallons."

"So, what if you had enough fuel to get home, plus say, oh, about fifteen gallons more so you could run around a bit when you got home?"

"That would be fifty-five gallons," the specialist said.

"Interesting coincidence, isn't it, that you need fifty-five gallons of gasoline, and that is exactly the amount that is in one of these barrels?"

"Yes," the specialist said. "Very interesting."

"So, are you going to help me to get my nineteen barrels loaded onto this truck or what?"

"Nineteen barrels?"

"Nineteen," Clay said.

The specialist smiled. "They are on pallets, five to a pallet. I'll get a forklift."

Clay pushed one of the barrels off one of the pallets. "Only four on this one."

"We'd better hurry," the specialist said, going toward the forklift.

Stagefield TAC-X

There are thirteen stagefields located around Fort Rucker. A stagefield is a facility that is somewhat remote from the main base, allowing student pilots to conduct flight and tactical operations there. TAC-X, or tactical operations training field X, was one of the thirteen, and though many Army aviators had trained here, it was no longer in operation.

When Clay approached the entrance to the stagefield, he saw that a double chain-link gate blocked the road. The gate was locked by process of a chain and padlock. A sign on the gate read:

U.S. GOVERNMENT PROPERTY
UNAUTHORIZED ENTRY PROHIBITED!

Clay got out of the truck and, using a pair of bolt cutters, cut the lock. A moment later he swung the gates open and drove the truck through. Stopping the truck, he got out and closed the gates behind him, passed the chain back through, and reset the lock so that it looked as if it was still secure. Then he drove to the largest of the four buildings, this one a hangar, and went through the same process of cutting that lock and swinging open the hangar door.

Something scurried past his legs, startling him, and he let out a little shout until he realized that it was nothing more than a raccoon. He backed the truck into the hangar, then rolled the barrels down the tail ramp. It took less than an hour to off-load every barrel of gasoline, roll them over into the corner, and set them upright. When every barrel was off-loaded he covered them with an old tarpaulin. With the tarp in place, he went around picking up trash from the hangar, a solvent bucket, some paint cans, an old oil pan, a couple of wooden boxes, and some Plexiglas and sheet metal, which he placed on top of the tarp. His crowning achievement was finding six empty barrels, which he placed in front of his handiwork.

He examined the area when he was finished. Even if someone came into the hangar and looked around, they would have no idea that there was a little over one thousand gallons of gasoline here.

Clay closed the hangar doors, then locked them

shut with his own padlock. Leaving stagefield TAC-X he did the same thing at the front gate, replacing the old lock with one of his own.

As he drove back to Ozark to turn in the truck, he called his daughter, who was a student about to graduate from Northwestern Louisiana University in Natchitoches, Louisiana. Although Clay had helped out as much as he could, she had held up her end by working as a waitress.

"Hello."

"Hi, Jenna. This is your dad."

"Hi, Daddy. I hope you are calling to tell me you can come to my graduation."

"Darlin', there's nothing I'd like more," Clay said. "But with the cost of fuel now—that is, when you can even get fuel—I just don't think I'll be able to. You can thank your president for that."

"I know you don't like him," Jenna said. "But that's because you haven't given him a chance. He is trying to do some things to make a real difference in the world."

"Yeah, like bringing all transportation to a halt."

"You aren't being fair. Mom and I are going to a pro-Ohmshidi rally tonight."

"Your mother still trying to save the world, is she?" Clay asked.

"Daddy, be fair. Just because you are a dinosaur doesn't mean you can't appreciate what Mom is trying to do."

Clay chuckled. "I will confess that your mother never met a cause she didn't support, or a movement she didn't join."

"And you never met a war you didn't love."

"I don't love war, darlin'."

"That would be hard to prove by me. You went to Iraq under the first President Bush, you went to Bosnia for Clinton, then two more times to Iraq and once to Afghanistan for the second President Bush. And you got medals for every one of them."

Clay lowered the phone from his ear and drummed his fingers on the dashboard for a moment. Why did Jenna have to sound exactly like her mother? Fortunately, she also looked like Carol, who was a beautiful woman.

"Daddy? Daddy, are you still there?"

Jenna's voice was tinny over the phone, and Clay raised it back to his ear. "I'm still here, darlin', but the traffic is getting a little heavier so I had better hang up. I'm very proud of you for graduating. And I love you, sweetheart."

"I love you too, Daddy. I just wish that you were a little more open-minded about things."

"Tell your mama I said hi," Clay said. "Bye."

"I will. Bye, Daddy."

Clay punched out of the call then dropped the phone back into his shirt pocket.

He thought of Carol, whose background was everything his wasn't. Whereas Clay's father was a Vietnam war veteran, Carol's mother had been a hippie, caught up in the free-spirit anti-war crowd. Carol, who was born in San Francisco, had no idea who her father was but, as she often assured Clay, she at least had the satisfaction of knowing that he was not a warrior.

There had been sparks between them from the moment they met, but underneath those sparks, or perhaps causing them, there was a very strong sexual attraction. In the end, though, the sexual attraction was not enough to save their marriage, and when Clay deployed to Iraq the second time, this time under George W. Bush, Carol left to protest that same war. In doing this, she was taking up where her mother had left off a generation earlier.

World Cable News—Thursday, May 10

> In Washington today, Congress passed by acclamation President Ohmshidi's Water Resources Act, a comprehensive law that gives the federal government absolute control over all coastal waters, bays, rivers, lakes—whether natural or man-made—springs, creeks, canals, drainage ditches, and ponds. Under the auspices of this act those bodies of water that now lie on private land will be confiscated, and their use for any reason, whether watering livestock, fishing, boating, or drinking water, will be subject to federal government approval and taxation.

> Congressman Hugh Langston of Alabama, who had led the fight against the Water Resources Act, protested the acclamation, claiming that the count was too close for a voice vote. Speaker of the House Nina Percy had Congressman Langston removed from the House floor.

> In other news, the National Chamber of Commerce estimates that the amount of money taken from the U.S. economy as a result of the petroleum

freeze, by virtue of lost revenue from the shortage of goods and services, as well as lost income from jobs that have been eliminated, to be in excess of five trillion dollars.

Despite severe rationing, and the steadily increasing cost of gasoline, our nation's supply of fuel has already reached the critical stage. Analysts are particularly concerned about those in the north who heat their homes with petroleum. If the winter is very severe, there will be extreme hardship throughout the Northeast.

CHAPTER EIGHT

One hundred eighty-five miles southwest of Fort Rucker, Bob Varney sat behind a table in the Page and Canvas bookstore. The Page and Canvas was a popular and well-known bookstore among authors because they could always count on a good turnout for their autographing sessions. Bob was here to autograph his book *Murder in Milwaukee*. His action and adventure books were consistent bestsellers and he always did well at book signings. In addition, he was considered a local author in Fairhope, even though he actually lived thirty miles south in an area called The Dunes, on the Gulf Beach, next to historic old Fort Morgan.

There were at least twenty people waiting for Bob before he started signing. The problem was, there were only four books available.

"I'm sorry, Mr. Varney," Shirley Grace, the owner

of the bookstore, said. "I had fifty books on order in plenty of time, but the distributor I have always worked with has gone out of business."

"Yes, that's been a problem over the last few years," Bob said. "The consolidation of distributors. Dozens of the regional distributors have gone out of business or sold out. Now there are only two or three major companies left."

Shirley shook her head. "There are none left," she said.

"What do you mean, none?"

"There are no book distributors left in business. Not one."

"Damn, I didn't know that. So, where are you going to get your books? Direct from the publisher?"

"I'm not going to get them from anywhere. As soon as this inventory is gone I'm closing my doors. She took in the books in her store with a wave of her hand. "The prices of the books are printed on the covers. I can't very well sell a seven-dollar book for fifty dollars, but at the current rate of inflation, that's what I would have to charge for them, just to break even."

"Tell me about it," Bob said. "I have three more books to do on this contract. I thought it was a good contract when I signed it—now what would have been a year's income will barely last a month. And my Army retirement and Social Security checks? They have been suspended, supposedly while DFAS reorganizes, and they haven't been restarted. Also, because I had more than one hundred thousand dollars in stock, I was not included in the one hundred thousand dollar giveaway."

Shirley wiped a tear away. "My grandfather started this store when he came home from World War Two," she said. "We have been in business since 1947. Ernest Hemingway, William Faulkner, Truman Capote, Eudora Welty, Willie Morris—they all signed books here. I can't believe it is all coming to an end."

"I'm so very sorry," Bob said. "I want you to know, Shirley, what an honor it has always been for me to sign here. I don't know where I'll be signing from now on, but I will very much miss this place."

"I don't know where you will be signing either," Shirley said. "I've talked to every bookstore owner in Baldwin and Mobile Counties. None are staying open."

"You're talking about the independents, though."

Shirley shook her head. "Not only independents but the big chain stores as well. By the end of this month, there won't be a bookstore left anywhere on the Gulf Coast, and I would be surprised if there were any left anywhere in America."

"When did all this happen?" Bob asked.

"Bob, I know you and the others down at Fort Morgan live almost like hermits. But you really should pay attention to what is going on around you. It's not only the bookstores; the entire country is coming down around us."

"I've been watching the news, but I never know what to believe. Even the news now is so slanted that it is difficult to discern the truth. The left-wing media says we are in a temporary recession and all will be well, while the right-wing media is all gloom and doom. I pass it all off as hyperbole and figure the truth is somewhere in the middle."

"It's not hyperbole. I wish it were, but it isn't."

"Maybe I should get out more," Bob said.

"No, you are probably better off holed up down there on the beach, away from everything. I would think that now is the time to just dig in and wait until this all blows over," Shirley said.

"I'll miss coming over here," Bob said. "And if you ever decide to reopen, let me know. I'll be your first guest author."

"If I ever reopen, yes," Shirley said wistfully. "It would be wonderful to think so."

As was his custom, Bob called his agent after the signing to tell him how the signing went.

"You have reached The Taylor Group Literary Agency. Please leave your name and telephone number."

Bob also knew Greg Taylor's personal cell number, so he called that.

"Hello, Bob," Greg answered.

"Hi, Greg. I forgot this was Saturday and I called the office," Bob said. "I didn't leave a message, but when you go in to the office Monday and check your missed calls, one will be from me, so you can just disregard it."

"I won't be going into the office Monday," Greg said. "No one will be. There is no office, there is no agency."

"What? What are you talking about?"

"You haven't checked your e-mail, have you?"

"No. What happened?"

"Ohmshidi is what happened," Greg said. "Bob, there is no agency, because there is no publishing. As of Monday morning, every publishing house in New York will be closing its doors."

"Every publishing house? You mean Kinston?"

"I mean Kinston, Berkline, Pelican; Pulman, Harkins and Role, Bantar; Dale, St. Morton—all of them, every publishing house in New York. The cost of fuel has shut down not only Ingerman, but every other distributor as well. And you know better than anyone that the book industry cannot survive without distribution. The only thing left now is online publishing. I tried to move the three books you have on contract with Kinston to Spindle press. Spindle agreed to take the books, but they are offering no advance, just royalties against the Internet sales. I told them I would talk to you, but to tell the truth, I don't think it's worth it. And since Kinston closed its doors, you are under no obligation to complete the three remaining books. I'd advise you to not to write any of them since you would be writing them for nothing."

Bob was silent for a long moment.

"Are you still there?"

"Yeah, I'm still here," Bob said.

"I wish I had better news for you."

"Yeah, so do I."

"It's been good working with you, Bob. I wish you all the best."

"Thanks, Greg. You too," Bob said. He punched the cell phone off and continued his drive to the Wash House Restaurant, where he was to meet his wife, Ellen, and their neighbors, James and Cille Laney, and Jerry and Gaye Cornett, from The Dunes at Fort Morgan.

Ellen was surprised when she saw Bob coming in.

"I thought you were signing books."

"I did sign them."

"Already? That was quick."

"There were only four books to sign."

"Only four books? That doesn't sound like Shirley. She always keeps a lot of your books on hand."

"Not today."

"You should call Gary right now, and tell him that she only received four books. He could probably find out what happened," Ellen said. Then, to the others, she added, "Gary Goldman is Bob's editor. He's been with Bob through three publishing houses, Bantar, Berkline, and now Kinston."

"I can't call Gary because there is no Kinston publishing anymore," Bob said, morosely.

"Oh, Bob! No!" Ellen said. "Kinston has gone out of business? But they are one of the strongest houses in New York. Well, is Greg going to try and put you somewhere else?"

"Greg closed the agency, and there is nowhere else."

"What—what do you mean?" Ellen asked in a small, frightened voice.

"There's no Bantar or Berkline or St. Morton,"

Bob said. "There are no publishing houses anywhere, and no distributors."

"If that is the case . . ." She let the sentence die, unable, or unwilling to finish it.

"If that's the case, I am out of work," Bob said, finishing the sentence for her.

"And with your retirement income halted," Ellen added. "Oh, Bob, what are we going to do?"

"We're going to do what every other American is doing," Bob said. "We are going to find some way to survive. And we can start by having lunch."

"I don't know," Ellen said. "Maybe we shouldn't be spending money eating out until we know where this is all going to go."

"We may as well spend the money," Bob said. "I have a feeling it will be worth about half as much tomorrow.

"This is getting bad for everyone," Jerry said. "I was talking to my broker yesterday; he said things are going to hell in a hand bucket on Wall Street. It's the total opposite of economic crisis in the past. Instead of the Dow going down, it is going up every day. But even though the Dow is now more than three hundred percent higher than it was when Ohmshidi was sworn in, its real value, according to my broker, is about one-fourth of what it was."

"I don't write books and I don't have any money in the stock market," James said. "All I have is my retirement from the power company, and it hasn't gone up one dime since all this began. Hell, my monthly income used to be enough to enable Cille and me to live comfortably. Now, it is going to take an entire month's retirement check, just to pay for this meal."

"James, maybe we shouldn't eat here," Cille said. "Maybe we should save our money, and go back home."

"Why?" James asked. "Bob is right. Whatever we spend today is probably worth twice as much as what it will be tomorrow. This may be our last meal out, so I say let's enjoy it."

Monday, May 28

Bob and Ellen Varney owned a house on the beach and a condo in St. Louis. They had a condo in St. Louis because they had a son who lived there with his wife and son. Every summer they rented out the beach house, earning enough rental income to pay for their St. Louis condo. The idea was that when they got too old to be able to live in the beach house, they would sell it, then move to St. Louis and live there full time.

Normally by this time of the year their house would be rented and they would already be in St. Louis. But so far not one person had booked their house for the summer. In fact, Sunrise Properties, who handled the rental for them, confided to Bob that not one of the thirty-six houses they managed had been rented.

Bob was sitting on the sofa in his living room, watching television. His wirehaired Jack Russell,

Charley, was on the sofa with him, lying up as close to Bob's leg as he could get. Bob was rubbing Charley behind his ears.

Bob watched World Cable News almost exclusively. His son, who was considerably more liberal in his thinking, had often teased Bob about watching the most conservative of all the cable news channels, but Bob believed, sincerely, that WCN was the most accurate in their reporting. Besides, WCN had George Gregoire, and Gregoire was Bob's favorite commentator. But Gregoire did not come on until six o'clock, and it was just a little after five, so Bob was watching the *Evening News Report* with Sherman Jones.

> *You are looking at pictures of the many Liberty Party rallies held across the country today. Although the Liberty Party has neither national organization nor officers, they have sprung up since the election of Ohmshidi to make their feelings known. This rally, held in Chicago, had well over two hundred thousand in attendance. Similar rallies have been held in Cleveland, Philadelphia, New York, and Houston so far, and they are planning a large rally in Washington, D.C. But if you didn't watch WCN, or didn't know someone, personally, who attended one of the rallies, you wouldn't know anything about it. Not one of the other networks has carried so much as one minute of news pertaining to the Liberty Party rallies.*
>
> *Well-known conservative talk show host Royal Peabody spoke at the rally in Houston.*

The picture moved from the rally in Chicago to the one in Houston. There were several signs on display:

Impeach The Foreign Imposter

We Need Fuel

Fuel Now

Royal Peabody was standing behind a podium on a flatbed trailer as he addressed the crowd.

We are the heart and soul of America; we are the voice of the people. Some are mocking us, saying that we are in the pocket of a political party, but I say no, a thousand times no! We are beholden to no political party or ideology other than the principle of freedom, common sense, and the right to pursue happiness.

You know what would make us happy now? Fuel!

Peabody shouted the word, and it came roaring back on two hundred thousand voices. *"Fuel!"*

There are literally hundreds of billions of barrels of recoverable oil in the Bakken range, and nearly that much oil in Anwar. In addition we have more usable coal than the rest of the world combined, to say nothing of our huge gas reserves.

Ladies and gentlemen, our nation is collapsing around us, while our salvation is before our very eyes. We have enough energy to last for one thousand years without importing so much as one drop of oil. We have forty trillion in pre-Ohmshidi dollars worth of energy.

We were at the beginning of a monetary windfall that would put to shame anything we have ever experienced before—then we elected Ohmshidi. My friends, Ohmshidi promised us change, and he has delivered on that promise. We have changed from boom to bust. Ohmshidi's misguided policies, his insane order to halt all drilling and refining, even the importation of fossil fuel, has snatched financial disaster from the jaws of economic boom.

"Supper's ready," Ellen said, and Bob muted the sound as he and Charley went into the kitchen. Though they had a dining room, they ate there only when they had company. When it was just the two of them, they ate across from each other at a small table in the kitchen.

"Bob, what's going to happen to us?" Ellen asked.

"Nothing. Except we will probably spend the summer here, instead of going up to St. Louis as we normally do. With the cost of fuel it would be foolish to go up there for no reason. Besides, if it actually comes down to a condition of survival, I think we could survive better here, than in St. Louis."

"It is going to come down to that, isn't it?" Ellen asked. "A condition of survival."

"I wouldn't have said this six months ago, but yes, I believe it is."

"Are you afraid?" Ellen asked.

"No."

Ellen smiled wanly, then reached across the table to put her hand over his.

"Good," she said. "As long as you are not afraid, then neither am I."

"I think we need to start getting ready, though."

"Getting ready, how?"

"You know how. Just like we do when we are getting ready for a hurricane. The only difference is, this time we are going to have to be prepared for a much longer time than we ever had to with any hurricane."

"We've got the freezer nearly full now."

Bob shook his head. "The freezer won't do it," he said. "When it goes, everything is going, including the electricity."

"But we've got our own generator, and one hundred-pound propane tank."

"Which, if we run it full time, will last us for about two weeks. I believe we are looking at a year of being totally on our own."

"A year?" Ellen gasped.

"Or longer," Bob said.

In the living room they could hear the TV still going.

A suicide bomber blew himself up today in Grand Central Station in New York. Nineteen were killed and at least thirty more were injured. That is the fourth terrorist attack in the continental

United States in the last twenty days, bringing the death toll total to eighty-six.

President Ohmshidi lodged a strong protest with the government of Yazikistan, but President Rafeek Syed dismissed the protest as the meaningless whining of a nation of kafirs, or unbelievers.

Chapter Nine

"Hello, Colonel Chambers," Karin said, putting on as cheerful a front as she could. The patient, Colonel Garrison J. Chambers, a veteran of World War II, was ninety years old. One week earlier he had cut his leg on a piece of rusty, corrugated tin. That cut had gotten infected and the infection was spreading. He should have been given penicillin, but there was no penicillin available.

Karin once read that honey had been used for hundreds of years to treat infected wounds and though the doctor told her she was being foolish when she suggested they try it, he had finally come around. Chambers's wound was being treated with honey.

Karin removed the bandage and looked at the wound. It might have been her imagination, but she believed she was seeing some improvement. She began cleansing the area around the wound.

"How does it look?" Colonel Chambers asked.

"It's looking good," Karin said.

Chambers lifted his head and looked down at his leg. "Captain, if you think that looks good, you are definitely a woman who isn't turned off by ugly. And that, my dear"—he pointed to the purple, putty wound—"has a serious case of ugly."

"Oh, it's all in the eyes of the beholder," Karin said.

"Hmm, where were you seventy years ago when I needed a woman who could overlook ugly?"

Karin laughed. "I'll bet you were a fine-looking young officer," she said. "I read in your records that you spent some time in Paris immediately after the war."

Karin knew that Colonel Chambers, as a company commander in the 101st Airborne, had also jumped into France on D-Day, and had been at Bastogne during the siege, where he was awarded the Silver Star and a Purple Heart.

"I was in Paris, yes."

"Now, be truthful, Colonel," she said, as she used peroxide-soaked cotton balls to dab gently around his wound. "Did you, or did you not have your share of beautiful young French ladies?"

"Ahh, you do bring up memories, my dear," Colonel Chambers said. "I seem to recall that there is one particularly pretty young lady who always sits down at the end of the bar at the Parisian Pony. Lovely thing she is, high-lifted breasts, long, smooth legs. I hope I'm not embarrassing you."

"Not at all, I'm enjoying the description," Karin replied.

Colonel Chambers was quiet for a moment. "I can see her now. She is so beautiful. Or was, I should say. My Lord, Chantal would be in her late eighties now. All of them. Every young woman I knew there. The soldiers too, the men who served with me, and under me. They were all so young then, and when I think of them, I remember them as they were, not as they must be now." He grew pensive.

"All memories are like that, Colonel."

"I suppose they are. If nobody has told you before, Captain, getting old—what is the term the young people use? Oh, yes, sucks. Getting old sucks."

"Yes, but consider the alternative," Karin said.

Colonel Chambers laughed out loud. "Good point, Captain, good point," he said.

"Tell me, my dear, when I get out of here, would you be too terribly embarrassed to have dinner with an old man?"

"Embarrassed? Not at all," Karin said. "I would love to have dinner with you."

"That is, assuming there is a restaurant still open somewhere by then. I've lived under eighteen presidents; none have frightened me as much as this one does." He reached up to take Karin's hand in his. "On the one hand, I am glad I am so old because I don't believe living under this president is going to be very pleasant. On the other hand, I defended this country for many years, and I almost feel as if it would be an act of betrayal on my part if I were to die now, and leave this mess behind me."

"Say what you want about yourself, Colonel, but don't ever feel that you have betrayed your country in any way."

"I notice by the lack of a ring that you aren't married. But do you have a young man?" Colonel Chambers asked.

"I do," Karin said. "But he wouldn't mind at all my having dinner with you."

"Ohh," Colonel Chambers said. "Darlin', when a pretty young girl says she will have dinner with you, and then says in the same breath that it won't matter to her beau, that's when you know you are getting very old."

Karin laughed, then leaned over and kissed him on the forehead before she left.

Environmental Flight Tactics

Jake was sitting at his desk reviewing the new curriculum, lesson plans, and objectives, as well as a new SOP, wondering what he could come up with next to keep the men busy. Sergeant Major Clay Matthews tapped lightly on the door to his office, then pushed it open.

"Major Lantz?"

"Yes, Sergeant Major, come on in," Jake said, pushing the written material to one side. "Have a seat," he offered.

"How are the new lesson plans?" Clay asked.

"They are good," Jake said. "They are surprisingly good. I just wish we could get the training going again so we could implement them. What's on your mind?"

"I thought you might like to know that I have everything on your list that you asked for."

"Including fuel? Jet fuel, I mean. I know you got the gasoline last month."

"Yes, sir, I got the jet fuel."

"I'm impressed," Jake said. "How did you do that?"

"I had General von Cairns sign for a fifty-barrel emergency reserve."

"And you convinced him to do that?"

"Not exactly," Clay said. "Turns out that Specialist Roswell, who works down at HQ, can sign the general's name as well as the general can. He signed an 1195 for me."

"You didn't tell him what this was about, did you?"

"No. I convinced him that I was going to sell it on the black market and give him half the profit."

"I don't know, Sergeant Major," Jake said. "If there is no sale and he doesn't get his share, it could cause us some trouble."

Clay shook his head. "Not really, sir," he said. "First of all, he's not going to be able to say that he signed the general's name without getting himself in a lot of trouble. And secondly, I have already sold fifteen barrels for five thousand dollars per barrel. I'm going to give Roswell the entire seventy-five thousand and tell him that's half."

"So, we have thirty-five barrels left?"

"No, sir, we have fifteen barrels left. I told the POL

sergeant that the general had really only requested thirty barrels, but I changed the number. That way he could have twenty barrels to do whatever he wants with. That expedited the operation and it also kept him from making any telephone calls back to the general to verify the requisition."

Jake chuckled, "I'm glad you are working for me, instead of against me."

"I would never work against you, Major," Clay said. He smiled. "I might be a thief, but I am a thief with honor."

"I can't argue with that, Sergeant Major."

"Oh, and I got a desalination device. Hand pump, not power. I figure we may not always have power."

"Good move," Jake said, just as the phone rang. He picked it up. "Environmental Flight Tactics, Major Lantz. All right, thank you. I'll be right there."

Hanging up the phone, he ran his finger down the scar on his cheek for a moment. "That was the general's office," he said. "He's issued an officers' call. I hope it's not . . ."

"It has nothing to do with our scrounging, sir," Clay said. "It is something else. Something entirely different."

"Do you know what it is?"

"Yes, sir, I think I do."

"What is it?"

"I'd rather not say, sir," Clay said. "I think you should hear it from the general himself."

"All right, I will," Jake said, standing up and

reaching for his black beret. "You did well, Clay. You did damn well."

"Thank you, sir."

Jake learned that this officers' call involved more than half of the officers on the post, including not just department heads and unit commanders, but all staff and faculty, hospital personnel, officers of the TO&E units, and even those officers who had returned from overseas and were now at Fort Rucker awaiting further assignment. The officers' call was held in the post theater, and every seat was filled.

"Gentlemen, the commanding general!" someone called, and all stood.

"Seats, gentlemen, seats," General von Cairns said as he strolled briskly onto the stage. Walking up to the podium, he tapped twice on the microphone, and was rewarded with a thumping sound that returned through the speakers and reverberated through the auditorium.

"Gentlemen, I will make this announcement short and sweet. I will take no questions afterward because I have no further information. I'm afraid you will just have to hear the announcement, then wait and see where it leads.

"This morning I was informed by the Department of the Army that, effective within the next thirty days, there will be a seventy five percent reduction in force in both officer and enlisted ranks. In short, gentlemen, one month from now, three out of four officers and men throughout the entire army, will be gone.

The theater rang with loud shouts of shock and dismay.

"No!"

"What the hell is going on?"

"What is the cutoff? What if we are within months of retirement?"

"I don't know that there is a cutoff," von Cairns said. "There was no mention of it. And, gentlemen, I'll be honest with you; I don't know that there will be any more retirements. I know that those who are currently retired have not received their retirement checks for some time, now."

"This isn't right!"

"This is the president's idea?"

"So I have been told," von Cairns replied.

"What's wrong with this man? Is he insane?

"This so-called president is destroying the Army. And with it, the nation," Colonel Haney said.

"Somebody needs to drop-kick that foreign son of a bitch from here back to Pakistan!" a chief warrant officer said.

"Gentlemen, please," von Cairns said, lifting his hands to request order. "I can only tell you what I know. And I know that this was soundly protested by the Department of Defense. By the way, disabuse yourself of any thought that the Army is taking this hit alone. Because this order does come directly from the president, it pertains to all branches of the service, active, reserve, and guard.

"I'm sorry, gentlemen, I wish I had better news for you. This meeting is dismissed."

As the officers filed out of the theater, still stunned from the general's announcement, Jake saw Karin standing with another group of nurses. He didn't want to intrude so he started to walk away, but, seeing him, she hurried over to join him.

"That was quite a shocker, wasn't it?" she asked as she fell in beside him.

"I'll be one of the first to leave," Jake said.

"What makes you think so? You have an exemplary military record, outstanding OERs, combat time, not only combat time but combat command time, with a Distinguished Flying Cross, Bronze Star, not to mention a Purple Heart."

"Karin, I have not had a student in over three months, and I have not flown so much as one hour in all that time. I can't see the Army paying me to sit behind a desk and drum my fingers. At least you have been kept busy."

"True, we have been busy at the hospital, but eighty percent of our workload has been with retirees and veterans, and we heard that hospital service for non-active duty personnel is about to be stopped. Nurses don't have any special protective status, and you heard what the general said. Seventy-five percent of us are going to be gone."

"Do you have any patients depending on you, this afternoon?"

Karin thought of Colonel Chambers. She had cleaned and doctored his wound this morning, and he was resting comfortably when she left. She had no other patients who were at a critical stage.

"No, not really," she said.

"Then don't go back to the hospital. Take the rest of the day off and let's go out to Lake Tholocco."

"What? You mean now? Just leave?"

"Why not?" Jake asked. "What are they going to do? Kick us out of the Army?"

Karin laughed. "You are right. What are they going to do?"

Leaving the theater, Jake drove not to the lake, but to the post commissary. When he parked the car, Karin started to get out, but Jake reached out to stop her.

"No, you stay here and listen to music," he said. "I'll be right back out."

"Are you sure? I know how you hate to shop. I'll be glad to help you."

"I may not want you to see what I'm buying."

"Oh, a mystery? I like mysteries."

Ten minutes later Jake came through the check-out line. When his purchase was rung up, it came to six hundred and fifty-two dollars.

"What, and no cents?" he asked with a sarcastic growl.

"We don't mess with anything less than a dollar anymore," the clerk replied with a straight face.

"Tell me something," Jake said. "How do the lower-ranking enlisted personnel handle this?"

"They don't. Since the one hundred thousand dollars everyone was given ran out, I haven't seen anyone below E-6 in here."

"Where do they go? As expensive as it is, groceries are still cheaper in the commissary than they are off post."

"Tell me about it," the clerk said. "I work here, but because I am a civilian, I can't buy here. And the truth is, I couldn't afford it if I could."

Jake returned to the car carrying all his purchases in one sack. He set the sack on the floor behind his seat.

"I thought you were going to listen to music. What is that noise you are listening to?" he asked.

"Top Dollar."

"That's not music."

"What do you call music?"

Jake punched a button to switch to a classical station.

"There you go," he said. "'Emperor Waltz.' That's music."

Lake Tholocco is a six hundred fifty-acre lake located entirely within the confines of Fort Rucker. The lake officers' club was at one time a favorite hangout for the young bachelor officers, but when the Army and the other branches of service did away with officers' clubs, the lake club lost some of its cachet.

The lake was still a popular place to go though, with swimming, skiing, boating, and even fishing.

There were also several rustic cabins around the lake in an area known as Singing Pines, and Jake pulled up in front of one of them.

"You have a key to this cabin?" Karin asked.

"Yes."

"You mean you planned to come out here? This wasn't a spur-of-the-moment thing?"

"Karin, you know me well enough to know that I plan everything," Jake answered.

There was a beautiful view of the lake from the cabin, and, because none of the other cabins were occupied, there was a great deal of privacy.

Getting out of the car, Jake reached into the back to retrieve his commissary purchases.

"When do I learn what you bought?" Karin asked, also exiting the car.

"Two steaks, two baking potatoes, two prepared salads, a loaf of French bread, garlic, salt, pepper, two root beers, and a bottle of cabernet sauvignon. You wanted romantic, I'm giving you romantic."

"Is a secluded cabin on the lake a part of that romantic scene?" Karin asked.

Jake smiled at her. "Yeah, it's the biggest part."

Jake made use of the charcoal grill outside the cabin to cook the two steaks. There was no charcoal available, but there were pine cones, and they made a suitable substitute. Karin put the potatoes in the oven and the salad and drinks in the refrigerator. That done, she came back outside to stand with Jake.

"I wish I had known we were coming to the lake,

I would have brought my bathing suit in to work this morning."

"You can always skinny-dip," Jake suggested.

"You tease, but as deserted as the lake is now, I believe I could do that. I know it is still duty hours, but there is almost always someone here. Where is everyone?"

"I wouldn't be surprised if half the people on the base were gone by now," Jake said.

"Gone where?"

"On their way home, wherever that is. Karin, did you know that Clay Matthews knew about this even before the general announced it?"

"How did he know?"

"It's the NCO underground," Jake said. "I learned a long time ago that NCOs and even the lower-ranking enlisted personnel tend to find out things a lot faster than the officers do. I doubt, very much, that there was one enlisted man on this base who did not know what the general was going to tell us, even before he told us this afternoon. There's no telling how many of them have packed up and left today."

"You mean they've already gotten their RIF orders?"

"No orders, they just left"

"Deserted, you mean."

"Who deserted, Karin? Did they desert the Army? Or did the Army desert them?"

"Yes, I see what you mean. When you think about it, I don't believe they deserted the Army, and I don't believe the Army deserted them," Karin said. "It is Ohmshidi who has deserted us all."

Jake lifted up one of the steaks to examine it; then he looked back at Karin. "That's about the size of it," he said.

They had an early dinner, then sat out front and watched the sun go down over the lake.

"Karin, have you given any thought to what lies ahead?" Jake asked.

"I try not to. Every time I think about it, I just get more frightened. Have you thought about it?"

"Yes, I have given it a great deal of thought. It's like flying, and always anticipating the worst so you can be prepared for what might happen. I believe we must think and plan ahead."

"Plan and think about what?"

"Survival."

"I know what you mean. Unemployment is now at thirty-six percent, or so they say. And I wouldn't be surprised if it is much higher than that. If we are riffed, it is going to be very hard to get a job in civilian life."

"I'm not talking about getting a job," Jake said. "Very soon there aren't going to be any jobs anywhere, for anyone. I'm talking about survival as in staying alive—the kind of survival when there is a complete and total collapse of civilization."

"Jake!" Karin gasped. "You don't mean that, do you?"

"I do mean it," Jake said. "Believe me; it cannot

go on like this. I believe our republic is going to have a complete breakdown."

"If that happens what will we do? What will anyone do?"

"I've already started," Jake said. "Actually, I started a couple of months ago, but I didn't say anything to you about it then, because I didn't want to worry you. As if you didn't have enough sense to be worried, just by listening to Ohmshidi."

"You already started what?" Karin asked.

"Do you remember when I told you I was going to see to it that you and I would survive? I am putting together a team," Jake said. "A team of survivors."

"By team, you mean there will be others?"

"Yes."

"Who do you have in mind?"

"Sergeant Major Clay Matthews, for one. I've already got him getting things ready. He is the kind of person I will be looking for, people who possess skills that can contribute to the survival of the team. Like your medical skills."

Karin hit him on the shoulder. "What? You mean the only reason you want me is because I'm a nurse? And here, all this time, I thought you wanted me because I am me," she said in mock mortification.

Jake laughed, and pulled her back to him. "Well, yes, that too," he said. "The steaks are done."

Jake returned to the grill and started picking up the steaks when he saw Karin just staring out at the lake.

"Karin, what is it?" he asked. "What's wrong?"

"This," she said, sweeping her hand across the lake.

"What? I think it's very nice here. Don't you like it?"

"Oh, I love it, Jake, but have you considered that this might be our last time like this? I mean, if things really do get worse, much worse, if we actually do have to go into a survival mode, something like this will be only in our memory."

Jake leaned over and kissed her, lightly. "Then, let's make this a good memory," he said.

"Yes."

They were just finishing their meal when Jake glanced at his watch. "It's about time for the news," he said.

"Are you sure you want to watch? I mean all the news is so depressing now."

"Do I want to watch? No, I don't," Jake said. He sighed. "But I don't think we have any choice. I am now morbidly obsessed with watching this man to see what he is going to do next. It's like being unable to turn away from a train wreck."

They moved over to the sofa, where Jake opened the wine, then poured each of them a glass. Handing a glass to Karin, he sat down beside her, then clicked on the TV.

Thirty-one people were killed and at least one hundred eighty injured when riots broke out in

Louisville today, protesting the lack of fuel, [the announcer said.] *This is the fifteenth riot this month, resulting in loss of life. The worst was the riot last week in Detroit, where one hundred and fifty-three were killed, and two hundred and forty-seven injured. The amount of damage done to private property as a result of the riots is incalculable, due to the fact that there is no longer a measureable value to the dollar.*

In Cleveland, a spokesman for the national trucking industry said that if an allocation of fuel is not set aside and administered just for trucks there will soon be a nationwide shortage of food. Such a shortage is already occurring in the smaller towns across the nation where trucks are their only source of supply. Governor Coleman of Missouri has asked that a state of emergency be declared for the small town of Advance, which he says is completely out of food.

On another front, the national commissioner of baseball announced today that after the games this Sunday, all league play will be suspended. Since the president ordered the fuel embargo, airline operations are at the lowest they have been at any time since 1931 when air travel was still a fledgling industry. The airlines have said they could not guarantee Major League Baseball that they could offer enough flights to maintain the team schedules. Plans are underway to have a truncated World Series between the two teams with the best record in the National and American Leagues. The commissioner admitted during a press conference that the future of Major League Baseball is uncertain. The winner of this series may well go down as the last World Series Champion in history, he said.

The National Football League and the NCAA have already announced that there will be no football season this fall, and are unable to make any predictions on the future. As these games are played a week apart, they might be able to continue their schedule by train, though Amtrak has cut its operations by more than half.

A NEWS BREAK notice flashed on the screen.

We have this just in. President Ohmshidi has asked for network time to make an announcement. We go now to the Oval Office in Washington, D.C.

Ohmshidi was staring at the camera, obviously waiting for the signal to proceed. A slight nod of his head indicated that the signal had been given, and he began speaking.

My fellow Americans. When I was elected president, I inherited a nation that was in chaos. Because of the reckless policies of the previous president, the gap between the haves and the have-nots had widened precipitously. We were seeing big business run amok, and greedy banks foreclosing on hardworking Americans. My predecessor made no real effort to stem our insatiable lust for oil; indeed he sat idly by as our environment was destroyed and global warming increased. In addition, by fighting unnecessary and unjust wars in which innocent women and children fell victim to American bombs, he made this country the most hated in the world.

I began immediately to tend to these shortfalls. My first step was in ordering the return of all American troops, and I am happy to report that no longer is the uniform of an American soldier seen anywhere beyond our borders. I also ordered a cessation to any new oil as a way of forcing scientists to develop a new and sustainable source of energy. And though our nation is going through a period of belt-tightening and some hardships, we are weathering this storm together, knowing that there is a bright and shining future ahead.

Last night, in a midnight session, I asked Congress to pass the Enabling Act. The act passed by an overwhelming majority, though I am sorry to say that the opposing party proved, once again, to be the party of no, because not one of them voted for it. To bring about the fundamental change the people of this country voted for, and to deal with the inherited problems I have enumerated, it has become necessary for me to ask for increased presidential powers. The Enabling Act gives me those powers.

You may ask, and well you should, what is the Enabling Act? Under this act the roles of the president and Congress are reversed. As it is now, I can propose a bill, but I must wait for Congress with all its petty jealousies and bickering to act upon it. The sheer number of people, egos, and differing ideas make it almost impossible to get a bill through, and

by the time it does come through Congress, there are
so many compromises and amendments that it
might bear scant resemblance to the bill I had pro-
posed. This is unacceptable. In this time of crisis, a
crisis I inherited from my predecessor, action must
be decisive and immediate. We wait for the
dawdling outcome of Congress at our own peril.
When the bill reaches my desk I may ratify it by af-
fixing my signature to the document, or I might
refuse it by veto. If I veto the bill it will require a
two-thirds majority to override that veto.

Under this new act this system will be reversed. I
will replace Congress in the order of bringing a bill
into law. There will be no need for bickering, com-
promise, amendment, or vote. Any proposal I make
will become law as soon as I declare it so, unless it
is vetoed by Congress, and that will require a two-
thirds majority of both the House and Senate.

A new era of government has begun and I,
Mehdi Ohmshidi, promise you efficiency and
progress such as this country has never seen before.

In conclusion, let me share with you three more
decisions I have made.

First, I have ordered that there be a one hundred
percent stand-down in our Strategic Defense Initia-
tive, better known as Sky Wars. I want every anti-
missile missile to be withdrawn and destroyed.
Secondly, I hereby order the immediate and unilat-
eral dismantling of all our nuclear weapons in
any guise, whether they be delivered by rocket, aircraft, or any other means.

And finally, I am, today, closing down the FBI,

the CIA, the Secret Service, and the Homeland Defense Agency. I am doing this because of all the questionable activities that have been carried on by these agencies over the years, from the persecution by the FBI of innocent citizens during the long, dark, and oppressive years of the Cold War, to the torture and murder perpetrated by the CIA, to the illegal spying and violation-of-privacy acts conducted by Homeland Security. I am creating a new agency, answerable only to me. This new agency shall be known as the State Protective Service, or, the SPS. This new agency will have, in addition to their other many responsibilities, the task of protecting your president. Therefore the Secret Service will no longer be required.

So as not to taint the SPS with any of the misdeeds of the former agencies, no one who was a member of those agencies will be authorized to wear the coveted uniform of the SPS.

I believe that the steps I have taken so far—the pullback of all U.S. military from overseas, the seventy-five percent reduction in the number of personnel in our armed forces, the dismantling of all offensive and defensive missiles, and yes, even the rejection of fossil fuels—have created an environment of peace that we will be able to enjoy for years to come.

Thank you, and good night.

Karin hit the mute button on the remote. "He can't do that, can he?" she asked, shocked by what she had just heard. "He's assuming dictatorial powers, and he can't do that. Surely the Supreme Court will stop it."

"Of course they will stop it," Jake said. "He's gone way too far now. Maybe this will all turn out for the good."

"Good? How can it be good?"

"I can't see any way that the Supreme Court will let this stand. They will stop it."

"Do you think so?"

"Yes, they have to. How can they not?" Jake asked. He leaned his head back and closed his eyes. "Or, maybe not," he added. "It may no longer be our problem."

"Why do you say that?"

"If we activate the survival team, we will be cutting ourselves off from the rest of the country."

"I know."

"I said I was choosing all the members of the team based upon their particular skills. You know what my particular skill is?" he asked.

"You have a lot of skills," Karin said. "You are one of the most accomplished men I know. You are rated in how many aircraft? You have instrument ratings, you are a qualified flight instructor, you know electronics, you are a whiz with the computer."

Jake started laughing, and he laughed so hard that tears came to his eyes.

"What is it? What did I say?" Karin asked.

"Think about it," Jake said.

Karin thought for a moment; then she shook her head. "Oh, wow," she said. "Am I really that dumb?

If there is a total breakdown, none of that will matter, will it?"

"My skill is the way I spent my youth," Jake said. "I never rode in an automobile until I was eighteen years old. You went to Lancaster with me, you know what my life was like. I was raised without electricity, without running water, without telephone, radio, or television. We farmed with mules, and what the mules couldn't do, we did with our bare hands and muscle. The first time I ever sat in an aircraft was when I went to flight school. I know how to live in a world that never even entered the twentieth century, let alone the twenty-first century."

"When we went to Pennsylvania for you to visit your family, I confess that I felt a little sorry for those people, dressed in plain clothes and riding around in a horse and buggy," Karin said. "I thought of how deprived they are. But now it holds a strange attraction for me. I could almost see myself living that life."

"Under circumstances like we are facing today, yes, the Life is very seductive," Jake said.

Karin smiled. "Seductive," she said. "Yes, you were very masculine, very seductive in your plain clothes."

"Who seduced who?" Jake asked, returning her smile.

"That isn't fair. You can't blame me. I was disoriented, not thinking straight, discombobulated."

"Really? You mean you just tolerated me in bed?"

"I had to. You outrank me," Karin teased.

"So, you will do anything I order you to do?"

Karin leaned into him, shut her eyes, and raised her lips to his, but stopping just short of a kiss.

"Captain Dawes, reporting for duty, sir," she mumbled.

Jake did not close the distance between their lips. Puzzled, Karin opened her eyes and looked at him.

"Haven't you heard? We are an all-volunteer army now," Jake said. "If we go any further, you are going to have to volunteer."

"Shut up and kiss me—sir," Karin said, pressing her lips against his.

"I need you, Karin," Jake said. "I don't think I've ever needed you more than I need you at this moment."

Karin stood, then started toward the bedroom. "Give me a moment."

"Make it a quick moment," Jake replied, his voice husky with desire.

CHAPTER TEN

Base hospital, Fort Rucker—Monday, June 18

"Captain Dawes?"

Looking up from her computer, on which she was filing a report, Karin saw Sergeant Julie Norton. Julie was a clerk in the office of the hospital commander.

"Yes, Sergeant Norton," Karin said, smiling at the young black woman. Julie was twenty-two years old and two years earlier, had been first runner-up in the Miss Georgia beauty contest.

"I thought you might like to know that Colonel Chambers just died," Julie said in a sad voice.

"I was afraid of that," Karin said. "He beat the infection, but then pneumonia set in, and he couldn't beat that. Pneumonia is hard to fight when you are young and strong. His body was weak; I'm surprised he lasted as long as he did."

"Yes, ma'am. The doctor said the only reason he

lasted as long as he did was because of the way you took care of him," Julie said.

"It's a shame," Karin said. "He was such a fascinating old man. And so pleasant."

"Did you know he listed you as his next of kin?" Julie asked.

"What? No, I had no idea. Why would he do something like that?"

"I don't know, either. Maybe it's because he doesn't have anyone else. I pulled his records after the doctor told me he had died, just like I do for everyone when they are being released, either discharged, or by dying. His wife died last year and their only son was killed in Vietnam."

"Oh, what a lonely man he must have been," Karin said.

"He left this letter for you."

Julie handed a sealed envelope to Karin. Opening it, she removed the letter. Despite the colonel's age, the penmanship was bold and very legible.

Dear Captain Dawes,

I want to thank you for the loving care you gave me during my time here in the hospital. The sad thing is, I know I will not survive this stay. It is not sad for me. I have lived more than my prescribed years, and I am ready to shuffle off this mortal coil. But it may be sad for you, because you invested so much of your time and effort in tending to an old man.

As you may already know from a perusal of my records, I was at Bastogne in December of 1944. I was a company commander for one of the forward units. The German commander sent a note to General McAuliffe demanding the surrender of the Americans. The general sent back a note that angered the German commander, and the German commander threw that note away.

I found that note and have kept it ever since. I am leaving that note to you.

Sincerely,
Garrison J. Chambers
Col U.S. Army (ret)

Karin looked back into the envelope and saw another piece of paper, folded into a square, the paper browning.

"Oh, my God, this can't be real," Karin said.

Karin removed the brown piece of paper, then opened it up. There were only nine words written on the paper, only one of which was the body of the note. But that one word had come down through American history as a symbol of duty, honor, and country.

To the German Commander

NUTS!

From the American Commander

The Dunes, Fort Morgan, Alabama—Monday, June 18

Bob Varney was standing on the beach looking out at the now deserted offshore gas drilling rigs. Until Ohmshidi halted all domestic drilling, the rigs were ablaze with lights each night as for twenty-four hours a day, every day; they pumped gas from the rich deposits just off the Alabama Gulf Coast. Now the rigs were dark and deserted.

Charley was busily digging up sand crabs. When he found one he would jerk it up out of the hole, then throw it. More often than not he would watch the crab scurry away quickly, then go to another hole to start the process all over again.

"Nothing has changed for you, has it, Charley Dog? As far as you are concerned, your world is still Ellen, me, this beach, and the sand crabs. You're not worried that I'm not writing anymore, or that my Army retirement and Social Security checks have stopped."

Charley came over to Bob and reared up, putting his front two feet on Bob's legs. Bob reached down and rubbed him behind the ears for a moment.

"Go find another crab," he said, and Charley took off on his mission.

Although normally at this time of the year the beach would be crowded with summer people, it was empty now. Bob wasn't surprised. Vacations cost money and with the cost of gasoline today—that is, when you could even find gasoline—it would be prohibitive for any family to make the long drive.

There were twenty-two houses in The Dunes compound. The houses that sat right on the beach were all huge, multimillion-dollar homes. Normally rented in the summer time, they were all empty now, as was every other house in The Dunes, except for the three houses that were occupied by permanent residents. Bob was a permanent resident and his house was on the third row, approximately three hundred yards from the beach.

In addition to the houses, there were two seven-story condominiums, The Dunes and The Indies. Not one unit in either of the two large condominiums was occupied. One mile farther down was Fort Morgan, an historic old fort that was built just after the War of 1812.

Bob turned toward the surf and shouted at the top of his voice. "It is I, Robinson Crusoe. Where is everyone?"

Charley came running back to him and looked up with a quizzical expression on his face.

"You think I'm losing my mind, do you, Charley Dog?" Bob asked. He shook his head. "No, I'm not losing my mind. I'm just losing my will.

"My will to what? Survive? No, I'll not lose my will to survive. I survived three combat tours as a helicopter pilot in Vietnam. If I could deal with long strings of green tracer rounds coming toward me, to say nothing of air-bursting flak, then I can damn well deal with what we are facing now.

"I think.

"Come on, Charley, I'm tired of walking. Be a good dog and lay a couple of turds for me so we can head back to the house."

Almost as if responding to Bob's request, Charley hunkered down to do his business. Once completed, he looked at his deposit as if proud of it, then came over to Bob to await the treat that was his reward for performance. Bob gave him a treat, then dug a hole in the sand and pushed Charley's effort into it. He used to pick it up in a plastic bag, then drop the bag in the trash can, but that was when Baldwin County was still picking up trash.

Due to fuel concerns, the letter from Baldwin County waste disposal said, *we will no longer be making our regular trash pickup. We apologize for any inconvenience this may cause.*

"You apologize," Bob said when he got the notice. "Well, as long as you apologize, I'm sure it will be all right."

They walked back on the boardwalk between the USA and Dreamweaver houses to the golf cart that was parked on the road. Charley ran to the cart, then jumped up on the seat.

Seeing Charley do this, exactly as he had done for the last ten years, Bob felt a lump in his throat. How he envied Charley's ignorance of the fact that everything was coming down around them.

He glanced at his watch. If he was going to get back home in time to watch George Gregoire, he was going to have to hurry.

Hello, America.

Last Friday we heard Mehdi Ohmshidi take the unprecedented act of declaring himself dictator of this nation. He did this with something called "the Enabling Act." Let me give you a history lesson. On March 23, 1933, the German Reichstag met in Berlin to consider passing a law that would end democracy in Germany, and establish the legal dictatorship of Adolph Hitler. This act was called the Enabling Act. It did pass, Hitler became dictator of Germany, and we all know what happened.

Is it just ironic coincidence that Ohmshidi chose the same name?

But, not to worry. The Enabling Act is clearly a violation of the United States Constitution, so the Supreme Court will overturn it. Right?

Not so fast. We now know that within moments after Ohmshidi made his announcement Friday night, the Supreme Court did meet in emergency session to consider the constitutionality of this new law.

What did they decide?

They decided nothing. They couldn't decide because before they even convened, federal agents descended upon the Supreme Court and took every justice of the Supreme Court into what is being called protective custody.

Who did this?

Not the FBI, not the CIA, not the Homeland Security. By dictatorial fiat, those agencies no longer exist. No, the arresting officers, we are told, belong to the newly organized agency, the State Protective Service.

A spokesman for the SPS has stated that the justices are not under arrest, but have been moved to an undisclosed site for their own safety. While there, the spokesman added, the justices will participate in a conference during which the details of the Enabling Act will be discussed.

America, we are seeing, before our very eyes, the

*total destruction of our republic. Misguided voters,
thinking it would be cool to vote a naturalized
American into office, flocked to the polls to show
the rest of the world what an unbiased and open-
minded nation we are. They voted for this man
without really knowing anything about him.*

And now, we are about to pay the piper.

The telephone rang and Ellen answered it.

"Hello? Oh, Tim, hi, sweetheart. Yes, he's here.
Okay, just a minute."

Ellen brought the phone over to Bob. "Tim
wants to talk to you," she said.

"Hello, Tim, what's up?" Bob asked.

"You were right, Dad," Tim said. His voice was
low and obviously strained.

"Right about what?"

"About everything," Tim said. "How could I have
ever been such a fool to vote for this man?"

"If it is any consolation to you, you aren't the
only one. He is president because more people
voted for him than against him. That's the way democracy works. Or at least, that is the way it used to
work. After his Enabling Act, and some of the other
things he's done, I don't know."

"Dad, I've pulled all your money out of the
market," Tim said. "Mine too."

"Why?"

"I've been in this business for ten years," Tim
said. "I can read the signs. The way things are going,

the stock market isn't going to last another year. I'm not sure it's going to last another month."

"But the market keeps going up," Bob said.

"Yes, it keeps going up, but the real value is plummeting. I'm going to do an electronic transfer of the money to your bank."

"How much is it?"

Tim chuckled. "It's a little over one and a half million," he said.

"Whoa, that's pretty good, isn't it? Last time I checked it was a little under three hundred thousand."

"I wish I could say that it was good, but the only thing it means is that money is losing its value faster than we can keep track."

"Tim, wait, don't do an electronic transfer," Bob said. "I won't be able to get it out of the bank. I can't draw out any more than ten thousand dollars at a time."

Tim laughed. "You haven't been keeping up, have you?"

"What do you mean?"

"The banks are no longer observing that limit. The value of the dollar has decreased so far that the FDIC insurance is virtually worthless now. That means that, though the Fed still has authority over the banks, they no longer have any leverage. The banks can do whatever they want and it doesn't matter."

"Tim, you know how far we are from town. Tell me truthfully, is the money even worth going into town for?"

"I don't know, Dad. I wish I could answer that. But if I were you, I would go into town and take it out, then buy as much as you can with it. The more you have in real property, such as food, bottled water, fuel, anything you can think of that you might need—and that you can actually find on the market—the better off you will be. The problem now is there are less and less goods and services still available."

"How are you doing?" Bob asked. "I mean, you are a broker, if the stock market really is going to go belly up, where does that leave you?"

Tim laughed, but it was a harsh, humorless laugh. "Dad, it leaves me in the same boat as everyone else in the country—up shit creek without a paddle."

"Are you, Pam, and Jack going to be all right?"

"You remember that place we bought on Lake of the Ozarks?"

"Yes."

"I've filled the SUV with survival gear. There's fresh water and game there. We're heading there tomorrow."

"Keep in touch with us," Bob said.

"I will for as long as I can," Tim said.

"You better talk to your mom now," Bob said. "You don't have to repeat all this. I'll fill her in on it later."

"Thanks, Dad."

Bob handed the phone over to Ellen. "He wants to talk to you," he said.

Because Ellen had been listening to one side of

the conversation, she knew that whatever it was wasn't pleasant, and her voice broke when she took the phone. "Hello?"

Fort Rucker—Monday, June 18

"My God," Jake said. "Do you know what you have here?" He was holding the McAuliffe note Karin had given him.

"Yes, it's the note General McAuliffe sent to the German commander," Karin said.

"It is a piece of American history," Jake said. "All the more important now that our history is being taken from us."

"It's amazing that Colonel Chambers held on to it all these years," Karin said. "It had to be worth a lot of money."

"I would say, conservatively, it was worth more than a million dollars back when a million dollars actually meant something. But I'm not surprised that he held on to it. He was there, so I'm sure that, to him, this note was worth more than any amount of money."

Karin nodded. "I didn't know him that long," she said. "But, from what I did know of him, I would say yes, he was that kind of a man."

"For someone who didn't know him all that long, you certainly made an impression on him," Jake said.

"Not nearly as much as the impression he made on me," Karin replied.

There was a light knock on the door and Sergeant Major Matthews stuck his head in.

"Excuse the intrusion, ma'am," Clay said. Then to Jake, "Major, I thought you might like to know that Sergeants Dagan, McMurtry, Jenkins, Pounders, and Vivian are gone."

"I'm surprised they stayed around as long as they did," Jake said. "Did you check with Staff and Faculty Company? Are they being reported missing on the morning report?"

"There is no morning report, Major. There is no first sergeant, there is no company commander. Nobody knows where Captain Poppell is. No one has seen him since the announcement of the RIF."

"I hope Dagan and the others get home all right," Jake said. "If that is where they are going. How many people do we have still reporting for work every day?"

"I'm not entirely sure, but I would say about twenty, sir."

"Twenty out of an authorized strength of seventy-two. Actually, that's better than I thought it would be."

"Yes, sir, well, I reckon they are pretty much like me, they don't have any place else to go."

"Are the mess halls still feeding?"

"A couple of them are. The consolidated mess is still serving meals."

"That's good. If the men are going to stay around, they should at least have someplace to eat."

"Yes, sir, that's pretty much what I think as well. When do you think they are going to start sending the RIF orders down?" Clay asked.

"From the looks of things, they aren't going to

need to send any orders down. Looks to me like the reduction in force is taking care of itself."

"Yes, sir, I would say that as well," Clay answered. "It almost makes you wonder if this isn't the way they planned it in the first place."

"Sergeant, in order to plan something, one must have enough sense to anticipate the outcome. It is clear to me that nobody in Washington, in or out of uniform, has that kind of sense."

Clay laughed out loud.

"I didn't say that for a joke, Clay, I said it as a matter of grave concern."

"Yes, sir, I know that, Major. But I figure that about the only way we are going to get through all this is if we learn to laugh at the stupidity."

Jake chuckled, and nodded his head. "You may have a point there, Sergeant Major. You may indeed have a point."

"Ma'am," Clay said before he withdrew.

"Sergeant Major, wait a moment," Jake said. "You come from an old Army family, don't you?"

"My Dad was in Korea and Vietnam, my grandpa was in World War Two, my great-grandpa was in World War One, and my great-great-grandpa was with Custer. Actually, he was with Benteen during the fight, or else I wouldn't be here."

"Then with that kind of background, you might appreciate this," Jake said. He handed the browned piece of paper to Clay.

Clay looked at it, then glanced up at Jake and Karin. "Is this real?" he asked.

"As far as we know, it is," Jake said.

"This is the note that McAuliffe sent to General Freiherr von Lüttwitz," Clay said. "I thought Colonel Chambers had it."

"You knew Colonel Chambers?" Karin asked, surprised by Clay's comment.

"Knew? You mean he has died?"

"Yes, this morning."

"I didn't know that," Clay said. "But yes, I knew him. My dad and my grandpa both served with him. He retired before I came into the Army, almost thirty years ago, but I remember him well. He was a fine old gentleman."

Karin showed Clay the letter Chambers had written before he died.

"Good for you, Captain," Clay said after he read the letter. "I can't think of anyone who would deserve it more."

Chapter Eleven

The Dunes, Fort Morgan—Wednesday, June 20

Bob wasn't able to get very much with the money that was transferred to his account. It wasn't that he didn't have enough money, though certainly what he did buy cost more than he could have possible imagined just one month ago. One pound of dry beans cost one thousand dollars; a five-pound bag of flour was fifteen hundred dollars.

Bob had more than a million dollars to work with, and he didn't mind spending it because he was sure it would be worth half as much the next day. What limited his purchases was not money, but availability. Most of the stores in Gulf Shores, and in Foley, had closed, and the few that remained open had less than ten percent of their normal items on the shelves.

When they returned to their house they loaded everything into the elevator to take it up to the kitchen.

"Look at that," Bob said, pointing to the groceries. "What we bought today cost more than the total amount of my last contract, and it doesn't even cover the whole floor of the elevator."

"At this rate, we are going to run out of money within a month," Ellen said.

"It won't matter."

"Of course it will matter. What do you mean it won't matter?"

"Ellen, one month from now we'll be using hundred dollar bills as toilet paper."

Bob helped Ellen put away the groceries; then he sat on the couch and picked up the remote. Charley jumped up beside him.

When the TV screen came up there was a huge letter *O* in the middle of the light blue screen. The *O* was green, with three horizontal, wavy blue lines at the bottom. Above the blue wavy lines was a green plant that looked for all the world like a marijuana plant.

The *O* went away, and the camera showed President Ohmshidi sitting at his desk in the Oval Office. There were some changes in the Oval Office from the last time Ohmshidi had made a public address—which was yesterday. The changes were immediately apparent. His desk was flanked, left and right, by two muscular and unsmiling black men, both members of the SPS. They were wearing forest-green uniforms with SPS gold collar pins; the two *S* letters, rendered as lightning bolts, were separated by the letter *P*, which resembled a one-sided hatchet.

Ohmshidi *O* logo armbands were around their left arm, and they stood at parade rest, staring unblinkingly straight ahead.

The American flag was missing. In its place was a white banner, which, because of the way it was hanging, did not display all its components.

> *My fellow citizens, as you know, in the past few days, since the establishment of the Enabling Act, the nation has been curious as to how the Supreme Court would act. I am pleased to report that this issue has now been resolved in my favor. All nine sitting justices have submitted their resignation and I have appointed a new court.*
>
> *This new court has unanimously approved the Enabling Act, as I knew they would. They have also ruled favorably upon other actions I have already taken, and will now explain to you.*
>
> *During my campaign, I had a logo developed for me that reflected my belief in this country, not what it is now, and certainly not what it has been in its odious past, but in the greatness that lies before us as we complete our fundamental change. As you recall that logo is my initial, the letter O in green. Inside this green circle are wavy blue lines that represent clean water, and a stylized green plant that symbolizes not only a green, clean world, but new growth.*
>
> *I'm going to ask the two officers of the SPS who are standing here to display one of the two banners that are behind me now.*

The two men removed one of the banners from its stand, then spread it out so it could be seen. The logo Ohmshidi had described was in the center of the flag.

This symbol, placed upon a pure white field, will be the new flag of our nation, proclaiming to the world that we are a nation of peace and a nation that safeguards our environment. For far too long, the red, white, and blue stars and stripes flag has, in song and story, represented us as a bellicose nation, too eager to go to war at the slightest, or even perceived, provocation.

I am ordering today that, with immediate effect, this new flag replace the Stars and Stripes as our national standard. I am further declaring that the display of the old flag, or any previous national symbol, such as the representation of an eagle, on public or private property, to be declared a seditious act. The wearing of a flag pin on the lapel is also prohibited. Accordingly, I have given orders to the SPS to arrest anyone who displays the old flag so that they may be brought to justice. Further, singing of the song "The Star-Spangled Banner" is hereby prohibited, and violators will be prosecuted. Any newspaper that publishes an article in opposition to this act will be shut down, and the author of the article, as well as the publisher of the newspaper will be arrested. Talk radio and opinionated television commentators are here and now cautioned that public protest over this will be regarded as an act of sedition and they will be arrested. In addition, any radio or television station that carries this seditious programming will be shut down, confiscated, and given to those citizens who are loyal to me, and to the new paradigm I am bringing about. This is absolutely necessary if we are to have a clean break with our troubled and misguided past.

And finally, I have changed the name of our country to the New World Collective. This is in keeping with my determination to make our nation a beacon to the rest of the world—a leader in peace, progress, and real equality for all humankind. I am ordering all government documents from henceforth to represent not only our new national symbol, but also our new name.

As I am sure you will understand, a new nation will require a new constitution. Accordingly I have declared the constitution of the nation once known at the United States of America to be null and void. I am having a new constitution written, one that will insure an equitable distribution of wealth among all its peoples, and one that will take into account the necessity of efficiency of government, by providing the president with absolute authority.

And now I make this promise to you. I will work tirelessly to make this new nation succeed, but I cannot do it alone. Much sacrifice will be required from you, so I ask all of you to do your part, and to report to the authorities anyone you see who, by word or deed, commission or omission, may be undermining the authority of your president.

I will close this broadcast with the words and music of the new national anthem, as sung by the Children's Choir of the Tranquility School of Baltimore.

Thank you, and long live the New World Collective.

The camera moved then to a group of children all wearing choir robes with the new *O* symbol upon their chests, singing what was to be the new national anthem. As they sang, the words rolled across the screen.

Unbreakable New World Collective
Our people loyal and true
To Ohmshidi, our Leader
We give all honor to you.

(Chorus) Glory to our great leader
May he remain right and strong
The party of the faithful
Ohmshidi to lead us on!

In the New World Collective,
We see the future of our dear land
And to the Ohmshidi banner,
In obedience shall we stand!

(Chorus) Glory to our great leader
May he remain right and strong
The party of the faithful
Ohmshidi to lead us on

"Jesus, Ellen, I never thought I would live to see something like this happen. This must be the way the Germans felt when they realized what Hitler was doing to them."

"Surely this can't go on," Ellen said. "Someone will stop it."

"Who?"

"I don't know. Congress? The Supreme Court?"

"He controls Congress, they don't control him. And he got rid of the Supreme Court and replaced it with his own court. And, you heard him say it yourself: he has declared the Constitution to be null and void."

"Then we will vote him out," Ellen said.

"You are assuming there is going to be another election," Bob said.

"He can't stop the elections, Bob. The people won't let him."

"Ohmshidi stopping the next election isn't the problem," Bob said. "The problem is we will no longer be a nation by the time the next election is due."

Fort Rucker—Thursday, June 21

At Fort Rucker the next morning the Stars and Stripes flag was run up the flagpole; then a cannon shot was fired and the bugle call for Retreat Ceremony was played. Normal procedure for retreat was for all soldiers, wherever on the base they may be, to stop what they were doing. If they were driving, they were required to stop alongside the road, get out, face the flag even if they couldn't see it, and salute.

That was exactly what was happening now, though many wondered if there was some sort of mistake. Retreat was at the end of the duty day, not at the beginning.

On the parade ground as Retreat sounded, a soldier slowly, and stately, lowered the Stars and Stripes. Then, very deliberately, and with as much dignity as could be mastered, two soldiers folded the flag into a triangle shape, so that only the blue field showed, without even a trace of the red. The flag was presented to a sergeant, who then presented it to General Clifton von Cairns. After presenting the flag, the sergeant took one step back and saluted. Von Cairns stuck the folded flag under his left arm, then returned the sergeant's salute.

"Sergeant, dismiss the detail," the general ordered.

"Shall we hoist the new flag, sir?" the sergeant replied.

"No. Dismiss the detail."

A broad grin spread across the sergeant's face. "Yes, sir!" he said, proudly. Then he did a smart about-face and called out, "Retreat detail dismissed!"

General von Cairns walked back into the headquarters building and into his office. Once inside his office, he closed the door, opened the drawer of his desk, took out a bottle of whiskey, removed the cap, then turned it up to his lips. He had long ago quit using a glass.

Base hospital, Fort Rucker—Wednesday, June 28

Colonel Ruben Sturgis, MC, the hospital commander, called his staff together. At one time there were twenty doctors, forty nurses, and sixty enlisted personnel on duty at the hospital. Today there were two doctors, three nurses, and one sergeant present for the meeting.

"Dr. Urban, you are the chief surgeon now, so this comes under your bailiwick. Effective immediately we are to provide no more care to retired personnel, nor to those who are qualified under VA," Colonel Sturgis said.

"What are we to do with those we have now?" Dr. Urban said.

"Discharge them," Sturgis said.

"Colonel, we have three in intensive care. If we discharge them immediately, they will die before nightfall."

"What is their prognosis?" Sturgis asked.

"I'll let Dr. Presley answer that," Urban said.

"Not good," the younger of the two doctors said. "The truth is, I doubt any of them will live to the end of the week. They are all three in extremis, and we simply don't have the medication to treat them."

Colonel Sturgis drummed his fingers on the table for a moment, then nodded. "Alright, keep them. Discharge the ones that we can, and admit no one new."

"Colonel, we have no orderlies left," Julie said.

"How many enlisted personnel do we have left?" Colonel Sturgis asked.

"I'm the only one."

"It isn't just the enlisted personnel," Karin said. "As far as I know, we are the only nurses left." Karin took in the other two nurses with a wave of her hand.

"How many patients do we have now?"

"We have seven," Julie said. "Four retired, two VA, and one active duty."

"What is the condition of the active-duty patient?"

"I took out his appendix yesterday," Dr. Presley said. "I was going to release him this afternoon."

"Release everyone, except the three who are in ICU," Sturgis said.

"Alright," Dr. Urban said.

Sturgis pursed his lips, then let out a long breath. "Just so you know, I have submitted my retirement papers. That was just a formality, I don't expect DA to act on them. Hell, I'm not even sure there is a DA anymore. I'm leaving tomorrow morning, no matter what. And if I leave, I don't intend to hold any of you here. Chances are we aren't going to even have an army within another month, if we last that long."

"We were going to ask you about that," one of the nurses said. "Linda and I were planning on leaving tomorrow."

"I'm going as well," Dr. Presley said.

"Will no one be here for the three ICU patients?" Sturgis asked.

"I'll stay until the end of the week," Dr. Urban said.

"I'll stay as well," Karin said.

"I'm not going anywhere," Julie said.

"Look, I'll stay too if you need me," Sturgis said. "I feel bad about deserting you at a time like this."

"We can handle it, Colonel," Dr. Urban said.

"Hell, there's nothing to do but watch them die anyway."

Sturgis looked at what was left of his staff, then nodded. "I don't know where we are going from here," he said. "But it has been a privilege to work with you. All of you."

CHAPTER TWELVE

Wednesday, July 4

Hello, Americans.

Today is Independence Day. For two hundred and thirty-four years, our nation honored this historic occasion. Even when our country was young, it was a cause for joy and celebration. In the great cities and small towns, parades were held, patriotic music was played, there were barbecues and fireworks, and baseball games.

When you think about it, Baseball was America, wasn't it? Babe Ruth, Stan Musial, Willie Mays, Hank Aaron, Derek Jeter.

George Gregoire paused for a long moment, his voice choking. He wiped a tear, then continued.

But—those days are no more.

It isn't just no more barbecues, no more fireworks, no more baseball. America itself, is no more.

When I first warned you of the danger we were facing under the evil, and yes, evil is the only word I can use to describe this tyrant, this evil Ohmshidi, I prayed long and hard that I would be wrong. But I wasn't wrong. In fact, if I made any mistake, it was in not being forceful enough.

Thomas Jefferson once said: "The tree of liberty must be refreshed from time to time with the blood of patriots and tyrants." Winston Churchill said: "If you will not fight for the right when you can easily win without bloodshed; if you will not fight when your victory will be sure and not too costly; you may come to the moment when you will have to fight with all the odds against you and only a small chance of survival. There may even be a worse case: you may have to fight when there is no hope of victory, because it is better to perish than to live as slaves."

My fellow Americans—yes, I said Americans, not World Collectives—that time has come! I am calling upon all Americans to rise up against the despot Ohmshidi!

The Stars and Stripes appeared on screen, with the music of "The Star-Spangled Banner." The flag was replaced with scenes of U.S. Air Force jets flying in a diamond formation; that was replaced with a Navy destroyer at sea; and that was replaced with Army tanks rushing across a desert.

Then, suddenly the music stopped and the screen went black. After a moment, a placard was placed on the screen.

**By order of Mehdi Ohmshidi,
Supreme Leader, New World Collective,
Broadcasting on this network has been
suspended for engaging in acts of sedition**

Fort Rucker—Monday, July 16

Although it had been some time since the president ordered a seventy-five percent reduction in force, no RIF orders had come down. That was understandable as there was almost a complete breakdown at all levels of the military, and the Pentagon was no longer issuing orders. Fort Rucker was a mere shadow of itself, practically a ghost town now, with only a few hundred soldiers still present for duty.

At this point, "Present for duty" was nothing more than an entry in the morning report, or it would have been if company clerks were still filing morning reports. But morning reports were no longer being filed because there were very few company clerks remaining and many of the clerks who did remain had no first sergeants or company commanders to validate the reports. Four fifths of the buildings on the base stood vacant, the classrooms and training facilities were empty, entire companies of the TO&E units were gone, and the base headquarters was just a shell with no more than two or three officers and NCOs still reporting for duty.

Those soldiers who were still reporting to their duty station did so as a matter of habit, and because they had nowhere else to go, or nothing else to do. They tried to hang on to a semblance of the lives they had before all this happened by coming to "work" though all they did was play hearts, bridge, poker, and blackjack. They gambled hundreds of dollars on every card, losing or winning with aplomb because, increasingly, money was losing its meaning. Most of the lower-ranking soldiers who did remain on the base did so only because the Army was still supplying them with quarters and food.

But even that was not a guarantee. The mess halls had not had a new delivery in the last two weeks, and the post was running critically low on provisions. Also there were few cooks remaining so, more often than not, the preparation of the food was being done by the soldiers themselves.

The stimulus package of one hundred thousand dollars issued by Ohmshidi, who now called himself Supreme Leader, to individuals to "jump-start" the economy, had long ago been used up. Those who cashed their checks immediately realized some benefit. Those who deposited their checks in the bank had money on paper, but not in reality, as a cascading closure of banks all across the country left much of the deposited money in limbo and un-accounted for.

By now, it made little difference what the money was worth anyway, as there was a steadily decreasing availability of goods and services. Automobile factories had shut down long ago, including foreign car companies, but the auto industry wasn't the only production stopped. No longer was there any major manufacturing of any kind, from aircraft, to household appliances, guns, and furniture, to clothing. In addition, food-processing plants had stopped so that no canned, frozen, or packaged food was being produced, and the food remaining in the nation's inventory was being used up at an alarming rate.

The value of stocks plummeted so far that there were no viable stocks remaining, and the market stopped all trading. Gasoline was rationed to five gallons per family, per week. The posted cost of gasoline, mandated by the government, was two hundred dollars per gallon, but the rationing and the cost were meaningless, as there were fewer and fewer service stations that actually had gasoline. Those few stations that did have gasoline would no longer sell for any amount of money, but would exchange it for something tangible. Bartering had become the new medium of exchange, and farmers and gardeners who had eggs, chickens, pigs, and vegetables became the new wealthy.

Unlike the Great Depression of the 1930s, when people who had cash were able to weather the storm, money meant nothing in this economy. Millionaires, and those billionaires who had managed to hide their money from Ohmshidi's "equalization" confiscation, discovered that it was all for naught. Those with assets in cash, stocks, and bonds, were totally wiped out.

Eventually all transportation came to a halt—the airlines halted operations, trains quit running, trucks stopped rolling. The interstate highway system had no traffic, though that wasn't to say that it had no cars. It had become the final resting place for millions of cars. There was a forced egalitarianism among automobiles, whether new and luxurious, or old and austere; they contributed equally to the national graveyard of vehicles, sitting alongside each other, abandoned right where they had run out of gas.

The trailers of the abandoned trucks had all been forced open and emptied of whatever cargo they might have been carrying. The state police no longer patrolled the roads and highways and, on those interstates not blocked off by parked cars, drivers who had gasoline, and who were foolish enough to waste it, could drive over one hundred miles per hour without worrying about a traffic ticket.

At Fort Rucker, as at nearly every other military base, the post exchange, commissary, and clubs were all closed. Aircraft sat unattended on the flight lines of all five Fort Rucker airfields. There was no traffic of military vehicles, and even the MPs, the few who remained, stayed in their quarters, or reported to the office only out of a sense of habit. Like the city and state police all across the nation, law enforcement was nonexistent.

The Daleville and Ozark gates were unattended, which meant the post could be entered by anyone, military or civilian, and there were increasing numbers of civilians wandering around the base to see what they could take, scavenging without opposition from any of the soldiers, most of whom were now scavenging for their own survival.

Nearly all of the local power-generating companies in and around Fort Rucker had gone off-line from their own resources, but had, so far, managed to maintain service by drawing electrical power from other grids around the nation. However, the condition was so precariously balanced that any unprogrammed surge could have catastrophic results. Fort Rucker was not affected because it was generating its own power, sufficient for the fort's use, though not enough to help the neighboring towns.

Tuesday, July 17

At the North American Electric Reliability Council, in an attempt to balance the electrical usage with decreasing fuel allocations, a switch was thrown, temporarily diverting so much power into the Ohio-based First Energy power lines that the system became overloaded. At the same time the warning system was short-circuited so that the monitors were unaware that a problem was developing.

1900 Zulu: A 689-megawatt coal plant in Eastlake, Ohio, went out of service.
2006 Zulu: A 345-kilovolt power line tripped off, putting strain on a neighboring line.
2032 Zulu: The power overload on the neighboring line caused it to sag and go out of service.

2115 Zulu: Two more 345-kilovolt lines failed within five minutes of each other.

2130 Zulu: Two 345-kilovolt lines in Michigan tripped off. A coal-fired plant near Grand Haven, Michigan went off-line.

2141 Zulu: A coal-fired power plant in Avon Lake, Ohio, went out of service.

2155 Zulu: The nuclear reactor in Perry, Ohio, shut down automatically, after losing power.

2200 Zulu: Systems from Detroit to New Jersey and Canada, including all of New York City, shut down.

That was followed by a massive power outage that first covered the northeast, then cascaded across all the power grids in the entire nation, so that by 2315 Zulu, or 6:15 P.M. Eastern Daylight Time, the entire nation from Canada to Mexico, and from the Atlantic to the Pacific, was blacked out. Only the tiniest communities that were not a part of the national grid, and who still had enough fuel to operate their generators, still had power. The loss of power took almost all television and radio broadcasts off the air. It also interrupted all communication between Fort Rucker and the Department of the Army. There was no longer any telephone, wire, or even Internet connection between Fort Rucker and the Department of Defense. Although the on-base telephones were still working, they were limited to on-base calls only. There was no longer any military cohesion. The few soldiers who remained wandered around the base without direction or purpose.

The Dunes, Fort Morgan—
6:14 P.M. CDT, Tuesday, July 17

Bob Varney was sitting on the couch in his living room watching the local news from the one television station that continued to operate in Mobile. How different the news was now with only one announcer and one camera. No longer were any of the features presented where the TV station would find people who had contributed to the news, either by participation in some newsworthy event, or by some odd little quirk that would often elicit a chuckle from the viewers. Those features had been eliminated because there was no longer enough fuel to allow the news reporters to go into the field.

> *Supreme Leader Ohmshidi announced today*
> *that he is asking the other nations of the world to*
> *come to our aid in this time of national crisis. He*
> *reminded the leaders of the other nations that we*
> *have always been quick to supply food, medicine,*
> *and humanitarian aid to other nations when they*
> *were in need. Now, according to Ohmshidi, the*
> *total mismanagement of the previous administra-*
> *tion has made it difficult to implement his policies,*
> *resulting in a nationwide food shortage. The*
> *nation of Yazikistan, once our enemy, has an-*
> *nounced that it will send three shiploads of food—*
> *proof, Ohmshidi says, that his policy of negotiation*
> *with the Muslim nations is paying dividends.*

"Jesus," Bob said in disgust. "We are begging now. Can you believe that, Ellen? Our country has been reduced to the point of begging. I never thought I would live to see this day."

"You shouldn't watch the news," Ellen said. "It gets you so upset that I'm afraid you might have a stroke."

"There is no baseball to watch anymore and the only thing else on the satellite channels—that is, the ones that are still broadcasting—are reruns. And there are virtually no commercials because there are so many companies out of business. Who would have ever thought that I would long for the time when there were commercials?"

In Mobile today—

The television suddenly went black.

"Bob, the power just went off," Ellen said from the kitchen.

"It will probably be back on in a minute or so," Bob replied. "There's no storm or anything, no reason why it went off."

"Why don't you start the generator, at least long enough for me to finish cooking supper?"

"I hate to waste the gas," Bob said. "Hurricane season is here. You know how it was with Ivan and Katrina. We were without power for two weeks."

"Yes, but I also know how hard it is to get food now," Ellen replied. "If I don't keep cooking this now, it won't be any good."

"All right, I'll start the generator."

The generator was all the way downstairs, run by

a large tank of propane gas. Bob started it, then came back upstairs.

"Stove going again?" he asked.

"Yes, thanks."

"Maybe I can watch the rest of the news now." He turned the TV back on, but the local television channel was black.

"Damn, they must be out of power in Mobile too. That's funny; we don't normally get power outages that go that far."

Bob swept through the channels but got nothing from any of them.

"I wonder if something happened to our satellite dish?"

"Try the radio," Ellen suggested.

Bob turned on the radio and got nothing on either the AM or the FM band.

"Damn, there's nothing on the radio either, not a thing. I'm going to try satellite radio."

Bob had a satellite radio upstairs in his office. It was there for two reasons: one, because it was the best place for his antenna, and the second, because he liked to listen to classical music as he was writing. As he started upstairs, Charley ran up the stairs ahead of him, then got into his position under the desk.

"I know, I know, I haven't written in a couple of weeks have I, Charley?" Bob said. "But I'm going to get back to it, I promise. Now I'm just going to see what I can find on the radio."

He found nothing.

"Something has happened," he said to Ellen as

he came back into the kitchen. "It's not normal that every radio and television station be off the air."

"It's not normal?" Ellen asked. "Tell me anything that has been normal since Ohmshidi took office."

Charley reared up to put his two front paws on Bob's leg. Bob picked him up and Charley began kissing him.

"Charley," Bob said. "Charley is normal."

"Supper is ready," Ellen said, putting the plates on the table.

"Fried chicken. Looks good," Bob said.

"That's the end of our chicken," Ellen said. "And I don't know if there will be any more. As you recall, when we were in the store it was practically empty. I got as much as I could because I think it's only going to get worse."

"I think so too," Bob said. He picked up a drumstick. "But I intend to enjoy it while we have it."

CHAPTER THIRTEEN

Fort Rucker—Wednesday, July 18

In the Post Headquarters, General von Cairns sat in his swivel chair staring out through the window at the open parade ground and empty flagpole. He took another pull from his bottle of whiskey.

"You drink too much," his wife had told him. "Ever since you came back from the war, you drink too much."

"It helps me forget."

"Forget what?"

"What I want to forget."

Those discussions about drinking were the beginning of the problems that only got worse in his marriage. Then, two years ago, Kitty left him. But because their daughter was already married and gone, the breakup wasn't that traumatic.

Von Cairns looked over at his bookshelf, filled with various artifacts that cataloged his time in the Army. There was a photo of him in his football uniform at West Point. Their record with Navy for the time von Cairns was a cadet was three losses and one tie, that game having been played before the NCAA had put in the tie-breaker system. Von Cairns had helped preserve the tie by intercepting a midshipman's pass in the end zone. Among the other items were a bent tail rotor from a helicopter crash he had survived, a captured Iraqi flag, silver cups from half a dozen stateside assignments, and a black, polished, knobbed shillelagh called a "Garryowen stick."

His first assignment out of West Point had been to the Seventh Cavalry, now at Fort Stewart, Georgia, but then he was stationed at Conn and Ledward Casernes in Schweinfurt, Germany. The Seventh Cavalry, "Custer's Own," had the nickname "Garryowen" and all the officers carried a swagger stick, the Garryowen stick.

There was something wonderful about being alive then, the tradition of being a part of such a storied unit, the pure joy of being a young single officer on flight status—they were still flying Hueys then—and being in Germany itself, the beer houses, the restaurants, and the outdoor markets, especially the flower markets. Germany was where he met Kitty, who had been, at the time, a schoolteacher in the American dependent children's school.

He remembered the first time he ever saw her. It was in the officers' club and she was sitting at a table with one of the other teachers. She had long dark brown hair and a wave of it kept falling across one eye, causing her to have to push it back. He thought she was absolutely beautiful, and he went over to introduce himself to her.

"I am Lieutenant Clifton von Cairns, and after I take you out to dinner tonight, you are going to write to your mother and tell her all about me."

Kitty laughed at him, but she did go to dinner with him that night, and several nights thereafter until the other teachers and other officers would always include the two of them for any planned event.

They were so in love then. They went to Paris together, to London, and to Rome. They were married in Germany, first a German civil marriage, because the U.S. has no reciprocal marriage agreements with foreign countries, then in the post chapel, exiting under arched sabers. They swore to each that their love would last forever. But that—like everything else—was gone.

"Where are you now, Kitty?" von Cairns asked, speaking aloud, but quietly. "What are you doing this minute? Are you recalling our days together in Germany? Do you have any memories of that time? Are all your memories bad ones?" he continued, speaking softly. "I still love you, you know. I can't tell you that. This is not the time for that. But I do hope that you have found happiness."

Von Cairns turned up his whiskey bottle for another drink, but there was none left. And the way things were now, there was not likely to be any more.

* * *

Back in the BOQ, Lieutenant Phil Patterson was contemplating his situation. He rarely reported to work now; General von Cairns had told him there was really no need for him to come in. He had nothing left to read, and nothing left to do. There was no radio to listen to, no TV to watch. Newspapers and magazines were no longer being published.

How differently things had turned out from what he had imagined when, as a boy, he had dreams of going to West Point. He remembered that June day of graduation, the sense of accomplishment, and the pride he had in receiving his commission. Part of his dream had been to fly, and he fulfilled that as well, though it had now been over four months since last he flew.

He was frightened. Not the kind of fear one might get when his life is in imminent danger. There was, with that kind of fear, also a charge of adrenalin, an awareness of life, an excitement.

This fear was intense, mind-numbing, and paralyzing. He had no idea what was going to happen, but he knew it was going to be bad. Very bad. And worse, he knew there was absolutely nothing he could do about it.

He had been thinking about it for several days now, and had even made preparations. Today he was going to leave.

Lieutenant Patterson drove down to the Headquarters Building and went into General von Cairns's office. He wasn't going to ask the general if he could leave; he was going to tell him that he was going to leave. It wasn't something he was proud of, but it was something he was going to do, and he knew that, realistically, there was nothing the general could do about it.

He saw that the general's chair was turned around and, as he often did, the general was staring through the window at the empty parade ground outside. He had been doing that more and more lately. And drinking—Patterson saw the empty whiskey bottle on the desk, just above the open drawer. At one point he wondered if he should make some comment about the general's drinking, being very subtle about it. But he was just a lieutenant, and such a thing wasn't his place.

"General," Patterson said. "General, sir, I'm sorry sir, I wanted to stay and do all I could, but, to be honest, I don't think there is anything left here I can do anymore. In fact, I don't think there is anything anyone can do. My mom is alone back in Arkansas, and I haven't heard from her in two weeks. I'm worried about her, and I'd like to go home. If you want me to just take a leave, I will do so. But, the way things are now, well, I hope you understand." Patterson paused, waiting for the general to turn around and reply.

"General?" Patterson said again.

When the general still didn't turn around, Patterson walked around the desk.

"Sir?"

Patterson stepped up to the general's chair, then gasped out loud. The general's head was back against the headrest and lolling over to one side. In his hand was an Army-issue M9 pistol. There was a black hole in his forehead, but a surprising lack of blood.

"I guess I'll just go," Patterson said in a quiet voice.

As he left the general's office and walked through the cavernous HQ building, he did not encounter a single soul.

His car was full of gasoline and he had two five-gallon cans in the trunk. He hoped that would be enough to get him to Blytheville, Arkansas.

Fort Rucker—Friday, July 20

Jake was playing a game of solitaire when the phone rang.

"EFT, Major Lantz."

"Major, this is Mr. Tadlock."

"Yes, Chief, what can I do for you?"

"I'm calling you from the General's office."

"Okay, put him on."

"Uh, no sir, I can't do that."

"Oh?"

"The reason I'm calling is I wonder if you could come over here."

"I guess I can. I hate to waste the gas, but if the general needs me for some reason . . ."

"It isn't the general who needs you, Major. I need you. Or at least, I need your advice. The general is dead."

"What?"

"Looks like he committed suicide. He's sittin' here in his chair and there's a pistol in his lap."

"Where's Lieutenant Patterson?"

"I don't know, Major. He wasn't here when I got here. Fact is, there's not a soul in the whole damn building."

"I'll be there as quick as I can."

Jake hung up the phone, then called out into the outer office. "Sergeant Major, are you out there?"

"Yes, sir," Clay answered.

Jake walked out into the outer office and saw Clay just getting up from his desk.

"I'd like you to come to the general's office with me if you would," he said.

"Damn! He hasn't caught on about the fuel requisitions, has he?"

"No. Ed Tadlock just called. The general is dead, Clay. Tadlock said he shot himself."

"I'll be damned. I thought von Cairns had more sand than that."

Chief Warrant Officer-3 Edward Tadlock was waiting just outside the door to the Post Headquarters building when Jake and Clay arrived in Jake's Jeep SUV.

"I waited out here," Tadlock said. "I don't mind telling you, it's creepy as hell in there."

"How do you know it was a suicide?" Jake asked. "Did he leave a note?"

"No, there was no note. But the pistol is still in his hand."

"Let's have a look."

The three men went back inside the building, which, as Tadlock had said, was completely deserted.

"I'm taking off," Tadlock said. "I'm going to Missouri. I own a small farm there, I'm going back to work it. My wife and kids are already there, waiting for me."

"Do you have enough fuel to make it all the way to Missouri?"

"I'm driving a diesel, and running it on jet fuel. I bought thirty gallons extra from someone. I didn't ask any questions as to where he got it."

"Well, good luck to you, Chief," Jake said.

When they stepped into the general's office, he was still sitting in his swivel chair, facing the window that looked out over the parade ground.

"I left him just the way I found him," Tadlock said.

Jake walked around to get a closer look at him. He shook his head. "Damn," he said. "He was a good man. I hate to see this."

"Ohmshidi killed him," Tadlock said. "Yeah, von Cairns may have pulled the trigger, but Ohmshidi killed him."

"I can't argue with that," Jake said.

"So now the question is, what do we do with him?"

"Does he have any next of kin?" Clay asked.

"He's divorced, I know that," Tadlock said.

"He has a daughter somewhere," Jake said. "If we looked through all his things, we could probably find out where she is. But then what? The way things are now, what could she do with him?"

"We can't leave him here," Tadlock said.

"Let's bury him out there on the parade ground, under the flagpole," Clay suggested.

"Damn good idea, Sergeant Major, damn good idea," Tadlock said.

Clay went to the general's quarters to get his dress blue uniform and he and Jake dressed the general, including all his medals. While they were doing that, Tadlock rounded up as many officers and men as he could, including seven men who would form a firing squadron to render last honors, and one bandsman who agreed to play taps.

Now the general lay in a main-rotor shipping case alongside a grave that three of the EM had dug. There were over fifty men and women present, in uniform, and in formation. The general was lowered into the grave, and Jake nodded at the firing team. The seven soldiers raised their rifles to their shoulders.

"Ready? Fire!"

The sound of the first volley echoed back from the buildings adjacent to the parade ground.

"Ready? Fire!"

Rifle fire, which, during his life, the general had heard in anger, now sounded in his honor.

"Ready? Fire!"

The last volley was fired, and those who were rendering hand salutes brought them down sharply.

The bandsman, a bespectacled specialist, raised a trumpet to his lips and with the first and third valves depressed, played taps.

Jake thought of the many times he had heard

this haunting bugle call, at night in the barracks while in basic training, and in OCS. He had also heard it played for too many of his friends, killed in combat or in aircraft accidents.

The young soldier played the call slowly and stately, holding the higher notes, gradually getting louder, then slowing the tempo as he reached the end, and holding the final, middle C longer than any other note before, he allowed it simply and sadly to . . . fade away.

CHAPTER FOURTEEN

The Dunes, Fort Morgan—Friday, July 27

Many of the houses at The Dunes had their own generators as a result of the long power outages following hurricanes. The problem was that at full usage the propane tanks could last for no more than a week. By rationing the usage, Bob was able to get ten days of service; then he, James, and Jerry began taking propane tanks from the unoccupied houses and using them for their own needs.

In addition to taking the propane tanks, they also took the food that many of the houses had in their freezer and pantries They ate the frozen food first so they would not have to keep it cold for too long— and at the beginning of their ordeal, they ate very well: steaks, roasts, lobster, shrimp, and fish.

For better utilization of the food the three families decided to take all their meals together.

"What is this? Leg of lamb?" Jerry asked as he cut into the meat.

"Yes. It came from Dr. Kelly's freezer," James said.

"You can say what you want about Dr. Kelly, the man does have good taste," Bob said. "That's also where we got the prime rib, isn't it?"

"And the lobster," James added.

James Laney did not have a college education, but he had worked himself up from general handy-man to plant manager of the Cobb County Electric Cooperative in Georgia. He accomplished this by mastering every job in the plant and even though he was now retired, he kept himself busy by taking care of the houses of the absentee owners: doing electrical repair, plumbing, carpentry, and paint-ing. Bob and Jerry had "elected" him mayor of The Dunes. The election was only partially in jest; James knew all the absentee owners, and had a key to every house.

James had married his wife Cille when he was seventeen and she was fifteen, and though every-thing seemed stacked against their marriage suc-ceeding, they had celebrated their fiftieth wedding anniversary earlier this year.

Jerry Cornett was a retired salesman and now the consummate outdoorsman who had fished and hunted around the world. He did his hunting with bows that he made himself, and was a champion bowman, having won so many bow shooting contests that the magazine *Bowhunt America* pronounced him "America's Senior Champion Archer." Jerry's wife, Gaye, was a retired hairstylist.

Until the collapse of the economy, Bob Varney had been a successful novelist. Success had come late for him—he had written over three hundred books, but most were ghostwriting projects for others. And while his ghostwriting paid well, it left him with a sense of frustration. He saw many of the books he had authored become bestsellers, but he was unable to take advantage of them. Then, two years ago he convinced his editor to let him write his own books. Those books had done very well and at long last, let him build his own career.

Ironically, the career that had taken him so long to build was now nonexistent due to the collapse of the U.S. economy.

Bob was also a retired Army officer who had done three tours in Vietnam as a helicopter pilot. It had been forty years since he last flew, and he often watched, with a bit of nostalgia, the service helicopters pass over his house as they flew out to the offshore gas rigs.

Because of his writing and research, he was practically a walking encyclopedia, fascinated by trivia, and he knew diverse facts ranging from the number of words in the King James Version of the Bible— 181,253—to the temperature of the sun at its core— twenty-seven million degrees. And he was a Custer expert who could name every officer who made that last scout with Custer, including those who were with Reno and Benteen, and tell what eventually happened to them.

Bob's only other talent was in cooking, but he excelled in that, his specialty being coming up with very satisfying meals by utilizing what was available.

Bob's wife, Ellen, was a retired schoolteacher, who, in her youth, had taught in Point Hope, Alaska. That remote experience was coming in handy now that the small Fort Morgan Dunes group was isolated from the rest of the world.

Hampton Roads, Virginia—Saturday, July 28

The United States had a long record of helping other countries in time of need—from the earthquakes in Haiti to the Indonesian tsunami, going all the way back to the Marshall Plan that helped Europe recover from World War Two. Because of that, countries around the world, many of whom had been helped by the U.S. at one time or another now rose to the occasion offering aid to the stricken nation that had fallen from such great heights.

Three cargo ships, the *Abdul,* the *Kishwan,* and the *Sahil,* their containers filled with food and goods, left Yazikistan bound for the United States. All three were flying proud banners proclaiming:

Friendship from the Islamic Republic of Yazikistan

After crossing the ocean together, the three ships parted company off the coast of the U.S., then sailed on for three separate destinations: Boston, New York, and Hampton Roads.

As the three ships separated, Ariz Khabir Jawwad, who was on the *Kishwan* bound for Hampton Roads, went to the container that was labeled RICE.

Buried in the rice inside this container was a Russian SS-25 nuclear warhead, with an effective charge of one hundred kilotons, which was eight times more powerful than the bomb that was dropped on Hiroshima. There was also a similar nuclear warhead on each of the other two relief ships.

Jawwad recalled the briefing he and the other two martyrs for Allah had received, prior to being dispatched on their mission.

"We expect the initial casualties from the three bombs to exceed one million in number. That figure does not include those deaths that will come indirectly from disease or other longer-term fatalities. The overall effect of an attack on this scale is particularly numbing. Anyone trying to flee will find themselves travelling through contaminated areas. The pollution of water supplies, destruction of homes, and general devastation will result in secondary problems with disease. Radiation reduces the body's ability to fight off illness. The final number of deaths from the martyrdom would then be much higher."

Jawwad thought of the others on board this ship, and the two other ships. They were completely unaware that one of the cargo containers held a nuclear bomb. When Jawwad detonated the bomb it would not only kill the American infidels, it would also kill everyone on board this ship and most of them were, like Jawwad, Muslims, true members of the faith. In addition, as Jawwad had been a crew member of the *Kishwan* for the last three years, he had made many close friends among the other crew members on board. When he had mentioned to his trainers that innocent Muslims would die, he was told that he would be doing them all a favor.

"They will be welcomed into heaven as martyrs who died for the faith. Worry not about them."

The *Kishwan* dropped anchor in Hampton Roads at 9 A.M. local time. It was a coordinated arrival; the *Abdul* would be in New York and the *Sahil* would be in Boston at exactly the same time. This had been carefully arranged so the mercy missions of the three ships would achieve maximum exposure in the world press.

Jawwad checked his watch. It had been agreed by the three martyrs that they would detonate the bombs at exactly nine-thirty. Jawwad watched the minute hand reach the number six, and waited fifteen seconds until the sweep hand reached the number twelve.

"Allah Akbar!" he shouted.

"Jawwad, why do you . . ."

The light was so brilliant that people as far away as Richmond saw it. A huge fireball rolled out across the water, touching the land on each side. The heat inside the fireball was hotter than the sun and the ship was vaporized.

At the same time the bomb at Hampton Roads was detonated, the bombs in New York and Boston also exploded.

Concurrent with the nuclear blasts in the U.S., one nuke was detonated in Spain, one in France, one in Germany, and one in Great Britain. Three nuclear-tipped missiles were launched into Israel.

The governments of Iran, Iraq, Libya, Syria, Afghanistan, Lebanon, and Saudi Arabia received a message from Caliph Rafeek Syed demanding that they recognize the Greater Islamic Caliphate of Allah, with him as the grand caliph. Every government contacted acquiesced to the demand.

Fort Rucker—Monday, July 30

Although it had been two days since the nuclear bombs had been detonated on American soil, Jake Lantz knew nothing about them. General von Cairns had been dead for almost two weeks, and not only had the Department of the Army not appointed a new base commander, Jake was convinced that DA didn't even know General von Cairns was dead. For that matter, Jake wasn't entirely convinced that there even was a Department of the Army anymore.

Lieutenant Colonel Dave Royal, who was director of the Aviation Maintenance Course, had contacted Jake shortly after the funeral, asking if Jake knew of anyone remaining on the base who might outrank him. When Jake said he did not, Colonel Royal asked if Jake thought he should assume command.

"I think it is entirely up to you, Dave," Jake replied. "The truth is, I know and you know there is nothing left to command. Most of the officers and nearly all of the men are gone now. The only people left behind are those who have no other place to go."

"I think you are right," Colonel Royal said. "But I'm not one who likes loose ends, so if you have no objection, I think I will assume command."

That was ten days ago, and Jake had heard nothing from Lieutenant Colonel Royal since that time, and wasn't even sure Royal was still on the base. And that brought Jake to the moment of truth. He knew that there was no longer any reason for him to stay. His Army career had come to an end, and it was time for him to activate his survival team.

Pulling a yellow tablet from his desk, Jake began studying the names he had written. He had personally chosen everyone whose name was on the tablet, using three things for his governing criteria. First, each must possess a skill set that would be beneficial to the team as a whole, since he was convinced that they would be completely self-contained for a long time. Second, they must all be single. He had nothing against married people, but he was going to limit this team to no more than eight members, and spouses would be excess baggage. Third, he had to know them personally, and he had to like them.

The first name on his list was Karin Dawes.

CAPTAIN KARIN DAWES

If you had asked any of Karin's childhood friends about her, they would all say that the last thing any of them ever expected was for Karin to wind up in the Army. Would they think of her as a nurse? Perhaps. All agreed that she was someone who tended to look out for others, but nobody expected her to become an Army nurse. And certainly no one ever thought of her being in a combat zone, though not because anyone questioned her courage or her physical stamina. Karin had always been very athletic.

Karin was a distance runner and a cheerleader, both in high school and at the University of Kentucky.

She continued to run after graduating from college and last year she came in first place among all women in both the Atlanta and the Chicago marathons.

While in college, Karin fell in love and planned to be married upon graduation. But only three days before the wedding, Tony Mason, her fiancé, was killed in a car wreck. Karin was so distraught by the event that she joined the Army. She was sent to Afghanistan immediately after her training, and there, she encountered a captain with severe wounds to his face, side, and leg. The wound in his leg got infected and there was a strong possibility that it would have to be amputated, but Karin made a special effort to tend to the wound, keeping him dosed with antibiotics, keeping it clean and aspirated, and treating it with antiseptic, sometimes spending the night in the room with the patient in order to attend to it. The captain's leg was saved. Dr. Metzger told the wounded officer, Captain Jake Lantz, that Karin had saved his leg.

It was not entirely by coincidence that when they returned to the States, they both wound up at Fort Rucker, Alabama. Karin thought she would never feel about another man as she had felt about Tony, but Jake Lantz had changed her mind. She would marry him in a minute if he would ask her, and if he didn't ask her, she might just ask him.

Sergeant Major Clay Matthews

Tactical officers in Officer Candidate School can be particularly brutal on the officer candidates, and if the TAC officers find some peculiarity, they can make it very hard. When the TACs learned that Jake had been raised Amish, they used it as a tool to try to break him. They called him "Amish boy" and asked if he knew how to drive a car, or turn on a light.

Sergeant Clay Matthews was a TAC NCO, and one day when the TAC officers were enjoying a field day with Jake, Sergeant Matthews called the young officer candidate to one side, telling the others that he would "get the candidate straight." When he was sure that the TAC officers were out of earshot, Clay spoke to Jake in a quiet and reassuring voice.

"Son, don't let these TACs get under your skin. They are paid to be assholes and they take their jobs seriously. But I've been watching you, and the truth is you've got more sand than anyone in this class, including the TACs. Stick with it; you are going to make a fine officer, one I would be proud to serve under."

Jake did graduate, then went almost immediately to college. After he got his degree he went to flight school, and after flight school he did serve with Sergeant Matthews in Iraq. During their service together, he took special pleasure in submitting Sergeant Matthews's name for the Silver Star when the sergeant pulled four of his fellow soldiers from a burning Humvee, then killed the six militants who had attacked them.

For the moment, Clay Matthews, who was forty-eight years old and divorced, was the noncommissioned officer in charge of Environmental Flight Tactics, Jake's department. At least he had been the NCOIC while EFT still existed.

Jake valued dependability above all else in the people he worked with, and Clay was the most dependable man, soldier or civilian, Jake had ever known. If you asked Clay to take care of a job, you could put that job out of your mind, because Clay would take care of it. He would be, Jake was sure, his most valuable asset in setting up a survivalist team. With him, Jake felt confident of success. Without him, it would be iffy at best.

Sergeants John Deedle and Marcus Warner

Deedle and Warner were helicopter mechanics who worked on the flight line. In all the time Jake had been in the Army he had never run across any who were better at their job, or any two men who better complemented each other's work. And their skills weren't limited just to aircraft maintenance. The two men were among the most resourceful he had ever met.

At twenty-four, Deedle was the younger of the two. By general consensus, John Deedle was the best mechanic on the base. Some swore he was the best in the Army. He was quick to diagnose problems, knew all the special tools and parts, and could, if asked, even though it was against Army procedures, disassemble and rebuild, fashioning parts if need be to fit any engine, transmission, or rotor component.

Marcus Warner was twenty-six and had been married, but was now divorced. He had no children and his wife had since remarried, so he had no obligations that would detract from his being a team member. Marcus Warner's mother had been born in Italy and immigrated to the U.S. when she was twelve. He grew up speaking Italian and English, but demonstrated a flair for languages early in his life. After he joined the Army he went to its language school at Presidio. He was fluent in Italian, Spanish, Portuguese, French, and German. But, since the Army had no particular need for any of those languages, he applied for, and was accepted into, the helicopter maintenance course. He had pulled two tours in Iraq, and was now a technical inspector for the school's fleet of aircraft.

SERGEANT FIRST CLASS WILLIE STARK

Willie Stark was thirty years old. An avionics specialist, Stark could practically build a radio from scratch. He not only knew all the inner workings and hidden mechanisms of any radio, he could read and send messages in Morse code. Stark, whom others referred to as an "electronics geek," was a wizard around radios and computers, but was too shy to have much experience with women. He had never been married, and had never even had a serious relationship with a woman.

SERGEANT DEON PRATT

Deon Pratt, twenty-five, was a powerfully built black man who was an instructor in the Escape and Evasion course at Fort Rucker. The consummate warrior, Deon was skilled in hand-to-hand combat.

He was also an expert in firearms and explosives. Deon had won a Silver Star in Afghanistan for killing fifteen enemy fighters and rescuing, under fire, his captain and first sergeant who had been wounded and were trapped beneath a collapsed building. Jake had thought long and hard about including a combat expert, but he realized that if there was a complete breakdown of civilization, Sergeant Pratt would be a good man to have on his side.

SERGEANT JULIE NORTON

Sergeant Norton was Karin's recommendation. She worked in the hospital with Karin, primarily as a clerk, but the beautiful twenty-two-year-old black woman was an organizing genius, an efficiency expert who had taken the post hospital from a barely functioning mess to one of the best-organized hospitals in the Army.

Julie was from a mill town in Georgia, and when she was still in high school, she volunteered to work in the poorest sections, holding fund-raisers to buy food, tutoring the young, helping single mothers to cope. One day playing softball with some of the children, she saw two thugs attack an older woman who had just cashed her Social Security check. While others stood by doing nothing, Julie took the ball bat and drove both of them off before they could get the money.

* * *

So far, Jake had not shared his idea of forming a survival team with anyone except Karin and Clay Matthews. He was very familiar with the people he was considering, respected all of them, and knew that they respected him. And although he had not yet asked them to join him, he was certain that they would come if asked. In fact, he was so certain, that he had not considered anyone else.

The ringing phone surprised Jake. As there was no business being conducted anywhere on the base, the telephones had been quiet.

"Environmental Flight, Major Lantz," he answered, mouthing the Army answering formula of name, rank, and unit, even though none of it mattered any longer.

"Jake? Have you heard?" Even in Karin's quiet voice, Jake could hear the fear coming through.

"Have I heard what?"

"There were three nuclear bombs detonated day before yesterday, one in Boston, one in New York, and one Norfolk, Virginia."

"What! How do you know?"

"Dr. Urban has a shortwave radio. He picked up a radio station in Canada."

"And the Canadian station said there were three nukes here?"

"Yes, but it wasn't just here. There were bombs in England, France, Germany, Spain, and Israel too."

"What are the casualties here?"

"I don't know, I haven't heard. But it has to be

several million. Jake, the worst has happened, the absolute worst."

"Come to my office, Karin. Bring Sergeant Norton. I'm going to call the others. I think it is time we assembled our team."

CHAPTER FIFTEEN

Jake had invited everyone on his team to come to his house for dinner. Since it was getting increasingly more difficult to come by food, the meal would have been incentive enough, even if they hadn't been interested in his idea of a survival team.

Jake served Meals Ready to Eat—or MREs. He also had several containers of fresh water, having taken that precaution before the water stopped running. There was no electricity in his house, but there were several candles on the dining room table so there was adequate light. He had two Coleman lanterns, but he wasn't using them because he wanted to be sparing of the fuel.

His house was ten miles from the base and he wasn't sure if all would be able to find transportation, but was relieved when he saw that Deedle, Warner, and Stark had arrived with Clay in his Jeep Liberty. Deon Pratt and Julie Norton arrived with Karin in her Camry.

"Oh, a candlelight soirée," John Deedle teased

when they came into the candlelit house. "Been a while since I went to one of them."

"Ha," Marcus Warner said. "I can just see you at a candlelight soirée."

"I'm sorry that I can only serve MREs," Jake said as he passed out the little packets.

"Major, I haven't eaten since yesterday morning," Deon Pratt said. "To me, this is like a Thanksgiving feast." Pratt tore into the packet, emptied the food on his plate, then began wolfing it down, ravenously.

Jake held up his hand. "That's another thing," he said. "The Army is no more, so I am no longer a major. I am Jake, to all of you."

"Now, Major—I mean, Jake, for an old lifer like me, that's goin' to take a little gettin' used to," Clay Matthews said. "I've been in this Army, man and boy, for thirty-one years."

"It ought to be easier for you than anyone else, Clay," Jake teased. "I remember when I was an offi-cer candidate and you used to chew my ass."

"Yes, sir, well, sometimes your ass needed chewin'," Clay replied, and the others laughed.

"I know that Clay, Marcus, Willie, and John all know each other. Karin, you and Julie know each other. Deon and I know each other, so what I'd like is for you all to get acquainted while you are enjoy-ing the delicious meal that I spent all day preparing for you. After that, I'll tell you why I've gathered you together, and what I think we should do. I'm going to need two things from you. I'm going to need your willingness to participate, and I'm going to need some input as to how best to accomplish what we need to do."

"I'll get us started," Clay said. Clay was just over six feet tall, with a square jaw and a flat-top haircut. Dark at one time, his hair was now gray. "My name is Clay Matthews. I am a fourth-generation soldier, born at the base hospital at Fort Benning, Georgia. However, there is absolutely no truth to the rumor that I was issued on a DA form 3161."

The others laughed.

"I've known the major—that is, Jake—for almost twelve years, and he is as fine an officer as I ever served with. He has shared with me what he has planned, and I am happy to be a part of it, but I'm getting a little long in the tooth, so I just hope I can pull my own weight."

Clay sat down.

"Clay, you were only about a year younger than you are now when you pulled four men out of a burning Hummer just before it exploded. I'm pretty sure you can pull your weight with us," Jake said.

"I'll go next," John Deedle said. Deedle was very short, and had a rather large nose on his narrow face. He had heavy brows and deep-set, dark eyes. "I'm a mechanic, and the way Sarge—uh, that is Clay—was born to the Army, I was born to maintenance. My dad owned a mechanic shop—he worked on cars, tractors, trucks, anything that had an engine. When I was no more than five years old, my dad would hold me by my heels and dangle me down into engine compartments because I was small and could get to nuts and bolts."

Willie Stark held up his hand, and Clay nodded.

Willie Stark was average height and weight with red hair and light blue eyes, which seemed slightly enlarged behind his glasses. "I'm Willie Stark, I'm in avionics—that is, I was in avionics until the Army had no further use for me. I'm also what you might call a computer geek, but there isn't a lot of call for that right now, either. But I do like radios, all kinds of radios, and I built my first complete radio with I was twelve years old. Before that, I built a crystal radio set."

"What's a crystal radio?" Julie Norton asked.

"It's a radio that doesn't use power, doesn't need a battery or electricity. It gets its power from the radio waves themselves."

Willie sat down, and Julie stood. Julie was tall and willowy, a black woman with blemish-free skin that was the same shade of golden brown as a piece of toast. She had huge, almond-shaped, very dark eyes under long black lashes, a physical attribute that had served her well in the beauty contests she used to enter.

"I'm not sure why I was invited to join this group, except maybe because I know Captain—uh, that is, Karin Dawes. And if that is the only thing that got me in, then I'm thankful for it. About the only thing I'm good for is keeping track of things. And since we no longer have anything to keep track of, not even that talent is worth anything now."

"I think just the opposite is true," Jake said. "It is when things are very scarce that we need to keep track. And if we are going to succeed, we are going to have to be organized. Karin tells me that you are the best at that of anyone she has ever seen."

"Yes, sir, well, I guess I get that from my mama. She worked for Mr. Simmons at the mill, kept all his books for him, kept his schedule too. He wound up making her his second in charge. Oh, did that make my grandmother proud. My grandmother had never been anything but a maid and here was her daughter, my mama, bossing around white men who used to boss my grandmother. Anyway, Mama started me out by making me keep my own things neat and in order, and it just sort of grew from there."

"You are my friend, Julie," Karin said. "But more than that, you are someone we are going to need."

"I second that," Jake said. "Marcus? Or do you prefer Mark?" Jake asked.

"I've always gone by Marcus."

"All right, Marcus, what do you bring to the table?"

"Hola, mi nombre es Marcus Warner. Soy mecánico de aviones, y hablo seis lenguas," Marcus began. When he saw the others looking at other in confusion, he laughed. "I just told you my name, explained that I was an aircraft mechanic, and could speak in four languages. I spoke to you in Spanish, but could have spoken to you in French, Italian, German, or Portuguese. I don't know that we will run into anyone from any of those other countries, but if we do, we will be able to talk to them."

"Deon?" Jake said.

Deon Pratt was dark-skinned with wide shoulders, powerful arms, and a flat, rock-hard stomach. "My field is weapons, explosives, hand-to-hand combat," Deon said. I'm a warrior without a war. Hell, I'm a warrior without even an army. But I'm glad to be with you guys, and I'll do whatever I can to make this thing work."

Karin was last to introduce herself, stressing only that, as a nurse, she would do what she could to keep everyone healthy.

"Thanks," Jake said when all had finished. "Now I suppose it is time for me to tell you what I have in mind, and I can say it in one word. Survival."

"I'm all for surviving," John said. "Where do we start?"

"What I propose now is that we spend the next several hours rounding up as much survival gear as we can. As soon as we are ready, we'll leave this area and set up a survival base."

"Where are we going?" Clay asked.

"Fort Morgan."

"Where?" Deon asked.

"It's an old fort, built long before the Civil War, down at Mobile Point, a little spit of land that separates Mobile Bay from the Gulf of Mexico. You may have heard the term, 'Damn the torpedoes, full speed ahead.' Fort Morgan is where Admiral Farragut was when he ran under the guns of the fort, and through the mines that blocked the entrance into Mobile Bay."

"What's at the fort now?" Willie asked.

"Now, there is nothing there but old casements and stone walls. But inside the fort is a rather large area of arable land, probably the only place down on the beach that has real soil, rather than sand. We could grow a substantial garden there."

"Sounds good to me," Julie said. "I use to love to work in my grandma's garden."

"I've chosen Fort Morgan for a number of reasons," Jake said. "Number-one reason is perhaps, the most obvious. It is a fort, and as conditions deteriorate even further in the country, I believe there are going to be armed bands of hooligans preying on anyone and everyone they think might have something they could use. As we are going to be well off, relatively speaking, we would be a prime target for such groups. The fort will provide us with protection.

"And as I said, there is arable land inside the fort where we can grow vegetables. Plus, there will be plenty of fish, and there is a considerable amount of game, from rabbits to possum to alligators."

"Alligators?" Marcus said. "Alligators as game?"

"Fried alligator tastes . . ."

"Like chicken, right?" Willie interrupted, and the others laughed.

"Wrong," Jake said. "It's a lot better than chicken."

"How are we going to get there?" John asked. "What I mean is, how will we get enough gas to drive that far? For that matter, if there are going to be these roving gangs you are talking about, I'm not sure I want to drive through them. I saw what IEDs could do in Afghanistan, and there we were in up-armored Humvees, or even armored personnel carriers. I wouldn't want to face one of them in a car."

"We aren't driving down, we're flying. We'll take one of the helicopters from Fort Rucker. I don't think the Army will miss it."

"We may have a problem there, sir—I mean, Jake," Marcus said. "For the last month, people have been stripping the helicopters down pretty good. I know for a fact that we don't have one flyable ship on the entire base."

"I know that too," Jake said. "But that's where you and John will earn your keep. We're going to take parts from as many aircraft as we need in order to get one that is flyable."

"What about fuel?" Marcus asked.

Jake chuckled. "Clay, you want to handle this?"

"Several weeks ago, when the major saw this coming, he asked me to find some way to put a little fuel aside as an emergency. I have fifteen fifty-five-gallon drums of JP-4 hidden away."

"Wow! That will top off the tanks, and give us one hundred ten gallons extra," John said.

"That's right," Jake replied.

"I have a question," Deon said. "There are already a lot more civilians roaming around the base than there are soldiers—looking to see what they can rip off. If they see us building a helicopter, they are likely to give us some trouble."

"We'll find a secure hangar to build the helicopter," Jake said. "And, from this day forward, we will wear no uniforms. That way if anyone sees us messing around out there, they'll think we are no different from them, we are just trying to find something to trade."

"May I make a suggestion?" Deon asked.

"Of course you can."

"Wherever this hangar is, I think I had better provide a little security."

Jake smiled. "I was hoping you would say that."

"You going to move out onto the base, Jake?" Clay asked. "Because if you don't, this drive back and forth to town is going to get long, and use up what gasoline you have left"

"I am going to move onto the base. In fact I think we should all bivouac together in the hangar. But before we leave town, I suggest we go on a scavenger mission. We need to round up as much useful supplies as we can."

"From what I have heard, people have been looting stores for the last three weeks. I doubt there is much left," Willie said.

"Mostly they have been stealing canned goods, packaged foods, that sort of thing. Some of them have even been stealing TV scts, though God only knows why since there is no more television," Jake said. "We need to be a little more discriminating on what we take."

"Like what?" John asked.

"I've made a list," Jake replied. Opening a drawer on the bar that separated the kitchen from the dining room, he began reading from the list. "A multi-tool knife, compass, flashlight with the windup generators, first-aid kits, blankets, matches, a lighter or lighters if we can come up with them, sunscreen, mosquito repellent, whistles and signal mirrors, nylon cord—that we can get from parachutes, and we'll use the parachute canopies as well. I already have two parachutes laid aside. Anyone have something they would like to add?"

"How about MREs?" Deon asked.

Jake smiled. "Are you enjoying these?"

"Yeah, but I'm weird, I always have liked MREs."

"Good, because we have fifteen cases of them down in the basement. That's one hundred eighty meals, which will last us for a little under two weeks if we have no more than two meals per day."

"What happens at the end of that two weeks? Marcus asked.

"Fish, game, whatever wild vegetables we can come up with. If we haven't found a way to be self-sustaining within two weeks, then we probably wouldn't make it anyway," Jake said. "Any other suggestions?"

"How about some tablets and pencils?" Julie asked.

"Yes, very good idea."

"How about toilet paper?" Karin added. "I mean this roughing it goes only so far."

"Toilet paper is good," Jake said. "But no matter how much of it we round up, there is going to come a time when we go through it. Then we'll have to come up with something else."

"Well, hell, Jake, if we can't find enough food, maybe we won't even be needing any toilet paper," Marcus said, and the others laughed.

"I'd rather face the problem of having to find toilet paper," Clay said.

"Me too," Willie agreed.

"If we are going to maintain this helicopter once we get down to Fort Morgan, we are going to need a full mechanic's toolbox, as well as some special tools," John said.

"If I have guessed right about you, you have your toolbox hidden away somewhere," Jake said.

John smiled. "Yeah, I do."

"We'll also be needing some replacement parts, especially filters, gaskets, and so forth," Marcus added.

"And at least one machine gun to mount in the doors," Deon said.

"You're right, an M240 machine gun might not be a bad thing to have once we get down to the fort," Clay said.

"Where are we going to find those?" Marcus asked. "Weapons were about the first things to go— a lot of soldiers sold them to civilians."

"I know where there is an untapped armory," Deon said. "M240s, M16s, pistols, ammunition. I don't know anything about repairing helicopters, and I don't know if we are going to have enough food to sustain us. But I know for a fact that we will be heavily armed."

"Good man," Jake said.

"What about radios?" Willie asked.

"I've been anticipating this for a while now," Jake said. "I have two Midland Radios, XT511 base camp emergency crank radios with GMRS two-way radio technology—AC, DC or hand-crank charger for BATT5R batteries."

"Wow, you went all out, didn't you?" Willie said.

"I'm reasonably sure there will be some, at least, shortwave radio out there. If there is, we will need to access it and, perhaps, to communicate with others like us."

"What about money?" Marcus asked.

Jake shook his head. "Money is only as good as the government that backs it," he said. "And as of now, we have no government."

"Gold coins?"

"No. Gold might be good if there was a viable market. We not only don't have a government, we don't have a market. When you go 'shopping' tonight, just take what you find, but don't take it from anyone else unless you barter something for it. I am all for our survival, but I'm not ready to put someone else at risk."

"When do we get started?" Clay asked.

"We start now," Jake replied. "We'll go into every store and abandoned building in town. Also, the mall. Clay, you want to pass out the arms?"

Clay nodded, then walked over to the corner to an olive-drab B-4 bag. "I don't have as big an armory as Deon is talking about, but I've got enough for us to get by right now." Opening the bag, he pulled out an M9 pistol and held it up. "I have one of these for each of us," he said. All eight pistols have full, fifteen-round magazines, plus I have five hundred additional rounds of nine millimeter ammunition."

"Carry these pistols with you," Jake said, "but use

them only if it is absolutely necessary to defend yourself."

"I've never fired one of these," Julie said as she was given the pistol.

"It's easy enough," Deon said. "Here is the safety. When the safety is off, all you have to do is pull the trigger."

"I also have four flashlights and four small RadioShack special two-way radios. The small limited-range two-way radios will serve us well for keeping touch with each other. And four is all we will need, as we will deploy in two-man teams," Jake said.

"Good idea. And it is probably safer that we deploy in two-man teams," Deon said.

"Thanks for the endorsement," Jake said. "Karin, you go with me, and Julie, I suggest you go with Deon. The rest of you team up however you want." Jake looked at his watch. "It is nineteen thirty hours now, we will rendezvous back here at twenty-four hundred. Any questions?"

"Yeah, I have one," John said. "When we get to the checkout counter, do we ask for plastic or paper bags?"

The others laughed.

"Major, these radios are pretty standard," Willie said. "That means that anyone who wants to can listen in. I suggest that we adopt call signs, rather than use names."

"Good idea, Willie. How about you assign them?"

"Okay. You'll be Vexation Six."

"Negative," Clay spoke up quickly. "Six designates the commander. Anyone out there listening who has ever been in the Army will recognize that in a heartbeat. I think we should keep the call signs as innocuous as we can."

"Yeah," Willie said. "You are right. Okay, how about Mickey Mouse one through four?"

"Alright. Jake, you and Karin are Mickey Mouse One; John, you and Marcus are Mickey Mouse Two; Deon, you and Julie are Three; and Clay and I will be Mickey Mouse Four," Willie said.

"Let's test them out," Jake suggested.

The four radios were checked; then radios, pistols, and flashlights were tucked into pockets.

"Back here at twenty-four hundred," Jake reminded them as they left on their appointed rounds.

CHAPTER SIXTEEN

By the time Jake and Karin arrived, there was very little left of the Wal-Mart Supercenter on South 231. The doors had been smashed in, and Karin started to step inside, but Jake held out his hand to stop her.

"Wait," he whispered. "Let's make sure nobody else is in here."

The two stood quietly just inside the store for a long moment. The store was so dark that they couldn't see two feet in front of them, which meant that if anyone was here they would have to be using a light, and the light could be seen.

They saw no light, and they heard no sound. After waiting about a minute, Jake turned on the large flashlight he was carrying.

"I think we've got it all to ourselves, such as it is," Jake said.

As the moved deeper inside they could see that what merchandise did remain was scattered around on the floor. There was a large yellow smiley face next to a sign that said SHOP WAL-MART.

Jake moved the light back and forth on the floor so they could see to pick their way through without tripping over anything.

Though the food products, clothing, and small utensils had been well cleaned out, the large-ticket items, TVs, etc., remained. Under ordinary circumstances, this would have been strange, but because there were no television stations broadcasting anywhere in America, at least as far as Jake knew, seeing the TV sets still sitting on the shelves wasn't at all surprising. However many of the TV sets had been smashed, not incidentally, but purposely, as an expression of anger and frustration.

Over each empty aisle in the food store were signs that told what product had once been there. Now the signs were little more than a tantalizing tease.

COOKIES, CRACKERS, CHIPS, AND SNACKS

RICE, BEANS, SPAGHETTI, NOODLES

SOUPS, CANNED MEAT

COLD AND HOT CEREALS

COFFEE, SOFT DRINKS

"Soft drinks," Karin said. "Do you think . . . ?"

"I bought the last root beer they had when they were still doing business," Jake said.

There was not one food item remaining anywhere in the store. Not even bulk, uncooked items, such as rice, flour, or beans.

In the book and magazine section, there were several soft-cover books scattered around on the floor.

"Let's grab as many of these as we can," Jake suggested. "Without TV or radio, I expect reading will be about our only source of entertainment."

"Good idea," Karin replied. "What do you like?"

"Westerns, action stories, just about anything, I guess. I think we are far beyond the ability to be choosy."

"Look, tablets and pencils," Karin said, scooping up several of them from the same aisle as the books. "This will please Julie."

As they moved on through the store, Jake saw a box underneath a turned-over stocking shelf. Pushing the shelf out of the way he saw that the box, though not completely full, had at least ten packages of "sandwich cookies, peanut-butter filling."

"Whoa, now this is going to be a treat," he said, stuffing the cookies down into the large, canvas bag.

"Where to now?" Karin asked.

"Let's go to the garden shop," Jake suggested.

Amazingly, the garden shop was virtually untouched. There, Jake found a wheelbarrow, which he loaded with a couple of watering cans, spades, rakes, and dozens of packets of seed from half a dozen vegetables. Here, too, he found insect repellent and he put as many cans as he could into the wheelbarrow.

"Wait," Jake said, stopping at one shelf. "These are the seeds we want."

"What do you mean? What's wrong with what we have?

"These are non-hybrid seeds. I can't believe there are so many of them."

"What are non-hybrid seeds?"

"Almost all the vegetables we see today are hybrids. Hybrid vegetables make the best vegetables, but they can't be counted on to produce seed that will reproduce. For that you need seeds in their original form. That's what this is."

Jake scooped up several packets, getting much more seed than he would need.

"If we can stay alive until these seeds produce, we'll be in good shape," Jake said.

Karin laughed. "Oh, great. All we have to do is stay alive? Yes, I'm for that."

Finally, with a completely stuffed B-4 bag on top of the filled wheelbarrow, Jake and Karin stepped back through the smashed doors and started across the nearly vacant parking lot toward Jake's Volvo.

Jake saw a pickup truck parked next to his car, and he knew, at once, that the pickup truck driver was either siphoning, or about to siphon, gas from his car. He heard a loud, crunching sound, and realized that the driver had not started yet because he had been held back by the locked cover over the gas cap.

Jake set the wheelbarrow down and ran quickly toward his car. The gas thief had a tire iron and was trying to pry up the cover. He was so intent on breaking into the gas tank that he had not seen Jake approach.

"Mister, I paid an arm and a leg for that gasoline and I don't intend to stand by and watch you steal it," Jake said.

Jake's voice startled the would-be thief, and he glanced up at Jake with a wild look in his eyes. He raised the tire iron he was using over his head.

"Stay back, Major," he said, remembering Jake's military rank. "Stay back or I'll lay your head open."

"You recognized me," Jake said. "Are you a soldier?"

"I was. But there ain't nobody a soldier no more, not even you," the wild-eyed young man said. "And you bein' a major don't mean jack shit to me no more. So you just stand over there—sir." He slurred the word *sir*, setting it apart to show his disdain. "And soon as I drain your tank, I'll be on my way."

Jake pulled his pistol and pointed it at the young man. "Son, you need to learn not to bring a tire iron to a gunfight. Now my recommendation to you is that you climb in your truck and you drive away. Otherwise I'll just have to shoot you."

Seeing the gun in Jake's hand, the young man's demeanor changed. No longer belligerent, he lowered the tire iron he had been using to pry open the gas-cap cover.

"All right, all right, I'm goin'," the young man said, holding one hand out in front of him, palm facing Jake as if by so doing, he could hold Jake off. He glanced at the right rear quarter of Jake's car. The paint was badly scratched and dented where he had been working to open the gas-cap cover. "I, uh, I'm sorry I messed up your car."

"Don't talk anymore," Jake said, coldly. "You piss me off every time you open your mouth. Just shut up, get in your truck, and drive away from here."

The young man threw the tire iron into the back of his truck, hurried around to the driver's side, got in, and drove away.

"Come on, Karin!" Jake shouted. "Let's get out of here."

By midnight everyone had returned to Jake's house and they put their acquisitions together to see how well they had done.

Clay and Marcus scored two five-gallon cans of gasoline. Jake didn't ask where, or how, they got it.

Deon and Julie returned with fifty pounds of flour, ten pounds of sugar, twenty pounds of rice, twenty-five pounds of dried beans, and five gallons of cooking oil.

"Where did you find this?" Jake asked. "I can't imagine any grocery store or warehouse still having any of this left."

"We got it from a VFW kitchen," Deon said.

"Whoa, good thinking."

"It was Julie's idea."

"My aunt used to work as a cook in the VFW back in Georgia," Julie said. "I know her kitchen was always well stocked and I thought there was a chance that nobody would think to look there."

"We also got this," Deon said, pulling something out of a sack. It was a bullhorn and he held it up to his mouth, then pulled the talk trigger.

"Jumpers in the air, you have a sixty-knot wind coming from your right!"

"Whoa!" Clay said, laughing. "That's a hell of a wind to be jumping into."

"Maybe for a leg," Deon teased. "Not for an airborne troop like me."

"I'm glad you came up with that thing," Jake said.

"Why, what are we going to use it for?" Karin asked.

"You heard Deon. What if we see some paratroopers in the air? We might have to give them directions."

The others laughed.

"Okay, you guys did well. You did very well in fact," Jake said. "So now, I suggest we spend the rest of the night here, then go out to the post in the morning. Our first order of business will be to find a hangar we can secure; second will be to find a helicopter we can put into flying condition."

The next morning the eight gathered for breakfast in Jake's dining room, again eating MREs though, as Jake explained, these were from a broken case and not part of the fifteen cases he had for their survival supplies.

Karin looked around the dining room, gray walls

set off by a large seascape painting, a dark blue carpet, and off-white upholstered chairs.

Jake saw where she was looking and he reached out to put his hand on hers. "You are thinking about this room and how we decorated it together, aren't you?"

"Jake, will we ever come back here?"

"I don't know," Jake replied. "I know that's not what you wanted to hear, but I have to be honest with you. I truly don't know if we will ever be able to come back or not. And if we do come back, what will we find?"

Karin nodded. "I know," she said. "And I'm okay with it."

Jake squeezed her hand, then looked over toward Willie.

"Willie, what do you say we crank up one of these radios and see if we can pick up any news on the shortwave bands?" he suggested.

"Good idea, yes, let's see what's out there," Clay agreed.

Willie cranked the radio for one minute; then he turned it on and started sweeping through the frequencies.

"Getting carrier waves," he said. "That's good."

"What does that mean?"

"That means there are some transmitting stations that are still up, just nobody talking on them right now."

Marcus continued to turn the dial until he picked up a woman's voice. She was clearly on the edge of panic.

"Someone, anyone," she was saying. "Can anyone hear me? This is Yellowbird. Can anyone hear me?"

Willie keyed the microphone.

"Yellowbird, this is Mickey Mouse. Over."

"Mickey Mouse, oh, thank God! There is someone out there!" The woman practically shouted in her excitement.

"Where are you, Yellowbird? What is your status? Over."

"I'm in Portsmouth, Virginia, real close to where the bomb went off."

"Are you safe?" Marcus asked.

"Safe? What is safe? We weren't hurt by the bomb, but I don't know about the radiation. We are so close."

"You say we. Who is we?"

"My husband, our two children, my brother and sister-in-law, and their three children."

"Are there others around?"

"Nobody that we want to associate with. There are a lot of men wandering around outside, shouting and breaking into houses and cars. We've heard screams and shooting. I've been trying to contact the police, but haven't been able to do so."

"What you need to do is get out of there," Willie said. "There are no police."

"How do you know there are no police? Oh!" In the background, Marcus could hear loud voices and the sound of shooting. "Can you hear that? Why don't the police come?"

"Yes, ma'am, I can hear it. But you can't count on the police. There has been a complete breakdown of all government agencics including the police. Do you have a car? And if so, do you have gasoline in your car?"

"I . . ." There was a long pause before the woman came back on the air. "My husband says I shouldn't answer that."

Now everyone was huddled around the radio listening to the woman's terrified voice from the other end, hearing, also, the shouts and the shooting.

"Your husband is correct, ma'am, you shouldn't tell," Willie said. "And I apologize for asking. But my advice to you is this. If you have a car with fuel, pack as much food, water, blankets, matches, and other such items as you might have, then get as far away from there as you can. The farther away from people you are, the safer you will be. Over."

There was a long silence, and Willie keyed the mic to speak again. "Yellowbird, do you read me? Over."

Still no reply.

"What happened?" Julie asked. "Why doesn't she answer?"

"I don't know." Willie keyed the mic again. "Yellowbird, if you can read me, pack as much food, water, blankets, matches, and other such items as you have, then get as far away from there as you can. Over."

"Good advice, dipshit," a man's gruff voice replied. "But the little lady and her family won't be needing it now. Over," he added with a malevolent laugh.

Willie did not respond. Instead he pinched the

bridge of his nose and shook his head. "Damn," he said quietly.

"See if you can find a broadcast somewhere," Jake suggested. "I mean a real news broadcast."

"Yeah," Willie said. "There's nothing we can do for Yellowbird."

Willie continued turning the dial, picking up whistles, static, sidetones, and carrier waves.

> *El gobierno Mexicano ha cerrado la frontera para impedir a Estadounidenses de inundar nuestro país.*

"What is he saying?" Jake asked Marcus.

Marcus chuckled. "How is this for irony? He is saying that the Mexican government has closed its borders to keep Americans from flooding into their country."

"See if you can find something in English," Clay said.

Willie turned the dial again, finally picking up an English broadcast.

> *. . . broadcasting over this shortwave frequency in the hope that there are some people out there with shortwave radios who can hear us.*

"Hey, that's George Gregoire," Jake said. "I recognized his voice."

"Damn, I used to watch him," Clay said. "I thought they drug him off and killed him."

"Evidently not. Let's see what he has to say," Jake said.

Everyone drew close to the radio.

Hello, America.

I can't tell you where I am. As I'm sure you know, I am now a wanted man. I never broadcast from the same place twice for fear of the SPS homing in on my radio signal. And to be honest with you, I don't even know if there is an SPS anymore.

I have a small group of dedicated people with me and they have been tuning in to shortwave broadcasts from around the world. We do that so we can keep you up to date on what is going on.

It has always been my belief that the peril we know is much less dangerous than the peril we don't know. And, as of now, this is what we know.

There were three nuclear bombs detonated on our soil. One in New York, one in Boston, and one in Virginia. These were not small bombs, certainly not the "suitcase" bombs that were, for so long, the stuff of novels and action movies. The bombs were huge, and the devastation is great. It is believed that the bombs were smuggled into the country inside large cargo containers on board container ships.

There has been no word from any official of the New World Collective government, that is assuming that there is a government. We don't know if the supreme leader of the New World . . ."

Gregoire paused in mid-broadcast for a moment; then, with a sigh, he continued.

To hell with that New World Collective nonsense, he said. *I intend to refer to our country, or what is left of it, as the United States. And I think I am perfectly safe in doing so, since if we do have any government left, they are totally impotent now. We have tried to make contact by shortwave with anyone in Washington, D.C., who could give us some information on the status of Ohmshidi— indeed, the status of our country. They say that there is a silver lining to every cloud. It is hard to find one to this cloud, but if there is, it is that the government, and if I may be so bold, Ohmshidi, are no longer functioning.*

As some of you may have heard on our initial broadcast, the United States was not the only nation to suffer these brutal nuclear attacks. Much of Europe seems to be in chaos right now, though they are not as bad as we are. We still don't know anything about Israel, other than the fact that they were hit by at least three, and maybe more, nuclear missiles.

America, is there any question as to how and why all this has happened? For nearly a century now, going back to the First World War, America has been the bulwark of freedom and democracy. We defended Europe in the First World War, we freed Europe in the Second World War, and we stood at their side during the long, frightening days of the Cold War.

But the first thing Ohmshidi did when he took office was pull all American soldiers back from their overseas assignments. Then he systematically disarmed us, while at the same time destroying our nation from within. Without a strong America, there is nothing left to stand between the world and the evil that would engulf the world.

I cannot but hope that there are groups of you hearing my voice now, groups of you who have taken the necessary steps to survive. And, once survival is assured, it is my hope that we will come together again, reclaim our nation, and once more be a united country under the Stars and Stripes.

And now, a word about who we are, and why and how we are broadcasting. As I am sure everyone within the sound of my voice is aware, there are no longer any television networks, or even television stations that are broadcasting. Those of us who are continuing with the shortwave 'casts are no longer employed, nor are we being compensated. But we do this because we are newsmen and women, first, last, and always. We do it because we must. And if providing news to a shattered people who are desperate for information serves a mission greater than ourselves, then we are compensated enough.

I am signing off now, but will broadcast again sometime tomorrow. I'm sorry I can't be more specific as to the time, but for now, I must err on the side of caution.

This is George Gregoire saying, good night, America, and God bless us all.

Chapter Seventeen

"Do we have a name?" Julie asked.

"A name?" Clay replied.

"This group," Julie said. "Do we have a name?"

"I don't know. I hadn't really thought of a name," Jake said.

"We've got to have a name," Julie said.

"All right. Do you have a suggestion?"

"Yes, as a matter of fact, I do have a suggestion," Julie said.

"What?"

"I think we should call ourselves Phoenix."

"Phoenix?" John asked.

"Julie explained. "I mean the United States of America, the country we all took an oath to serve, is dead as far as most people are concerned. Except us—we're going to make it rise from the ashes."

"Yeah," Deon said. "I like it."

"Phoenix," Clay said. He nodded. "It does have a ring to it."

"I like it," Karin said.

"Me, too," Marcus added.

"Alright," Jake said, smiling. "Hereinafter, we will be known as Phoenix."

"Well then, in that case we should change our radio call sign from Mickey Mouse to Phoenix," Willie suggested.

"I agree," Jake said. "From now on my call sign is Phoenix One."

"I've got somethin' else to bring up," Clay said.

"Now's the time to do it," Jake replied.

"Major—I mean, Jake, I know you said we aren't in the Army anymore. But the truth is, while we were in the Army, we had a standard operating procedure. And even if we aren't in the Army, I think we still need some structure. I mean, all you have to do is look at what's going on all around us now to know that we must have some SOP. I know you don't want to be a major anymore, but how about you taking charge, as a civilian, of our group?"

"We are all together in this," Jake said. "I don't want to presume."

"You wouldn't be presuming, and I agree with Clay," John said. "We do need some SOP, and you are the one who started Phoenix, so I think it only makes sense that you be our leader. We can still remain on a first-name basis." John smiled. "I sort of like calling officers by their first names."

"I concur," Marcus said. "Jake should be our leader."

"Count me in," Deon added.

Willie, Julie, and Karin quickly added their own support for the idea.

"Alright," Jake said. "I accept. Now, what do you say we get back out to the post and get busy?"

"Go out to the post and get busy? Jesus, give the man a little authority and he goes all power mad on us," John said.

The others laughed.

The Dunes, Fort Morgan—Tuesday, July 30

"Ellen, where is my typewriter?" Bob Varney asked.

"It's in the very back of the storeroom off your office," Ellen said. "Way in the back. Why do you ask?"

"I'm going to write," Bob said.

"I really . . ." Ellen started to say that she really thought it would be a waste of time, but she stopped in midsentence. She had lived with this man for over forty years and she knew him inside out. And she knew that he needed to write, and if truth be told, she needed it as well. She needed a sense of continuity to her life, and having her husband write books, whether they were ever published or not, was that continuity.

"I really think that is a good idea," she said.

Bob leaned over to kiss her. "Thanks for not trying to talk me out of it," he said.

It had been almost thirty years since Bob Varney last used a typewriter, but he had kept his old Smith-Corona portable all those years, keeping it in good shape, and keeping it in fresh typewriter ribbons. Retrieving it from the back of the storeroom, he opened the case, then blew and brushed the dust and cobwebs away. That done, he rolled two pieces of paper into the typewriter, using the second page as a pad against the platen because when he took typing in high school his typing teacher, Miss Sidwell, had told her students to do that.

Using the lever, he counted down eleven double-spaces before he typed:

                    Lilies Are for Dying
                              by
                        Robert Varney
                        Chapter One

John Hughes had what is called a very
structured personality. Every morning he had
one soft-boiled egg, a dry piece of toast, and
half a grapefruit. He drove to work by the
same route every day, and crossed the
intersection of Greer and Elm at exactly
the same time. That's why he was passing
Elmer's Liquor Store just in time to see
Elmer being shot.

"Charley, listen to this and tell me what you think," Bob said to his dog. He read the opening paragraph aloud. "Is that a grabber?"

Charley was lying under the desk with his head on Bob's foot. This was the normal position for writer and dog when a book was in progress. But that was the only normal thing about the setup. Bob was writing this book on a typewriter, and he knew this book was going nowhere.

His agent had told him that he need not waste his time writing any of the three books that remained on his contact, but his agent didn't understand. Bob didn't write because it was his job, Bob wrote because he *had* to write.

He returned to the book, listening to the tap, tap, tap of the keys, remembering that sound from years ago and, oddly, being comforted by it, as if it could take him back to another time and another place when things were as they should be.

As he continued to write through the morning, the pages began to pile up on the right side of the typewriter, and he remembered that as well, recalling the sense of satisfaction he got from watching the pile of pages grow. He had mentioned to his father once how he enjoyed watching the pile of pages grow, and his father, who had been a farmer, compared it to watching a crop being "made," as in "Are you making any cotton?" It's funny, Bob didn't realize until now, how much he missed watching the pile of pages grow. Seeing the word-count number increase at the bottom of the computer screen was never the same thing.

From his office he could see the Gulf through the front windows and Mobile Bay through the back windows. He saw a boat about a mile offshore and figured it must be a fishing boat. Was he catching fish to eat? Or to barter? Probably a little of both, he decided.

"It is good to see you writing, again," Ellen said, coming up behind him and putting her hands on his shoulders.

"You do realize that it is a complete exercise in futility, don't you?" Bob asked.

"Not futile," Ellen said. "It doesn't matter that it isn't going anywhere, it is restoring a sense of balance to our lives. It gives the illusion that everything is as it was, and I need that. We need it."

Bob lifted her hand to his lips and kissed it. "We were born twenty years too late," he said.

"Why do you say that?"

"If we had been born twenty years earlier, we would more than likely be gone by now, and we would have left the world while it was still sane."

"What's going to happen to us, Bob?"

"Nothing," Bob said. "We're going to ride it out and, in the long run, we'll be okay. Just don't be planning any trips to New York or Chicago. Or even into Gulf Shores," he said.

"Maybe I'll start my romance novel," Ellen said.

"Ha! You've been saying you were going to write a romance novel for the last forty-five years."

"I know, but other things kept coming up," Ellen said. "This time I'm going to do it, for sure. I've got a bunch of yellow tablets and a bunch of pencils. And the time to do it."

"Good for you," Bob said. "You start it. If you need help, just ask."

Fort Rucker—Wednesday, August 1

Jake and Karin were the last two to leave Ozark and head out to Fort Rucker, the others having left two days earlier. They were halfway to the post when they saw a pickup truck with a trailer, crossways on the road, blocking any possibility of passage.

"I wonder what this is?" Karin said.

The truck and the trailer were both filled with furniture, bedding, boxes, barrels, and crates.

"Looks like someone is trying to move all their belongings," Jake replied as he stopped the car and put it in park. "My guess is they were trying to turn around and got hung up with the trailer. I'll see if I can help."

Getting out of the car, Jake started toward the pickup truck. That was when someone stepped around the front of the truck. The man was wearing black pants, a black T-shirt, and a black headband. He also had a holstered pistol strapped to his belt. That didn't concern Jake—many had taken to wearing pistols since the total collapse of the republic. Jake was also carrying a pistol, but it was under the flap of his shirt and so not immediately visible.

"Can I help you?" Jake asked.

"Oh, yeah, you can help me," the man replied.

"What can I do for you?"

"Well, it's like this. You see this truck? It don't have enough gas in it to even get me back to Ozark. But seein' as you was drivin' your car, it looks to me like you do have gas. So what I'm goin' to do is, I'm gonna give you a can and a rubber hose." He put his hand on his pistol and patted it a couple of times. "And what you are going to do for me is siphon out all the gas that's in your tank and fill this can."

Jake pulled his pistol and pointed at the man. "No, I don't think so," he said.

"Whoa, I didn't know you were carrying," the man said, holding both hands up, palms facing Jake.

"Apparently not. Now, I'm going to ask you real nice to get that truck off the road and out of my way," Jake said.

To Jake's surprise, the man dropped his hands and chuckled. "You don't seem to understand what's at stake here," he said. "I don't know if that pretty little woman back there is your girlfriend or your wife, but if you don't do what I told you to do, my friend is going to put a bullet through her head."

Jake turned back toward his car and saw that Karin was now out on the road, standing just in front of a man who was holding a pistol to her head. This man, like the one who had confronted Jake, was wearing black pants, a black T-shirt, and a black headband.

"Better do what my friend says, mister, unless you want to see this woman's brains on the highway."

"You would shoot an innocent woman over a can of gasoline?" Jake asked.

"Oh, yeah, you can count on it," the man replied.

"I'm sorry, Jake," Karin said. "He must have been lying in the ditch alongside the road. I didn't see him come up."

"Let her go," Jake said, pointing his pistol at the man who was holding his gun to Karin's head.

"Ha! Is that pistol supposed to scare me?" the man replied. "You're a good sixty feet away from me—I'm only about six inches away from your woman. You really think you are good enough to shoot me, without hitting her?"

"How about those Kentucky Wildcats?" Jake asked.

"Say what?" the man with the gun replied.

"I like the cheerleaders," Jake said.

"Man, are you crazy or what? Can't you see I've got your woman here? Now are you going to fill that gas can or . . ."

At first Karin was confused by Jake's comment; then she smiled as she knew exactly what he meant. Suddenly Karin did a backflip, vaulting completely over the head of the man who was holding a gun on her.

"What the . . . ?"

That was as far as the gunman got because as he turned toward Karin, Jake took his shot. Blood and brain matter spewed out from the entry wound in the temple.

Because Jake had turned to take his shot, his back was now to the man standing in front of the pickup truck.

"You son of a bitch!" the man yelled.

Jake whirled back on the would-be gasoline thief, shooting him between the eyes even as the man was bringing his own pistol up.

"Are you all right?" Jake called back to Karin.

"Yes," Karin replied. She looked down at the man who had been holding his gun on her; then she walked up to Jake. "It took me a second to figure out what you were saying."

"You figured it out quickly enough. You did well."

"Were they soldiers, do you think?" Karin asked.

"There are no soldiers anymore," Jake answered.

Karin knew that Jake did not want to think that he had shot two men who may have, just recently, served in the same army with him, so she didn't press the issue any further.

"I'll get the truck out of the way," Jake said. Climbing in behind the wheel, he turned on the key and saw that the gas gauge didn't even come up to the E mark.

"I hope there's enough fuel to get it off the road," he said. He hit the starter and the engine kicked over. He drove it off the road and down into the ditch. Then, exiting the truck, he climbed back up to the road.

"What are we going to do with them?" Karin asked.

"What do you want to do with them?"

"I don't know. Somehow it doesn't feel right to just leave them both lying in the middle of the road."

"All right. I'll get them out of the road," Jake promised.

Grabbing one of them by his feet, Jake dragged him down into the ditch and left him by the truck. Then he returned and did the same thing to the other man. He started to go through their pockets to see if they had any identification, but stopped short because he realized that he didn't want to know who they were.

Returning to his car, he slid in behind the steering wheel and glanced over at Karin. She looked a bit queasy so she reached over to put his hand on hers.

"You did well," he said again.

"Jake, has it come to this?" Karin asked. "Is it going to be dog-eat-dog?"

"I'm afraid it is," Jake said. "But dogs run in packs. And we have our pack now."

Karin smiled, wanly. "Phoenix," she said.

"Phoenix," Jake repeated.

Three miles farther on Jake and Karin saw two people lying alongside the road. Jake slowed down enough to get a good look at them. It was an old man and a woman.

"Jake, stop." Karin said. "I have to check on them."

Jake stopped and Karin, getting out of the car, hurried over to the couple. She squatted down and felt for a pulse in each of them. "The woman is dead, but the man is alive," she said.

Both the man and the woman had been shot.

"Sir, what happened?" Jake asked.

"The sons of bitches took my truck," the old man said, straining to talk. "They took my truck and trailer. Had all our belongin's on it."

Jake looked at Karin and she shook her head, to tell him that the man didn't have long left.

"They shot Suzie," the man said. "Then they shot me. Dressed like pirates they were, all in black. The sons of bitches." He coughed a couple of times, then took one last rattling breath.

Karin tried his pulse again.

"He's dead," she said.

"Those murdering bastards," Jake said. "If I was feeling any twinge of regret before, I don't now."

"What are we going to do with them?" Karin asked. "We can't just leave them here like we did the other two. After what the other two did, they can lie out on the road until the buzzards pick them clean as far as I'm concerned. But these folks are innocent. They didn't do anything to bring this on."

"I've got an entrenching tool in the car," Jake said. "We sure can't give them anything like a proper burial, but you're right. We don't need to leave them out here, exposed to the elements."

Forty-five minutes later Jake and Karin stood over a fresh mound. Jake buried them both in the same grave. It kept him from having to dig two graves, but he was fairly certain they would have wanted to be buried together anyway. Before he buried them, he took the old man's billfold. It had pictures, a driver's license, but no money. But it didn't matter that there was no money, since money was worthless anyway. And at least now, he knew who they were.

"Mr. Theodore Fuller, Mrs. Suzie Fuller, I don't think I'll be able to find any of your next of kin to let them know what happened to you, but I hope there is some comfort that you didn't leave this world without someone knowing your names," Jake said. "I'm sorry your lives ended up like this. On the other hand, you did go out together, and you'll be together for all eternity now. And truth to tell, with what the rest of us are facing, you may well be the lucky ones."

Karin reached over and squeezed Jake's hand.

"You might be right," she said. "They might be the lucky ones."

"Come on, the others will be worrying about us. Let's go see if John and Marcus have found a helicopter we can put back together."

CHAPTER EIGHTEEN

The Ozark gate at Fort Rucker was unmanned, but it had been unmanned for several days now. There was, however, still a sign attached to the MP shack that read VISITORS MUST OBTAIN PASS.

After going through the gate they passed several abandoned vehicles, and as they moved farther onto the base, Jake was surprised to see that many of the base housing units were still occupied. But then, as he thought more about it, it wasn't surprising at all. These houses were home to the married soldiers. Like the houses in Ozark, Enterprise, and Dothan, these houses had no electricity or water, but they did provide shelter. Where else would they go?

One man walking alongside the road saw the blue post sticker on Jake's windshield indicating that he was an officer and automatically saluted. Just as automatically, Jake returned the man's salute; then, as he passed, he looked in the mirror as the man continued his long, lonely walk.

"Oh," Karin said quietly, and glancing toward

her, Jake saw a tear sliding down her face. "Where will he go? What will he eat? We are trained to look out for our troops but—oh, Jake, I feel so helpless."

Jake squeezed her hand again. "We are looking out for six of them," he said. "That's a start."

"They are looking out for us, just as much," Karin replied.

"That's true."

When he turned off Hatch Road onto Hanchey Field Road, Jake felt a sudden twinge of melancholy. So many times over the years of his multiple assignments to "Mother Rucker," he had made this same turn on the way to log flight time. At first glance Hanchey Field didn't look too much different from how it always did. More than one hundred helicopters were parked at the huge heliport. However, a closer examination of the helicopters showed that nearly all had been stripped of anything of value. Many were missing rotor blades—others had been stripped clean of sheet metal so that nothing but the skeletal frame remained.

"I don't know," Jake said as they drove toward the hangars. "From the looks of things, I'm not sure we can find enough to assemble even one flyable helicopter. Give them a call. We ought to be in range."

Karin keyed the two-way radio. "Phoenix Base, this is Phoenix One, over."

There was a moment's delay; then they heard, "Phoenix One, this is Phoenix Base. Where are you?"

"We're on the field."

"Phoenix One, do you remember Dewey Alain and the foam generator?"

Jake smiled, then nodded. "Tell him yes."

"I remember," Karin said.

"That's where we are. Call when you approach. I'll open the doors and let you in."

"Phoenix One, out," Karin said. She looked over at Jake, who was still chuckling. "What is this about the foam generator?"

"We had a hangar fire drill once," Jake said. "Sergeant Alain was supposed to simulate hitting the big red button that would activate the foam generator and flood the hangar. But he didn't simulate, he actually did it, and the hangar was filled waist high with foam. It took two days to clean it all up."

Karin laughed.

"Wait, that's not the half of it," he said. "Two weeks later, there was a report of survey done for the damage, and the inspection team wanted to know what happened. Sergeant Alain explained about the fire drill, told them his job was to simulate hitting the foam button. 'But I didn't simulate it,' he said. 'I actually hit it.'" Jake laughed. "Then he . . ."

"Don't tell me, he hit it again?" Karin asked, laughing.

Now Jake was laughing so hard that tears came to his eyes. "If I'm lyin' I'm dyin'," he said. "He hit it again."

Jake started toward the hangar. "That's the one," he said.

"Phoenix Base, hit the foam generator."

"Ha, he told you," John replied. The hangar door started up, and as they came closer, they saw Marcus pulling the chain to raise the door. As soon as they were inside, the door went back down.

Jake parked his dark gray Volvo next to Clay's red Liberty. As he exited the car he looked at the Black-hawk helicopter they had selected. At first glance it looked as if he could climb in, light the engine, and pull pitch, but he knew that looks were deceiving. "It looks good," he said. "What does the logbook say about it?"

John shook his head. "We have no idea. The log-books are all stored on the mainframe server and with the server down, we have no way of accessing the records."

"There is something to be said for hard-copy log-books," Jake said.

"You got that right. But we are doing a very thorough periodic inspection, so we are finding and correcting all the faults."

"Do we have any idea as to the total hours?"

"Onboard system says twenty-seven hundred and fifteen hours, but of course, that's just the airframe. We have no idea of the total hours on the engine, engine components, transmission, or rotor system."

"There has been a lot of cannibalization on this aircraft," Marcus added. "Neither engine has a fuel control. Igniters are missing on engine number two. No filters anywhere, engine or transmission. We're missing a pitch change link on the main rotor."

"Why would anyone take a pitch change link?" Jake asked. "What on earth would they use it for?"

"Beats me. But we've got almost a hundred helicopters to draw from, I'm pretty sure we'll find one we can use.

"Have any trouble coming in?" Clay asked.

Jake and Karin exchanged looks.

"You did, didn't you?" Clay said. "What happened?"

Jake told about their encounter on the road with the two young men who had stopped them.

"There's going to be a lot more of that," Clay said. "Especially if anyone finds out how much fuel we have."

"But we have jet fuel, don't we? What good would that do in a car?" Karin asked.

"A gasoline engine will not run on jet fuel, but a diesel engine will," Jake explained.

Clay pointed to his Jeep Liberty. "That will not only run on jet fuel, it is running on jet fuel."

"I was going to suggest that," Jake said. "I am just about out of gasoline, so any running around we have to do in the next few days is going to have to be in your vehicle."

"We could go out to TAC-X," Clay suggested.

"No, not yet," Jake said. "We'll keep that as an emergency supply. There may come a time when we will be in desperate need of it."

"You're probably right," Clay replied.

The others expressed some curiosity in what Jake and Clay were talking about, but none of them asked any questions, and neither Jake nor Clay made any attempt to satisfy their curiosity.

Saturday, August 4

"I need some Kleenex," John said. "At least six boxes."

"Six boxes? Wow, you must have some runny nose," Deon said.

"Not for my nose. We aren't going to be able to find any new filters, so I'm going to have to make some. Kleenex tissues will work."

"Alright," Clay said. "I'll check the commissary and the PX. If I can't find any there I'll run in to town."

"Better try Enterprise or Dothan. I know there aren't any in Ozark," John said. "We looked yesterday."

Clay started toward his Jeep SUV.

"Deon, go with him," Jake said. "After what Karin and I ran into on the way out here today, there's no telling who or what might be waiting for you."

"All right," Deon said. He walked over to the wall where their weapons were, picked up two M-16s, then put them both back down. Instead, he picked up an M-240, a machine gun.

"You plan on starting a war?" Julie asked.

"No," Deon said. "I don't plan to start one, but if I happen to get into one, I damn sure plan on winning it."

"I like the way that man thinks," Clay said.

* * *

Although they passed several abandoned vehicles on the way in to Dothan, and even more once they reached the city, they did not run into any trouble. Seeing a Winn-Dixie on Westgate Parkway, Clay pulled into the parking lot, weaving around abandoned cars and trucks. He pulled all the way up onto the wide sidewalk in front of the store.

"Let's see what we can find in here," Clay suggested.

The inside of the store was a jumbled mess— overturned shelves and counters, broken glass, empty boxes, shredded paper, and signs that mocked with their cheery false promises.

Winn✓Dixie Brings You the *Freshest* Produce!

"We aren't goin' to find anything in here," Deon said.

"Doesn't look like it," Clay admitted. "But we may as well give it a try. If there is anything, it will more than likely be over here," he said, pointing toward a sign that said PAPER PRODUCTS.

The two men looked through the residue under the sign. Suddenly Deon raised up and pointed. "Is that what I think it is?" he asked.

Clay looked in the direction Deon was pointing. There, on the floor, was a huge pile of currency in denominations from ones to one-hundred-dollar bills.

"How much do you think is there?" Deon asked.

"I don't know. A couple hundred thousand dollars, probably."

"It's just lying here. You know there've been hundreds of people that have picked through this store since everything collapsed, but nobody took any of the money."

"You want to take some of it?" Clay asked.

"No. What good is it?"

"There you go, that's why nobody has taken any of it," Clay said. "We better try someplace else. We aren't going to find anything here."

The next place they stopped was a Bruno's store, and there they found several boxes of a house-brand tissue that were water damaged.

"What do you think?" Deon asked.

"I think this will have to do."

John had only asked for six boxes, but they found ten boxes that looked to be in pretty good shape, figuring that the extra boxes might make up for any that were too damaged to be of use.

On the way back to Fort Rucker, they saw a pickup truck parked across the road in a blocking position. There were four armed men, and three of them were pointing their weapons at them, while the fourth held up his hand in a signal for them to stop.

"Uh-oh," Clay said.

"Stop here," Deon said.

"What for? We're goin' to have to face them so we may as well see what they want."

"You know damn well what they want," Deon

said. "They either want this vehicle or the fuel. Stop here; let me get up on top."

Deon reached in the back and picked up the machine gun; then he got out of the jeep and climbed up on top. He loaded the weapon, chambered a round, lay down on top of the car facing forward, braced his feet on the top railing, then hit his hand on the roof.

"Let's go!" he called.

Seeing that the Jeep wasn't going to stop, the three men with weapons—two rifles and a pistol—began firing.

Deon opened fire with the machine gun and the two men with rifles went down. The one with the pistol threw his weapon on the ground and put his hands up.

"Drive on through!" Deon called down to Clay.

Clay accelerated, then left the road to go around the block when he got there.

"You boys have a nice day now, you hear?" Deon shouted as they drove by.

The two who were still on their feet glared back, but said nothing.

"Oh, yeah, this will work just fine," John said when he saw the tissues they had brought back. "I'll have these filters better than new. Marcus, how are you coming on the hydro mechanical unit?"

"I've about got the HMU up and running. I've got the variable geometry actuator, the compressor inlet sensor, and the high-pressure fuel pump installed," he said.

"Good, good, we're cookin' with gas now."

"Cooking with gas? I thought this helicopter used jet fuel," Julie said.

"It does. When we say cooking with gas we mean . . ."

Julie started laughing.

"I think Julie is pulling a couple of legs," Karin said.

For the next several minutes John and Marcus worked on the helicopter engine while the others watched and handed them tools when asked. Deon took a pair of binoculars and an M-16 with him, then went up into the tower where he would have a panoramic view of the entire airfield.

"Phoenix," he called down a few moments after he left. "There are some people over in the far northeast corner of the field."

"What are they doing?"

"Looks like they are trying to find a helicopter that still has some fuel."

"Keep an eye on them, but don't do anything unless they start something."

"Roger."

That night they scheduled a guard detail. John was first on, and he went up into the tower to keep watch while the others spread out their sleeping bags. Willie cranked up one of the radios and after some searching, found a broadcast. The voice they heard was that of Ohmshidi.

"Damn, you mean that son of a bitch is still around?" Clay asked.

> *To my fellow citizens of the great commonwealth of the New World Collective, I send my greetings, and my assurances that I am well, and I am working very hard to restore order and hasten the recovery.*
>
> *As I am sure all within the sound of this broadcast know, there were three nuclear detonations upon our soil. While I believe my peace overtures to the Islamic nations were bearing fruit, I neglected the danger from within. It is my sincere belief that the bombs were detonated not by foreign enemies but by domestic terrorists incited to do so by the seditious broadcasts of George Gregoire. I have declared Gregoire to be an enemy of the state, and hereby grant to any citizen who comes in contact with Gregoire the authority to shoot him on sight.*
>
> *This may seem like a drastic measure, but under our current situation, drastic measures are allowed—indeed, even required.*
>
> *Since the nuclear attack against us, I have, under the authority granted me by the Enabling Act, taken additional action to insure our security. So that there may be efficiency of operation, I have dissolved the government. Congress, as you once knew it, no longer exists, nor does the Supreme Court. Under the aegis of the Enabling Act I have taken on the total responsibility of the government. I assure you this is only a temporary condition and*

as soon as order is restored and I am assured that recovery is well underway, I will authorize new elections to replace the Congress. I will then, on a gradual basis, return some of the authority I have assumed to the newly elected body, which shall be known as the People's Collective. I have also dissolved the entire military, from the chairman of the Joint Chiefs of Staff, down to the lowest-ranking private. If you are in the military, and you hear this broadcast, you may take this as your authority to leave the post, base, or ship to which you are assigned. You are free to go home, or to anyplace you wish. I thank you for your service. All police and military authority now rests with me, and me alone, to be carried out by the SPS units, which I will be expanding.

Because of the unrest that is rampant throughout the country, and as a matter of personal security, I will tell you that I am no longer in New World City, the place once known as Washington, D.C., but have established the capital in a location that, for now, I shall not disclose. But, as you can tell by this broadcast, the government, through me, is still functioning, and that means that the NWC is still a member nation in the world of nations.

Thank you, and good night.

CHAPTER NINETEEN

"Holy crap, can you believe that?" Willie said. "He has actually dismissed the entire Army."

"It is a stupid and empty gesture," Jake said. "He destroyed the Army with his incompetent meddling, so there is no more Army anyway. He is just saying this to make it appear as if he is still in charge."

"Who were the idiots who voted for this man?" Clay asked. "How could we have possibly elected someone like this?"

"When more than half the voting public got their news and opinions from stand-up comedians, what did you expect?" Jake asked.

"I don't know," Clay replied. "But I sure didn't expect anything like this."

"Always before, when our country got into serious straits someone would say something like, 'We are Americans, we've been through hard times before. We got through that, and we'll get through this,'" John said. He shook his head. "But I don't think we have ever been through anything like this."

"Anybody else broadcasting?" Jake asked.

"There's nothing left on this frequency but carrier wave," Willie said. "Let me see what else I can find."

El huracán hará la recalada en Point de Mobile antes de medianoche esta noche. Es ahora una categoría cinco, pero disminuirá en la fuerza antes de la recalada a categoría tres . . .

"I'll see if I can find something in English," Willie said.

"No, wait! It's a hurricane!" Marcus said, holding his hand out to stop Willie.

"A hurricane? Where? When?"

"It's in the Gulf now, should make landfall by midnight tonight at Mobile Point."

"Mobile Point? Isn't that where Fort Morgan is?" John asked.

"Yes," Jake said. "Marcus, what's the strength, did he say?"

"It's a cat five now," Marcus said. "They are saying it should be a three by landfall."

"Whoa, that's quite a storm."

"Does that change our plans any?" Deon asked. "I mean, do we still plan to go to Fort Morgan?"

"Fort Morgan has been there since 1834," Jake said. "I imagine it has gone through its share of storms. We're still going. But we are going to get a lot of rain and wind here tonight, so we need to be ready for it."

Willie continued to search the dial, stopping

when he heard English being spoken. It was not only English, it was English with a British accent.

This is the BBC World Broadcast on 5.110 megahertz. Now, here is the news.

Authorities in Southampton have stopped looking for survivors and are now cordoning off the entire area to prevent entry into the contaminated area. The final count of casualties is believed to be a little over one hundred fifty thousand dead, with another one hundred thousand injured. There is no way of knowing the number of people who will ultimately die of radiation exposure, though it is thought to be very high.

There is little news out of Germany or Spain, we know only that they, too, had nuclear bombs explode in their countries. France reports an expected death total of one and one half million. So far there has been no news of any sort from Israel—indeed, we do not know if the country yet exists.

Caliph Rafeek Syed has announced the formation of the Greater Islamic Caliphate of Allah, composed of the former nations of Iraq, Iran, Syria, Libya, Lebanon, Saudi Arabia, and Yazikistan. That association, if true, would constitute a greater power than all of Europe, and what is left of the New World Collective.

We now know that every bomb that exploded in Europe, as well as the three that exploded in the New World Collective, were delivered on board ships. The Greater Islamic Caliphate of Allah has taken credit for the blasts, and has declared that the suicide bombers, as well as the unsuspecting crewmen of all three ships, are martyrs and now in paradise.

Supreme Leader Ohmshidi is no longer in New World City, but continues to make pronouncements from undisclosed locations. In his latest broadcast, he announced the dissolution of Congress and the Supreme Court, though such action is meaningless at the present, since the United States, or the New World Collective as the country is now known, has ceased to exist as a nation.

In addition to the loss of life and extreme damage wrought by the three atomic bombs, the rest of the former United States is in far more dire straits than any of the European Union countries. For all intent and purposes, the U.S. no longer has a functioning government. It has no viable currency, which doesn't matter as there is no longer a commercial enterprise in operation within the borders of what was once the United States. All transportation has come to a halt and the supply of food is becoming very critical in all areas of the country. Electricity and running water have been terminated, as has all telephone service. There are no broadcast facilities in operation, not even at the local level, though we have picked up some short-wave transmissions, including those of one-time right-wing television host, George Gregoire. There are no policemen on duty anywhere in the entire nation, nor is there martial law. There can be no martial law because there is no military.

At a NATO meeting yesterday, it was decided that those nations who have not suffered a nuclear

attack would make an attempt to send food and
supplies to the stricken nations as soon as possible.
There was also some discussion as to whether NATO
should send a contingent of military to the NWC
to help in restoring and maintaining order in the
affected nations, though no action was taken.

Prime Minister Corey Wellington said yesterday
that while he is confident that the United Kingdom
will survive the single nuclear bomb blast that oc-
curred on British soil, he fears that the nuclear
explosions in the United States, on top of what the
nation was already experiencing there, will make
recovery impossible. He is personally saddened by
the terrible conditions of what was "once the preem-
inent superpower of the world."

"The United States was always the leader in,
and set the standard for, aid to countries in need,"
the prime minister said. "How sad it is that such a
powerful and benevolent nation could have been
brought to its knees by an inept and ultimately de-
structive president. We cannot, and we will not
turn our back on our American cousins."

This is BBC and this has been the news.

"Damn," Clay said. "It looks now like the whole
world is going to hell in a handbasket."

"What happened has happened," Jake said. "But
we can't look back now. We have to keep our eyes
on what is in front of us. We have to survive."

"Survive, then what?" Karin said. "What do we
do then? Do we just live out the rest of our lives in
isolation?"

"You heard Gregoire. There will be others like us," Jake said. "We will establish contact with them."

"And once we establish contact, then what?"

"We're not ready yet to decide then what," Jake said. "As I said, our first duty is to survive. And we do that by facing one challenge at a time, one day at a time."

The Dunes, Fort Morgan—Saturday, August 4

James Laney stood on the roof of The Indies, a seven-story condo built ten years earlier for people who wanted a vacation beach home for themselves, and also for those who wanted investment rental property.

Not one unit was occupied now, as many had been taken over by the bank in foreclosures. Even those units that were owned outright stood empty now because there was no fuel available for the owners to come down, nor incentive to do so, since there was neither electricity nor running water.

A few minutes earlier James had climbed the stairs to the top of The Indies in order to have a better view of the Gulf and, more importantly, the sky over the Gulf.

"We've got a hurricane comin'," he had announced that morning to Jerry Cornett and Bob Varney. "I can feel it in my ankles and in my knees."

Since James had accurately forecasted both Hurricanes Ivan and Katrina, Jerry and Bob took him seriously. They were sitting at a table on the deck behind James's house when he came back.

"Did you see anything?" Jerry asked.

"No," James said. "But I know damn well one is out there."

"What are we going to do?" Bob asked.

"What can we do? If we combined what fuel we have left and all crowded into the same car, it would not be enough to get us away from the storm," James said. "And even if we did we wouldn't have enough fuel to come back here. We don't have any choice. We are going to ride it out."

"I thought we said that, after Katrina, we weren't going to ride another one out," Bob said.

"Yeah, we did say that," James agreed. "But I don't think we have a choice now."

"James is right," Jerry said. "We don't have any choice."

"Jerry, your house is right down on the front line," James said. "You and Gaye might be better off coming here to stay with Cille and me."

"Yeah, I think we will. What about you, Bob?"

"We're a little farther back from the beach than James, even," Bob said. "We'll ride it out there, then come back over here after it passes."

Because there was no functioning TV or radio, Bob and the others of the little group had no news on the hurricane with regard to either its strength, or its name. They took it upon themselves to name the storm, calling it Hurricane Ohmshidi, declaring that no matter how strong it was, it couldn't possibly do more damage than the president had already done.

Bob convinced Ellen that they, and Charley, should ride out the storm in their minivan. "It presents less of a surface to the wind," he explained. "Besides, if you can drive a car at a hundred miles an hour on the highway, it seems reasonable to assume that the car can withstand one-hundred-mile-per-hour winds."

The wind started increasing in strength at about six o'clock that evening, getting progressively stronger until midnight. Bob, Ellen, and Charley were in their Toyota Sienna, looking through the windshield onto the street in front of their house. The wind was howling like the engines of a jet airliner sitting on the end of the runway just starting its takeoff run, and the minivan was buffeted about like an airplane flying through rough air.

The rain that pelted the windshield made it very difficult to see, because each drop of rain was filled with sand that had blown up from the beach. When they could see, they saw roofs from houses, balconies, outside steps, and large pieces of wood tumbling by in front of them. Bob had parked under his house, so the van had some protection from the tumbling debris by the large doubly braced stilts upon which his house set.

At midnight the eye passed over them and everything stilled. With no rain nor wind, Bob flashed on the lights so they could see. The street was piled high with wreckage from houses that had fallen before the storm.

Bob had a small, handheld, two-way radio. He depressed the talk button. "James, do you hear me?"

"Yeah, I hear you."

"You folks making out all right over there?"

"We're fine," James said. "But there is water all the way up to the back of my property line. There's water from here all the way down to the Gulf. How are you folks doing?"

"The car is getting buffeted around quite a bit, but other than that we are doing fine."

"You can always come over here if you want."

"No, we've come this far, we'll ride the rest of it out. Fact is, I don't want to go outside now, anyway, because the wind is picking up again."

"All right, we'll see you in the morning."

When the rain started again, Bob put his seat back down.

"What are you doing?" Ellen asked.

"I'm going to sleep."

"In this? How can you sleep in this?"

"What else is there to do?" Bob asked.

Charley had been sitting on Ellen's lap, but he jumped over onto Bob and lay down on top of him. He was shaking badly.

"You don't need to be afraid, Charley Dog," Bob said. "You aren't going to get wet or blown away."

"I hope that's true for all of us," Ellen said.

Bob reached up to take her hand. "It could be worse," he said.

"How could it be worse?"

"This could be ten years ago when my mother and your mother were still alive, and they could both be in the backseat."

Ellen laughed. "You're right," she said. "It could be worse."

Though the noise of the storm and the wind continued unabated for at least seven more hours, from midnight until seven o'clock the next morning, Bob went to sleep. He didn't wake until Ellen shook his shoulder.

"What is it?"

"The storm has stopped," Ellen said.

"Good," Bob said. He put his seat back up. "Did you get any sleep?"

"No."

"Why not?"

"Someone had to stay awake."

"Why?"

"I don't know why," Ellen said. "It's just that somebody needed to stay awake."

"I appreciate your dedication to duty," Bob said.

The rain had stopped, and they could see, but the wind, while no longer at hurricane strength, was still blowing very hard. However, the wind had stilled enough that large pieces of debris were no longer flying by.

"Let's go over and see how the others fared," Bob suggested.

Walking was difficult, but by leaning into the wind, they were able to stay on their feet. Charley could not stand up against it, and was rolled up by the wind, so Bob had to carry him. When they reached James's house, they saw that the water had come up to the very edge of his property. Every other house in the compound, at least those that remained standing, were in water that was halfway up the stilts upon which all the houses were mounted. They were surprised to see two women with James and the others.

James introduced them as Sarah Miller, who was twenty-one, and Becky Jackson, her aunt. Though she was Sarah's aunt, Becky was only twenty-three.

"They were in the Carpe Diem house," James explained. "That's where they rode out the storm last night."

"Whoa, Carpe Diem is under water up to the first floor, isn't it?" Bob asked.

"Yes," Becky said.

"I'll bet it was a frightening night."

"I've never been so afraid in my life," Sarah said.

"We thought we were the only ones out here, until Mr. Laney came over in his boat to get us this morning," Becky said.

"What in the world were you doing there?"

"We had a gift shop in Mobile, but when everything started going bad, we had to close our shop. Then things got a little dangerous there. My folks have this place down here so we came down, thinking it would be safer," Becky said.

"Of course, without TV or radio, we had no idea we were coming right into the middle of a hurricane. We got here yesterday morning, the hurricane hit last night," Sarah added.

"You're lucky the house didn't blow away," Cille said. "So many of them have."

"Nineteen in The Dunes alone," James said. "Including Jerry's house."

"I'm sorry, Jerry," Bob said.

"It could've been worse," Jerry said. "Gaye and I could have been in it."

"I guess that's right."

"Wait until you see the front of The Indies condo," James said. "The entire front wall came down last night. It looks like a giant dollhouse. You can see into every unit in the building."

"And we're going to have to live with this a long time," Bob said. "It's not like it was with Katrina and Ivan when everyone started rebuilding right away."

"At least we don't have to worry about the power coming back," Jerry said. "Because it never is coming back."

"I'd love to know what's going on in the world," Bob said. "It would be nice if they've impeached Ohmshidi. Surely, by now, those idiots in Washington have figured out that this idiot is the one who totally destroyed our economy."

"We don't have a government anymore," Becky said.

"You can say that again. I mean if they are just going to sit by and watch Ohmshidi destroy us without doing a thing to stop him . . ."

"No, I mean seriously. Since the three atom bombs, Ohmshidi has dissolved the government."

"Three atom bombs? Government dissolved? What are you talking about?" Bob asked.

"And where are you getting all this information?" Jerry added.

"There is a man in Mobile who lives close to us, who has a shortwave radio," Becky said. "Boston, New York, and, I think Norfolk, were all hit with nuclear bombs."

"Son of a bitch!" Jerry said. "It's not enough I've lost my house. We're losing our entire country."

"Losing our country?" James said. "Sounds to me like we have lost it."

"Well, there's one good thing," Bob said.

"What's that?"

"It can't get any worse."

Despite himself, Jerry laughed. "And that's a good thing?"

"Any port in a storm."

"Oh, don't talk any more about storms," Becky said. "The one we had last night was enough."

"Well, we all made it through, so what do you say we have some breakfast?" Jerry suggested.

"Sounds good to me," Cille said.

"How about biscuits and gravy?" Bob asked.

"Biscuits and gravy? You've got biscuits and gravy?" Becky asked. "How? I mean, where did you get it?"

"You just don't know my talent," Bob said. "I can make something out of nothing."

Ellen laughed. "He's telling you a big one. But he is good at making do. And since nearly every house out here had a well-stocked pantry and there is nobody here anymore, we have sort of inherited it. Flour, cornmeal, canned vegetables, condensed milk, and several canned meat products."

"What about water?"

"Every house out here has a hot water tank. Some of them have two tanks," James said. "We're okay on water for a while."

"What happens when you run out?"

"As you may have noticed, last night we get a lot of rain. We'll build a catchment and storage system when we need it."

A little less than an hour later all eight sat down to a bountiful breakfast of biscuits, gravy, and fried Spam.

"Oh," Sarah said as she took her first bite. "This is good!"

"Life is good," Bob said. He chuckled. "Or, at least as good as it can be under the present circumstances."

CHAPTER TWENTY

Fort Rucker—Sunday, August 5

Although Fort Rucker wasn't hit with the full force of the hurricane, there were sustained winds of sixty miles per hour as well as torrential rains, and the wind and rain pounded the walls of the hangar throughout the long night. When Jake and the others emerged from the hangar the next morning they were surprised at the amount of damage the storm had done. Because none of the helicopters on the field had been tied down, many of them had been overturned, or pushed into other helicopters nearby.

"I'm glad we found a helicopter when we did," John said. "Look at that mess. I doubt there is one airframe left that could be used."

"Yes," Willie agreed. "It's a good thing we moved the zero-seven-seventeen inside."

"The only thing we have left is to connect the servo, right?" Jake asked.

"That's it."

"How long will that take?"

"No more than twenty minutes to connect it and bleed it," John said. "Then it'll be ready for a test flight."

"Why test fly it?" Marcus asked. "Let's just climb on it and go."

"No," Jake said. "If this thing is going to fall apart in the air, I'm going to be the only one on board. I won't do a complete, by-the-book test flight, but I do want to make sure everything is okay before I risk anyone's life but my own."

Half an hour later, Karin and Julie pulled on the chain to raise the door as the men pushed the helicopter out of the hangar and onto the tarmac. Although the U-60 is a twin-engine aircraft, they had made the decision to disconnect the left engine from the freewheeling clutch at the transmission. That way they were able to cannibalize it for the other engine. It meant that the helicopter would have less power and would fly slower with less of a payload, but it also meant it would use just over half as much fuel.

"All right, Jake, why don't you climb in and see what we have?" John said.

"You don't mind if I do a pre-flight, do you?" Jake asked.

"Have at it," John said.

Jake did a thorough walk-around inspection, checking all fluid levels, as well as the rotor system for any loose or missing items. He looked at the blades to make certain there was no damage or separation of the laminated surfaces. After that, he started checking for leaks in the engine, transmission, gearboxes for the tail rotor drive train, hydraulics, and blade grips. Everything checked out.

After the walk around, Jake climbed in to the right seat to start his cockpit checks. He put on his SPH4 flight helmet, then plugged in the radio jack. Once he had a good start with the engine and rotor coming up to flight idle speed quite nicely, he checked to see that all of the gauges were in the green. Smiling, he gave John a thumbs-up.

"Alright!" John said, returning the thumbs-up salute.

After the engine was running, Jake went through a number of other checks, including turning on and checking the inverters, checking the generator, and turning off the hydraulic system to check control travel, then turning it back on to insure that there were no stuck valves that might bring trouble, including even a hydrostatic lock, which could result in a loss of control.

It was now well over four months since Jake had sat behind the controls of a functioning helicopter, and he felt a strong sense of satisfaction at being there again. With the rotor blades spinning at full speed, he moved the cyclic around to check the rotor plane. It dipped exactly as it was supposed to, and he felt no falloff of rotor control as a result of John's jury-rigged pitch change link.

Automatically, he set the radios to departure

frequency, then keyed the transmit switch before he realized he had nobody to contact. He released the radio transmit switch, and pulled up on the collective pitch control, causing the helicopter to lift from the ground. He stabilized it, then pulled the collective and pushed the cyclic forward. The helicopter took off easily and he climbed to five hundred feet as he passed over the edge of Hanchey Field. He did a complete circle around the field, looking down at the hangar and the little group of people who were gathered anxiously, awaiting his return.

He had just started shooting his approach to the tarmac right in front of the hangar when he saw a pickup truck coming quickly up Hanchey Road. He expedited the approach, sat down, then killed the engine.

"How did it go?" John asked, running over and sticking his head in through the open window.

"The flight was perfect," Jake said. "But it looks like we're about to have company. Deon!" he called.

"What's up?" Deon asked, sprinting over to him.

"There is a pickup truck full of men coming this way, fast," Jake replied. "It may not mean anything, but there is no sense in taking a chance."

"I'll get a machine gun up in the tower," Deon said.

"Good idea. But don't do anything unless you get word from me," Jake said. "Or unless they start shooting."

Deon nodded; then, grabbing the M-240 and

an ammo box, he hurried up the outside steps into the tower.

"What is your plan?" Clay asked.

"Get everyone into the hangar, but have them armed, just in case," Jake said.

"Are you going to stay out here?"

"Yes. I intend to see what they want."

"I'm going to stay with you."

"No need," Jake said.

"I'd feel better. I'm going to be standing right beside you with an M-16."

"All right," Jake said. "If you say so."

Clay hurried back into the hangar, then returned with the rifle just as the red Dodge Ram pulled onto the airfield and started toward them.

The pickup truck approached at full speed.

"What the hell?" Clay said. "They plan to run us down!"

Clay raised his rifle to fire, but there were two men in the back of the truck, with their rifles resting on the top. They opened fire and Clay was hit.

"Clay!" Jake shouted and reached for him.

"No! Get out of the way!" Clay yelled, and he shoved Jake hard, knocking him down, but getting him out of the way of the onrushing truck. Even as Jake hit the ground, he heard a sickening thump when the truck ran Clay over. The driver slammed on the brakes, then swung the truck around. In the meantime, the two gunners opened up on Jake. Jake was still on the ground and he rolled hard to his right as the bullets ricocheted off the blacktop just beside him. Deon opened up with the M-240 and Jake saw the tracer rounds streaming into the truck. Then he saw the driver lose control, and crash into the helicopter. Both helicopter and truck exploded into a huge ball of fire. Neither the driver, nor the two shooters got out.

Jake moved quickly to check Clay, but jerked his face away when he saw that Clay's head had been smashed by one of the wheels. Steeling himself, he turned back to his longtime friend, removed Clay's shirt, and spread it over his head. There was no need for either of the women to see this, and even though Karin was a nurse, this was more than anything she would ordinarily see.

Deon came down from the tower as the others came out of the hangar.

"What happened?" Karin said, then seeing Clay lying on the ground, his head covered by his shirt and blood pooling underneath, she gasped. "Oh my God," she said.

"Damn," Willie said. "The sergeant major got through Iraq and Afghanistan, only to have some homegrown bastard kill him."

There were some secondary explosions from the burning truck and helicopter.

"Think anyone survived that?" Marcus asked.

"I hope they did," Willie answered. "I hope the sons of bitches are roasting alive. They may as well get a taste of what it's like before they go to hell."

"I doubt anyone survived," Jake said.

"Including the helicopter," Deon said. "We're going to have to start over from scratch."

"Scratch is right," John said. "Because there

isn't anything left we can build from. We are, as they say, SOL."

"What about one of the other airfields?" Marcus suggested.

"No good," Jake said, shaking his hand. "One of the last things we did while the post was still functioning was move all the UH-sixties to Hanchey. If we can't put together another one from what we have here, we are going to have to come up with another plan."

"A Chinook?" Marcus suggested.

"I don't think so," John said. "They've got more parts than a Blackhawk; it'll be harder coming up with all we need for them than it was for the zero-seven-seventeen."

"What are we going to do with Sergeant Major Matthews?" Karin asked.

"We're going to bury him," Jake said.

"Where? How? There is nothing here but black-top and cement," Marcus said.

"There's real ground behind the hangar," Jake said. "And an old warrior like Clay would probably want to be buried on an Army base, even if there is no Army anymore. If a couple of you will help me carry Sarge around back."

"We'll get him," Marcus said, nodding toward the others.

Willie and Marcus took Clay's arms, Deon and John took his feet. Jake, Karin, and Julie followed them around the side of the hangar.

The rain from the storm made the ground soft, so it took no more than half an hour to dig a grave for Clay. With his blood-soaked shirt still wrapped around his head, they lowered him gently into the grave.

"I wish we had a flag to drape over him," Karin said.

"We do!" Deon said with a big smile. "I saw one while I was up in the tower. I'll go get it."

"You knew the sergeant major a long time, didn't you, sir?" Marcus asked. For the moment, the rank and military courtesy seemed appropriate.

"Yes," Jake answered. "I don't think I would have gotten through Officer Candidate School without him."

A moment later Deon returned with the flag. It was a storm flag rather than a garrison flag, so it was considerably smaller.

"It's not big enough to drape over him," Julie said.

"We'll fold it into the triangle, then put it in his hands. He will like that," Jake said.

"I've often wondered why we fold a flag like that," Julie said. "It has to be symbolic of something."

"It is," Jake said. "Folded properly, it takes exactly thirteen folds, two lengthwise and eleven triangular. That represents the thirteen original states."

Willie and John folded the flag into the triangle.

"Now," Jake said, holding out the flag. "This triangle resembles a cocked hat, representing every solder, sailor, marine, and airman who has ever served. And finally, you can see that there are now only four stars visible. Those four stars stand for 'In God we trust.'"

"I'll put the flag in his hands," Deon offered, and taking the flag from Jake, he leaned down over the open grave and placed the flag so that Clay was holding it over his heart, with his hands over it. It was almost as if the sergeant major was actually holding on to the flag.

"I'm going to have a little service for him, if you don't mind," Jake said.

"Who would mind?" Deon asked. "I think it is entirely appropriate."

"So do I," Karin said.

Jake lowered his head, and the others did as well. "Dear Lord," Jake began. "We commit into your keeping Sergeant Major Clayton Bertis Matthews the Third. Clay served his country and his fellow man with honor and valor. He took up arms to defend all that good men find dear: life, liberty, and the pursuit of happiness. He lived his life according to those ideals, and, moreover, he imparted that dedication and his wisdom to others. He was my mentor, my friend, and my strength. We leave him here now, secure in the knowledge that you hold him in the palm of your hand. Amen."

"Amen," the others repeated.

As they left, the others, one at a time, passed by Clay's grave. Willie and Marcus both signed themselves with the cross.

CHAPTER TWENTY-ONE

By the time they returned to the front of the hangar the fire had burned out and all that was left was the smoldering wreckage of the truck and helicopter. No longer red, the truck had rusted out in the flames. The tires had been burned off and the aluminum wheels were no more than molten slag. Inside the truck a charred body was draped over what was left of the steering wheel. The two gunners had been thrown forward over the cab of the truck and their charred remains lay in the blackened residue of what had been the helicopter.

"How much fuel was on board?" Jake asked.

"Unfortunately, we had it topped off," John said.

"That leaves us just under four hundred gallons. If we can put another one together, we won't be able to top off the tank, but we'll have enough fuel to get to where we are going."

"*If* we can put another one together," John said. "I'm going to take Clay's Jeep and drive around the field to see if I can find something we can use to start over."

"I've been thinking," Jake said.

"Well, Major, that's why the Army pays you the big bucks," Deon said, and the others, including Jake, laughed.

"John, while you are looking at the other helicopters, I suggest that the rest of us build some hasty fortifications of some sort. That way if this happens again, we'll be ready for them."

"Good idea," Marcus said.

"I'm glad you think it's a good idea," Jake said. "Because now that I have suggested that, I have no idea what we can use for the fortification."

"There are ten fifty-five-gallon drums over in the hangar next door," John said. "They are empty, but if we put dirt in them . . ."

"Yes," Jake said interrupting him. "We did that in Iraq, built up around our Quonset huts. It worked well."

"You'll have to cut the tops off to get the dirt in," John said. "I've got a hacksaw and some blades here."

"Won't you need that if you find something out on the line?" Jake asked.

"If it isn't something I can take off using a wrench or a screwdriver, then it's not likely to be anything we can use. Take the hacksaw."

"All right. Let's get started," Jake said.

"A suggestion, sir?" Marcus offered.

"Any suggestion is welcomed."

"As soon as we get the top off one of the barrels,

I suggest that one of us saw, while the rest of us fill the empty with sand."

"Good idea."

An hour later they had only two barrels filled with sand. Jake raised up from digging and wiped the back of his hand across his forehead.

"You know, when I said that we did this in Iraq—I forgot. There was no 'we' to it. We hired local contractors for the job."

"Yeah, I was wondering where you got that 'we,'" Deon said.

By nightfall, they had the ten barrels in a V shape in front of the personnel door. Back inside, they wondered aloud whether or not John would find anything they could use.

It was almost an hour later before John returned, and when he came into the hangar, the expression on his face told everything.

"We're stopped cold," John said. "There is nothing left that is salvageable."

"Do you mean to say that out of a hundred or more helicopters, that you can't put together one that is flyable?" Jake asked.

"I'm not saying that," John said. "But what I am saying is that there is so little salvageable remaining on each of the aircraft that it would take days, maybe weeks, to put one together. The biggest problem is with the airframes. Those that haven't been destroyed by all the scavengers are too badly damaged by the storm. I wish I had better news for you, but I don't."

"What do we do now?" Karin asked.

"What about the museum?" Deon asked.

"The museum? What about the museum? What are you talking about?" John asked.

"During the Vietnam War my dad was a door gunner on a Huey. There is a Huey on display at the museum just like the one he was on. I've seen it a dozen times—it looks like it's ready to fly."

"I wonder if the engine and transmission are in it." John said.

"They are," Jake said with a wide smile. "I remember reading an article in the *Flyer* last year about when it was brought to the museum. It was landed out front, then moved inside."

"How long has it been there?" John asked.

"I don't know, twenty years, maybe a little longer."

"And it was flyable when it arrived?"

"Yes, in the article I read, they had a big ceremony about it. The pilot who flew it in was one of the last Vietnam veterans still on active duty. Do you think you could make it flyable?"

"We could come a hell of a lot closer with it than I can with anything that's out here," John said. "All of the parts should still be there, but after all this time there will be dried-out bushings, filters, gaskets, and so forth. We'll have to rehydrate them, if we can."

"Question is, how do we get it here?" Marcus asked.

"We'll get it here in Clay's Jeep," Jake said.

"What? You can't get a helicopter in that Jeep."

"We could if we took the body off. Then we could set the helicopter on the Jeep's frame. The tail cone will stick out, but it's on skids, not wheels, so we can tie it down securely without worrying about it falling off."

"Yeah!" Deon said. "Damn right."

"Thing is, I hate doing that to Clay's car," Marcus said.

"Believe me, Marcus, I knew Clay better than anyone here. And if Clay were still alive, he would be the first one to say do it," Jake said.

"Yeah," John said. "I think he would too. All right, let's get this buggy stripped down."

It was a tired bunch who ate their supper that night, but before they turned in, they drew little slips of paper upon which times were recorded, the times determining who and when they would pull guard duty.

The next morning, with nothing left of Clay's Jeep but the frame, the men drove over to the Army Aviation Museum. Like all the other buildings on the fort, the museum had been vandalized and stripped of anything that could be construed to be of value. But the display of a Huey, depicting an LZ in Vietnam, was still intact. John opened the cowl and took a quick glance at the engine.

"All right!" he said. "Looks like nobody has messed with it. I think we've got a shot at getting this thing going!"

The hardest thing was going to be getting the helicopter loaded onto the back of the Jeep, but anticipating that, they had brought a crane and pulley system from the hangar and, after half an hour getting everything rigged up, John climbed up onto the engine deck and screwed a lifting eye onto the top of the mast. This was exactly the kind of lifting eye that was used by the aircraft recovery teams when they were sent in to pick up a downed helicopter on the battlefield.

When everything was rigged up, they began cranking on the crane and pulley system until the helicopter was lifted from the place it had occupied on the display for nearly twenty years, then swung over to the Jeep frame and lowered. The skids were lashed in place, and everyone but Deon, who was driving the Jeep, climbed into the helicopter for the drive back to Hanchey Field.

Once they had the helicopter in the hangar, John began a more thorough examination.

"Damn!" he said. "How did I not see this?"

"What?"

"We're missing a drag brace."

"How important is that?" Deon asked.

"Not all that important, if you don't mind throwing a rotor blade," John said.

"Anything out there we can use?" Jake asked.

John shook his head. "No, they are very precise."

"John, isn't there a Cobra helicopter there in the museum?" Marcus asked.

A huge smile spread across John's face. "Yes! And they share the same rotor system!"

"Let's go back."

"Deon, go with them," Jake said. "It's getting a

lot more antsy out there. I don't know what they might run into."

"All right," Deon said. "Willie, the M-two-forty is still in the tower. How about you going up there and keeping an eye open while I'm gone?"

"Good idea," Willie said.

John, Marcus, and Deon climbed back onto what was left of the Jeep, as Willie went back up into the tower. That left Jake, Karin, and Julie alone in the hangar.

"If you don't mind, I'm going to see if we can get anything else on the radio," Julie said.

"You know how to do it?" Karin asked.

"Oh, yeah, I've been watching Willie."

Julie turned the crank to build up the power; then she turned the radio and started moving the dial through all the frequencies.

. . . establish contact. We have to be very careful in this, because the IRE, the Islamic Republic of Enlightenment, has their spies everywhere. No doubt they are monitoring this very transmission. Well, I've got news for you, IRE, there are millions of us out here. We've been knocked down, but we aren't knocked out. We have survivalist groups coalescing all over the country and the time is going to come, and soon, when we get together and reconstitute the United States of America.

To my fellow American patriots, find safe ways to contact each other, make yourselves strong, grow in strength, until we are able to join together as one unbeatable band. Until then, this is General Francis

*Marion of the Brotherhood of Liberty, and I'm
using that term in its most generic sense, because
we welcome our sister patriots with open arms. And
in the Brotherhood of Liberty, men and women,
black, white, Asian, American Indian, Protestant,
Catholic, Christian, Jew, freedom-loving secular-
ists, we are united, we are strong, and we will be
victorious. I am asking you to grow strong, hold on,
and wait until that glorious day when we will take
our country back. God bless America!*

Oh, do you think that's real?" Karin asked.

"I don't know if it is for real or not," Jake said.
"But his name is obviously false."

"Why do you say that?"

"Because Francis Marion was in the American
Revolution. He was the first guerrilla fighter."

"Are we going to try and make contact with them?"

"We'll play that by ear," Jake said. "For now our
primary objective is to survive."

CHAPTER TWENTY-TWO

When John, Marcus, and Deon returned a couple of hours later, they began unloading parts.

"We took everything we might possibly need," John said. "We got both drag braces, the dampers, the pitch change links, the igniters, the fuel pump and fuel control, the hydraulic pump, the servos, the tail rotor gearboxes, the hangar bearings, everything we could get."

"We'll have this sucker up and flying in no time," Marcus said confidently.

"No trouble, I take it?"

"Not really," Deon said.

"What do you mean by not really? Was there trouble or not?"

"The place is crawling with scavengers," Deon said. "And they are getting frustrated."

"How do you know they are getting frustrated?"

"They've been setting fire to all the buildings." He looked at Karin and Julie. "The hospital is burned down," he said.

"Why would they burn the hospital?" Julic asked.

"My guess is they were after drugs, if not for themselves, to use in barter," Deon said. "But you know, for sure, that there were no drugs of any value left in the hospital when it was abandoned."

"You're right," Karin said. "As a matter of fact there was nothing lcft even before the hospital was abandoned. For the last two months, the strongest thing we had was aspirin."

"There are others like us out there," Julie said, happily.

"I'm sure there are," Deon said.

"No, I mean for real, like us," Julie said. "We heard them on the radio."

"Did you?"

"They call themselves the Brotherhood of Liberty," Julie said.

"They've asked us to join them," Karin added.

Deon and the others looked directly at Jake. "Are we?" Deon asked.

"Are we what?"

"Are we going to join them?"

"Maybe, someday," Jake said. "If they are legitimate."

"Why would you think they would not be legitimate?"

"The way I look at it there is a fifty–fifty chance that it is legitimate. It could either be set up by the SPS to reel in the revolutionaries, or it could be legitimate. When the time comes, we may check it out. But this is not the time."

Wednesday, August 8

Because the helicopter had been flyable when it was put on display in the museum, work on it proceeded much faster than it had on the original Blackhawk. They had a little trouble with the drag brace because, as it turned out, the chord of the blade was a little wider than they thought, which meant the drag brace was a little longer, so they had to compensate by repositioning it slightly.

They replaced the drag brace and a couple of hanger bearings on the tail rotor driveshaft. In addition, they removed every gasket, seal, and filter, soaked them all in solvent, then oil. In that way they were able to reconstitute all but two. And those two they were able to replace by reworking gaskets they found on the helicopters that were still out on the airfield. Finally, they found a battery from one of the helicopters on the field that they were able to install, with some adjustment, into the Huey.

Finally they had everything put back, and were about ready to use the positioning wheels on the skids to roll the helicopter out of the hangar when a call came over the radio from Deon.

"Yeah, Deon, go ahead," Marcus said.

"We've got company coming," Deon said. "And it doesn't look like any social call. They came up on motorcycles, but they left them on the other side of the field. They are armed, and they are moving toward the hangar in combat advance."

"How many are there?" Marcus asked.

"A shitwad load," Deon said.

"That many?"

"At least."

"Alright, grab your weapons. Let's get outside and into position," Jake called to the others. He took the radio from Marcus. "Deon, stay alert, but keep out of sight as much as you can."

"Roger."

Jake and the others rushed outside, then took up positions behind the V of sand barrels. "John, you take the right end of the V. Willie, you take the left end. Marcus, you and I will have the point. Ladies, one of you on each side," Jake directed.

Jake waited until everyone was in position; then he raised his head just above the barricade and brought the bullhorn to his lips.

"Those of you coming across the field. Turn around and go back. Do not come any closer," he said over the loudspeaker.

"What have you got in the hangar?" someone shouted back.

"Nothing that concerns you. Turn around and go back."

"You got gasoline in there?"

"No."

"You're lyin'! Let us take a look."

"No."

"I don't believe you. I think you've got gasoline in there, and we're going to take it."

"I told you, we don't have gasoline. Look around out on the field, take what you want, but do not come any closer. This is your last warning. If you come closer, we will shoot."

The answer this time was a rifle shot. The bullet whistled by just overhead, then punched through the hangar wall.

"Turn around and go back!" Jake said over the bullhorn. "There's nothing here for you."

This time two of the scavengers fired.

"Jake, I have the shooters in sight," Deon said. "Permission to fire?"

Two more shots were fired by the scavengers, and one of the bullets hit the top of a barrel, and sent a little shard of steel into Marcus's face.

"Damn, I'm hit!" Marcus said.

Jake looked at him, then laughed. "You've cut yourself worse, shaving," he said. He picked up the little radio. "Deon, fire at will," he said.

Deon opened up with the M-240 from the top of the control tower. Jake could see the tracer rounds slashing down, and he heard one of the scavengers let out a yell of pain.

This time there were more than a couple of rounds fired—several scavengers opened fire, and some had M-16s, as evidenced by the automatic fire. They started maneuvering toward the hangar and as they worked their way forward, Jake counted at least twelve.

The Phoenix group was outnumbered, but they had position, and with Deon and the M-240, superior firepower.

The firefight was intense for several minutes; then it died off. It was quiet for a moment. Then Jake and the others could hear the motorcycle engines start. A moment later, they could hear the Doppler effect of motorcycles riding away.

"They're gone," Marcus said.

"Maybe," Jake replied. He leaned his rifle against one of the barrels, then pulled his pistol. He thumbed the magazine out, checked it, then slid it back into the handle. "But I'm going to have to find out."

"You going out there alone?" Marcus asked.

"Yes, no sense in risking more than one of us."

"You're not going out there alone," John said. "If something happens to you, we're all up shit creek. You're the only one who can fly this thing."

"John's right," Deon said. Deon had come down from the tower to join the others. "We can't risk you. I'll go out."

"You can go out with me," Jake said. "But I'm going out."

"Pulling rank on us, are you—*Major*?" John asked, coming down hard on the last word.

"I told you, we don't have rank," Jake started to say; then he paused. "All right, mea culpa. Deon, do what you have to do."

"Want company, Deon?" John asked.

"No. No offense, but you are a wrench turner. I can do better if I don't have you to worry about."

John smiled. "Okay, Rambo, fine by me. I was just putting on a brave front for the ladies."

Deon came back after about fifteen minutes with his report. "Six dead, one wounded."

"How badly is he wounded?" Karin asked.

"He was hit in the thigh, but I don't think he's going to die."

"He could if he gets an infection. Or at the minimum, lose his leg. I'd better go take a look."

"Why?" John asked. "Half an hour ago the son of a bitch was trying to kill us."

"He's probably a soldier, John, just like us," Karin said. "If the situation was normal, you would pass him in the PX and never blink an eye."

"Yeah, you're right," John said.

"I'd better go with you," Deon said.

"Wait until I get my kit."

The wounded scavenger looked to be in his late twenties. He was wearing BDUs, but there was no rank visible. He was sitting up, holding a belt tourniquet around his leg.

"No," Karin said. "You don't want to use a tourniquet unless you are unable to stop the bleeding by direct pressure. Otherwise you could get tissue damage. Let me take a look."

"You a doctor?"

"What difference does it make to you who she is?" Deon asked. "Half an hour ago you were trying to kill her. Now she's here to help you, though why she is willing to do that beats the hell out of me."

Karin removed the tourniquet and looked at the wound. "I've got to get the bullet out," she said.

"How are you going to do that?"

"I'm going to pull it out," she said, removing a forceps from the kit she had brought with her. She stuck the forceps down into the wound until she came in contact with the bullet. Then, grabbing the bullet, she pulled it out.

"Damn, it hurt more coming out than it did going in," the wounded man said.

"Good," Deon said. "If it was up to me you'd be dead now. So if you're goin' to live, I at least want you to hurt some."

"The problem is going to be if any of the cloth from your pants went into the hole with the bullet," she said.

"How are you going to know?"

"I'm going to look for it," she said. She took another instrument from her kit that looked like an oversized pair of tweezers from her kit. She put this down into the wound and clamped it shut. "Ahh, feels like I got something."

Pulling the tweezers out, she saw a small piece of cloth clamped between the arms.

"Good," she said.

By now the bleeding had stopped and Karin took out a bottle of alcohol. "This is going to hurt a little," she said.

"It already hurts," the wounded man said.

Karin poured alcohol onto the wound.

"Damn, damn, damn!" the wounded man said, shutting his eyes and wincing in pain.

Karin used a cotton ball to clean the wound. Then, she soaked a second cotton ball in alcohol and stuffed it into the bullet hole. Finally, she wrapped a compression bandage around the wound and secured it tightly.

"Don't take this off for at least seventy-two hours,"

she said. She stood up. "I'm ready to go back," she said to Deon.

"What? Are you just going to leave me here?" the wounded man asked.

"I've done all I can for you," Karin said.

"But what do I do now? Where do I go?"

"You can go anywhere you want," Karin said. "And if you keep the wound clean, it should heal without any difficulty."

"I left my bike on the other side. I can't walk. Will you bring it to me? It's the green . . ." He paused and looked over toward the body of one of the other scavengers. "I mean it's the Purple Honda VTX-1800," he said. "Only thing is, Cootie, over there, has the keys."

"All right," Deon said.

"Deon, you know that isn't his, don't you?"

Deon shrugged. "What difference does it make now?"

Karin chuckled. "I guess you're right."

"Hey," the wounded man said. "Thanks for patching me up."

Karin nodded, but said nothing.

"Listen, 'cause you helped me? I'm going to tell you something. They'll be back. And now they know about the machine gun and they know you've built a barricade in front of the hangar. They'll be back, and this time, there will be a lot more of them. They know you have fuel."

"We don't have any gasoline," Karin said.

"Doesn't matter. You've got jet fuel, and it'll

trade just as well. I hear you're building a helicopter in there."

"Where'd you hear that?" Deon asked, coming back with the keys.

"Word gets around. If I was you, I'd get out of here as soon as you can."

"Thanks for the warning," Karin said.

"Yeah, well, I guess I owe you," the wounded man said.

Deon jogged back to get the motorcycle as Karin returned to the hangar. She heard the motorcycle start just as she reached the fortifications.

Deon waited until the wounded man drove off. Then he returned to join the others. "Did you tell them what he said?" he asked Karin.

"Yes."

"I think we're all set now," John said. "You've never flown a Huey before, have you, Jake? You think you can fly it all right?"

"Have you ever worked on a Huey before, John?"

"No, I never have. But the principles of maintenance aren't that much different. A helicopter is a . . ." John stopped in midsentence, then smiled. "Okay, I get your point. Have at it, Jake, your chariot awaits," John said, holding his hand out invitingly, toward the helicopter.

"I hope this jury-rigged battery works," Jake said. "Cross your fingers that we don't get a hung start or hot start."

He checked battery voltage and placed the starter-generator switch in the starter position, turned on the main fuel pump, then opened the throttle to a point just below the flight idle detent. He pulled the starter trigger on the pilot's collective pitch control and heard the igniters pop in his earphones as the engine started spooling up, monitoring his gauges closely. He was gratified to see everything move into the green. With a big smile, he gave a thumbs-up to those waiting outside. His test flight, which was nothing more than a sweep around the airfield, went well. He saw the one motorcycle going up Hatch Road, and he saw no one coming toward them. He landed and killed the engine.

"Let's get it loaded and get out of here," he said.

CHAPTER TWENTY-THREE

The Dunes, Fort Morgan—Wednesday, August 8

"Lookie here," James said as he, Bob, and Jerry were poking around in the refuse left by the hurricane.

"What?" Jerry said.

"This a solar panel power setup. Or, what's left of it after the storm."

"You think we can reconstruct it?" Bob asked.

"Let me see what's here," James said. "We've got the panels. We're going to need to poke around and see if we can find everything else we need."

"What would that be?" Jerry asked.

"We need a current regulator, something that will keep the batteries from overcharging, or draining in case the current tries to run backward."

"Like a reverse current relay between a battery and a generator?" Bob asked.

"Yes. And if we're going to use it in a house, we'll also need a converter that changes DC to AC."

"Why do we even need to mess with it?" Jerry asked. "I mean, as long as we've got propane, we have power."

"What happens when we run out of propane?" Bob asked. "Where are we going to get more?"

"Oh, yeah, I see what you mean. Okay, let's see if we can find everything that you need," Jerry said.

"Problem is," James said, "this setup will only power one house."

"No problem. When the time comes and we've run out of propane, we'll just choose the house we want, and we'll all move in together," Bob said.

"Or build us a new house," James said. "One that will accommodate three families, and make maximum use of the electricity we can generate this way."

"Whoa, I don't know. I'm not much at house building," Bob said.

"James and I will build it. You can be the gofer," Jerry suggested.

Fort Rucker—Wednesday, August 8

With all their survival gear on board, Jake pulled pitch and the helicopter took off. As they passed over the golf course they saw two people playing golf, and Jake laughed.

"What is it?" John asked. John was in the left seat and, like Jake, was wearing a flight helmet. Jake keyed the mic switch to the first indent, which was intercom. "I always heard that come hell or high water, a committed golfer was going to play. Look down there."

Jake made a circle around the Silver Wings Golf Course, and the two players waved up at him.

As they flew south toward the Gulf, they saw, as they expected, the highways littered with cars and trucks. Then he heard Karin's voice on the intercom. She was also wearing a headset and was plugged in to the crew chief's section.

"Jake, look down there," Karin said.

When Jake looked around, Karin pointed to something on the ground. There, below, in white paint on the grass behind a farmhouse were the words:

HELP
We Need Food
Medical Care

"Can't we land so I can see if I can help?" Karin asked.

"They probably need food more than they need medical care," Jake replied.

"Maybe we could give them a case of MREs," Karin suggested.

"It's all right with me if you can get the others to agree," Jake said.

Karin discussed it with the others, then a moment later keyed her mic again.

"Everyone else says it is okay," she said.

"All right, we'll land and see what we can do for them."

Jake circled back, then started his descent. The rotor blades popped loudly as they cavitated down through their own rotor wash.

Just as he was flaring out to land, two men ran of the house. Both were carrying M-16s and they began shooting.

Jake terminated the descent, pushed the cyclic forward, and jerked up on the collective. The helicopter leaped up over the house; then he lowered pitch, flying nap of the earth and putting the house between them and the two gunmen on the ground.

He continued flying at a low level, popping up just high enough to clear the ground obstacles. Finally, when he was more than two miles away, he climbed back up to altitude.

The blades were now making a whistling sound and the helicopter had picked up a slight vertical bounce.

"Damn," John said. "We've got a whistle and a one-to-one vertical."

"Yeah, I've been through this before," Jake said. "We took a round, or maybe a couple of rounds, through the rotor blades."

"They didn't really need help, did they?"

"No. They were using it to lure a helicopter down so they could do to them exactly what they tried to do to us."

"Yeah, but, you've got to wonder just how many helicopters there are flying around right now," John said.

"Can't be too many, I don't think," Jake said. "As far as I know we are the only ones to fly out of Rucker in the last six weeks, and I can't think of anyplace that would be more likely to launch a helicopter than us. Bless their hearts, we were about their only chance and they blew it."

John laughed so hard that tears began rolling down his face, and only Karin, who also had a head-set, knew what he was laughing about. The others looked at her quizzically, and she tried to explain what they were laughing at, but it wasn't the same.

The flight down was almost two hours in length, and all along the route they saw vehicles abandoned on the road, towns with their business districts deserted, and burned-out houses. They also saw several bodies, some alongside the roads, some on the streets of the town, and others lying out in open fields.

"There it is, the Gulf," Jake said.

Before them the Gulf spread from horizon to horizon, blue and sparkling in the sunshine. Jake turned right and they saw a long peninsula stretch-ing toward the west. The peninsula was quite narrow and it separated the Gulf of Mexico from Mobile Bay.

"Where is this place we're going?" John asked.

"It's at the very end of this peninsula."

"It's an island," Karin said. "They call it Pleasure Island."

"How can it be an island? It isn't surrounded by water," John said.

"Yeah, technically it is," Jake said. "We just crossed the intercoastal canal. That cuts the penin-sula off from the mainland and makes it an island."

Jake dropped down to about five hundred feet, then flew right along the surf. As they looked out onto the very expensive houses along the beach they could see the extent of damage from the recent hurricane. At least one out of every three houses was completely destroyed, and half of the ones still standing were damaged by degrees from light to severe. The farther west they flew, the greater the damage.

"Look at these houses," Karin said. "They are million-dollar-plus houses."

"Yeah," Jake said. "And that was back when a million dollars meant something."

The Dunes, Fort Morgan

Bob Varney was on page one hundred thirteen of his work in progress. One thing he did miss about the computer was the word-count feature. He estimated that he was just under twenty-five thousand words, using his old method of counting at two-hundred-twenty words per page.

After he finished the book, he would have to go back through the first draft as he did in the pre-computer days, marking up typos, and making editorial adjustments. That would require retyping the entire manuscript. It was hard to believe that he wrote his first one hundred books that way.

Suddenly Bob heard a sound that took him forty years back in time. For a moment, he wasn't in the third-floor office of his beach home, he was in the BOQ at Tan Son Nhut in Saigon. He was typing on this very typewriter, and passing overhead was a UH-1 helicopter returning to the base.

Bob had been hearing helicopters pass overhead for the last ten years, but he had not heard anything like this in a long time. The UH-1 has a very unique sound. Put any Vietnam veteran in an open field, blindfold him, and fly ten helicopters overhead but only one Huey, and the veteran will be able to tell which one is the Huey.

"Damn, Charley, that's a Huey!" Bob shouted. Getting up from his desk, he stepped onto the front deck and saw, flying at an altitude of about five hundred feet over the surf, a U.S. Army UH-1D helicopter, in the muted colors that were used for such aircraft in Vietnam.

"*Choi oi*," Bob said, using the Vietnamese expression that covers everything from mild surprise to total shock. "It *is* a Huey! What is it doing down here?"

Charley looked at him quizzically.

"You don't understand, do you?" Bob said. "Well, here's the thing, see. I used to fly that very same kind of helicopter. Oh, this was long before you were born, Charley Dog. And the thing is, this is definitely an Army helicopter, but the Army doesn't fly them anymore. And, even if they did, what is it doing down here?"

Bob watched the UH-1D as it headed west, still over the surf; then he saw the pilot make a climbing turn out over the water, gaining another two hundred feet or so as he continued the turn through two hundred seventy degrees. Then the helicopter started descending.

"Where is he going, Charley?"

Bob ran back into the house. "Ellen!" he called. "A Huey!"

"What?"

"Didn't you hear the helicopter?"

"Yes. What about it? Isn't it going out to one of the offshore rigs?"

"No, it wasn't a civilian helicopter. It's Army. It was a Huey, a UH-1D model."

"Maybe the Army sent someone down here to check on the damage from the hurricane."

"This isn't the Army."

"I thought you just said that it was."

"I meant it was an Army helicopter, but not the kind they use now. This was a Huey, like I flew in Vietnam. Only it's been thirty years since the Army flew them, so who is flying it, and what is it doing down here?"

Fort Morgan

Jake circled over Fort Morgan so everyone could get a good look at it.

"Wow," John said. "It's shaped like a star."

"Yes, that's the way forts were built then."

"What is it doing here?"

"It has been preserved as an historical land-mark," Jake said. "This very fort is considered the finest example of military architecture in the Western Hemisphere."

"It sure looks old."

"It is old. Well over one hundred fifty years old. It was a very important fort during the Civil War."

Jake made a wide circle out over the sea, nearly as far out as the old Mobile Point Lighthouse; then he turned back toward the fort, setting up a 500-feet-per-minute rate of descent. He made a long, shallow approach to the fort until he cleared the walls. Then he arrested his forward motion, moved into a hover, and finally made a vertical descent for the last fifty feet. The rotor wash blew up bits of grass and some of the sand that had been blown in by the recent hurricane. He touched down, then killed the engine, and the blades coasted down until they stopped.

For a long moment after the aircraft sat down and the rotors stopped, nobody got out. They all sat there in awe and silence, listening to the descending hum of the instrument gyros as they spun down.

"And this is where we are going to live?" Julie asked.

"This is it. You can consider this place your home sweet home," Jake said. He loosened his seat and harness. "What do you say we step outside and have a look around?"

The ground inside the fort was amazingly green with well-nourished grass. The sandstone walls were high, and gray, and foreboding looking. There were several sally ports that led from the field to the outside of the walls, and into the walls of the fort itself. They looked around for a bit. Then Jake pointed to one of the sally ports. "What do you say we take a look in there?" he suggested.

They walked across the grass, then stepped up onto the paving stones and walked in to the arched passage way. Once out of the sun, it became much cooler. Coming off the sally port and branching off to one side was a large, all-brick room.

"What do you think this was?" Willie asked.

"My guess would be that it was an ammo casement," Jake said.

"Casement? You mean like casement windows?" Julie asked.

"No, a casement is also a secure room for storing arms and ammunition."

"Secure, huh? Well, you can't get much more secure than this," Marcus said. "Look at this thing."

They left the first casement and began exploring the others. The brick rooms were large, dank, and dark, lit only by the door off the sally port and tiny slits that were more for ventilation than for light.

"This looks like a dungeon," Karin said. "I can almost close my eyes and see someone hanging from the walls."

"Oooh," Julie replied with a shiver. "That's a pleasant thought."

"Ah, hang a few pictures, put up some curtains, throw a carpet on the floor, and we'll have it looking really homey in no time," Jake said, and the others laughed.

"Is this really going to be our quarters?" Marcus asked.

"Until we can come up with something better," Jake replied. "And we can grow a garden. Did you see how green the grass is?"

"It's too late to plant anything now, isn't it?" Willie asked.

"I don't think so. It doesn't get cold down here until mid-December. That leaves us almost five months, if we get the garden in soon."

"We'll get it in soon," John said. "What else do we have to do?"

"I'd like to take a look at that gun on top," John said. "It doesn't look like a Civil War cannon to me."

"It isn't," Jake said. "It's an eight-inch coastal artillery gun."

"What's it doing here?"

"This fort was manned until the beginning of World War Two," Jake said.

"Ha! Did they think the Germans were going to attack us by ship?" John asked.

"They did attack us by ship. Or at least, by submarine. There were fifty-six ships sunk in the Gulf by German submarines. Some of the people who lived on the coast then could actually watch the attacks."

"So, that big gun up top was used, huh?"

"No, it would have only been good against surface vessels, and if any of the German surface ships came into the Gulf, they never came close enough to the coast to be seen. Only thing to come this close were the submarines, and there were an awfully lot of them."

When Jake and the others went back out into the open area of the fort, they were surprised to see three men standing there by bicycles. All three men looked to be in their late sixties and none of them were armed.

"Who are you?" Jake asked.

"My name is Bob Varney, and we were about to ask you the same thing."

"I'm Jacob Lantz," Jake said.

"What are you doing here, Jake?"

"What business is it of yours what we are doing here?" Willie asked.

Jake held his hand out. "They aren't armed, Willie. I don't think they mean us any trouble." He turned back to Bob Varney. "It got a little too difficult to stay where we were, so we decided to come down here. We're going to live here for a while."

"You're going to live here? In the fort?" one of the men with Bob asked.

"Yes. Who are you?"

"My name is James Laney. Bob, Jerry Cornett, and I live here, with our wives."

Jake looked surprised. "You live here, in the fort?"

"No, not in the fort. Just back down the road a ways, to the first bunch of houses."

"It looked to me like nearly all the houses were destroyed by the hurricane," Jake said.

"They just about were."

"Are you the only ones out here?"

"We always were the only ones who lived here full time," Jerry said. "Then, when the economy got so bad, nobody else could afford to come down here, so for the last few months we've been here all alone."

"Do you have any idea about what's going on in the rest of the country?" Bob asked. "Since there is no radio or TV, we are completely in the dark. But we heard that there were some nuclear bombs dropped."

"They weren't dropped," Jake said. "They were smuggled in on board cargo ships."

"Damn. So, what's being done about it? Are we under martial law?" Bob asked.

Jake shook his head. "You would have to have a military in order to have martial law," he said. "And thanks to Ohmshidi, we no longer have a military. We are all military—or at least as close to the military as you are going to get. Also you have to have a government to declare martial law, and we no longer have a government."

"And you are?" Bob asked.

"Sergeant—that is, John. John Deedle." John introduced the others in the group.

"We call ourselves Phoenix," Julie said.

"Good name."

"Bob's an author," James said.

"Bob Varney—yes, Robert Varney," Jake said. "I've read some of your books."

"Don't hold that against me," Bob said with a self-deprecating smile.

"No, I enjoyed them. Seriously. You are a very skilled writer."

"Perhaps, but you can understand, I am sure, that of all the skills needed for survival, a writer's skill contributes the least."

"What are you planning to do here?" James asked.

"We are establishing our base here," Karin added.

"Firebase Phoenix," Bob suggested.

Karin smiled broadly. "What a great name!" she said. "Yes, this is Firebase Phoenix."

"All right, so tell me. What happened to the president? What happened to Congress?"

"As far as Congress is concerned, Ohmshidi dismissed Congress, and the Supreme Court, so they were already long gone," Jake said. "And as far as the president is concerned, that cowardly bastard is hiding out somewhere."

"Or he's dead," John said.

"No such luck," Deon put in.

As the others continued conversing among themselves, Bob walked over to the Huey and looked at it.

"What do you think?" Jake asked.

"I thought the Army retired the last Huey thirty years ago."

"They did. We stole this one from the museum."

"And put it back in flying shape. You must have some pretty good maintenance men."

"They're the best."

Bob looked up at the rotor head. "That's not the original drag brace. But evidently it held, all right. What is it? Off a five-forty rotor head?"

"A five-forty rotor head?" Jake asked.

"This is a D model. The C model and the Cobra both have five hundred forty rotor systems. Slightly different."

"Yes, we took the drag brace from a Cobra," John said.

"That's what I thought. Looks like you did a good job of adapting it."

"You seem to know your helicopters," Jake said.

"Well, I certainly know the UH1-D model," Bob said. "And probably just about every other one you saw in the museum."

"Were you an Army aviator?"

"Yes, I have a little over six thousand hours, thirty-six hundred hours in one just like this. I flew three tours in Vietnam, and I taught maintenance test flight procedures at AMOC in Fort Eustis. Chief Warrant Officer-four, retired."

Jake extended his hand again. "Major Lantz, and I didn't get a chance to retire. Ostensibly I'm still on active duty since I never got any orders relieving me. We are all in the same boat. Karin is a captain, an Army nurse, the rest are sergeants."

"Welcome to Fort Morgan," Bob said. "It'll be good to have neighbors again."

CHAPTER TWENTY-FOUR

When Bob, James, and Jerry returned to The Dunes after their visit to Fort Morgan, they found that all the women in James's house were in a condition of shock and fear. Becky was lying on the couch and the other women were gathered around her. She had a black eye and a split lip.

"What happened?" Bob asked.

"We've been robbed," Ellen said.

"Robbed? How did that happen?"

"Four armed men came through the gate," Ellen said. "When they found out we were living here, they broke in to the house and took as much as they could carry from the pantry and from the freezer."

"They also took the propane tanks," Cille said.

"We have no food or electricity," Gaye added.

"What happened to Becky?"

"We don't really know," Ellen said. "She had gone with Sarah, so they weren't here when the men came. It wasn't until after the men left that we found her."

"You found her?"

"She was down by the swimming pool. She was lying in the road and at first we were afraid she was dead. But she came to, and we helped her back. We asked her what happened, but she can't remember."

"What's the last thing you remember?" Bob asked.

"Walking on the beach with Sarah," Becky said.

"Where is Sarah now?"

"I don't know," Becky said. "I don't even know how I wound up at the swimming pool. One minute I was walking on the beach, and the next minute Ellen and Cille were asking me how I feel."

"We are a little worried about Sarah," Cille said.

"Maybe more than a little worried," Gaye said.

"I'll go look for her," James offered.

"Was there anyone down at the fort?" Ellen asked.

"Yes. And that reminds me," Bob said. "Becky, why don't you come with me? One of the people in the helicopter that landed down at the fort is an Army nurse. I think maybe she should look you over."

"You don't need to do that."

"You were knocked out, weren't you?"

"I guess I was. I don't know why else I would be lying in the road next to the swimming pool."

"That means that, at the very least, you have a concussion," Bob said. "I think it would be good for her to look you over."

"All right."

"If you and James are both going to be gone,

I think I should stay here with the women," Jerry said.

"I think that's probably a good idea. Why don't you go over to my house and look in the top drawer of the chest of drawers in the bedroom. I have a P-thirty-eight pistol there, with a full magazine."

"Right," Jerry said.

"Becky, do you feel up to walking down to the golf cart? We'll take that down to the fort."

"I think so," Becky said. She sat up, but when she tried to stand, she fell back on the sofa. "I don't know, maybe I can't."

"Tell you what. We'll set you in a kitchen chair," Bob said. "I'll hold the back and Jerry can take the legs. We can get you down the stairs that way."

Cille brought a chair over and they helped Becky onto it. Then the two men carried her downstairs, all the way to the golf cart. She was able to move from the chair to the golf cart on her own.

"I think I've got enough charge left to get us there and back," Bob said as he put the cart in gear.

"Jake!" Deon called down from the top of the wall. "It's that warrant officer and some woman, coming up on a golf cart."

"Wave them on in," Jake said.

Deon was standing on the north parapet of the fort and he waved at the two on the golf cart, inviting them in.

Jake and Karin went out to meet them.

"Hi, Bob what brings you back so quickly?" Jake said. Then he noticed Becky. "Good Lord, what happened?"

"She doesn't know, exactly," Bob said. "But while we were here visiting, some men broke into our place. They took all our food and our propane. After they left, the women found Becky unconscious on the road near the house. I remembered that the captain here was a nurse."

"Yes, I am," Karin said. "A nurse, I mean. None of us have rank anymore."

"I was wondering if you would take a look at her."

"I'd be glad to. Becky, is it?"

"Yes, ma'am," Becky replied.

"I'm Karin. Bob, why don't you get down and let me drive her into one of the casements so we can have a little privacy."

"All right."

"You say you were robbed?" Jake asked, after Karin drove off.

"The women were, yes. They took almost all of our food."

"Look, we don't have much, but we could let you have a case of MREs. That's not going to last you very long, though."

"We've got a couple of people who are pretty good at hunting and fishing," Bob said. "We'll get along all right."

"They're good at it, you say?"

"Yes, very good. With wild game and fish, and seaweed for our vegetable, we'll survive."

"I wonder if you would be interested in something," Jake said.

"What is that?"

"Moving in with us. I know that you are probably much more comfortable in your own house right now, but I'll be honest with you, Bob. If you have been holed up here for the last six weeks or two months, you don't have any idea what is going on out there. You are likely to have more unwanted company, and they might do more than just rob you. If you are with us, you would at least be safe."

"That is something to consider," Bob said. "Let me take it up with the others. If it were just Ellen and me, I would take you up on it in a military minute. But I don't want to abandon the others."

"I understand," Jake said. "Talk with the others and see what they say."

"I can see the advantage we might have in moving in here, for security purposes," Bob said. "But what would you get out of it?"

"The more of us there are, the more security that is for all of us," Jake said. "And, to be honest, I'm intrigued by the fact that you say James and Jerry are very good at hunting and fishing. We have enough food and MREs to last us a few weeks, somewhat less if you join us; then we are going to have to supply our own food. I see there is chickweed here. That's edible. And, as you say, seaweed."

"Across the road there are some scuppernongs," Bob said.

"Scuppernongs?"

"It's a wild grape. It's good raw, and it makes a really good jelly."

"We've brought seeds," Jake said. "And they are pure seeds, not hybrid. I plan to get a garden in as soon as I can. If it stays warm long enough, we'll have some homegrown vegetables in six to eight weeks."

"Sounds good. What have you got?"

"Several kinds of beans, peas, corn, beets, carrots, cucumber, radish, spinach, cabbage, lettuce, tomato, onion, bell peppers, jalapeno peppers, watermelon, and cantaloupe. I also have a dozen potatoes that we can use the eyes from."

"I can make a great possum stew with potatoes, onion, carrots, and jalapeño peppers," Bob said. "I can't wait until the garden grows."

Karin drove the golf cart back out into the central area then. Becky was crying, quietly. Bob looked at her quizzically, but Karin got out of the cart and signaled for Bob to step away from the others.

"What is it?" Bob asked.

"She was raped," Karin said.

"Raped?" Bob gasped. He looked back toward her. "Those bastards!"

"She doesn't remember it, but while I was examining her, she told me she felt pain there. She isn't wearing panties under her dress, though she insists that she had them on when she and the other girl left. She isn't wearing them now, and there are abrasions and semen residue."

"Damn," Bob said.

"She's very upset, as I'm sure you can understand. She's likely to go through some serious depression over the next several days, at least until she learns whether or not she was made pregnant."

"The poor girl," Bob said. "Oh, what about her dizziness?"

"She had a concussion, that is for certain," Karin said. "But I don't think she had a skull fracture. I treated her lacerations. If she keeps the wounds clean, they shouldn't give her any trouble."

"Thanks, Karin," Bob said. He walked back over to the golf cart, then spoke to Jake. "I'll talk to the others soon as I get back," he said. "For now, we have a girl missing. James is out looking for her."

Becky was quiet for half of the trip back from the fort. Then she spoke, so quietly that Bob could barely hear her.

"Don't tell the others," she said. "Don't tell the others I was raped. I'm so ashamed." She began to cry.

"Becky, you have absolutely nothing to be ashamed of," Bob said.

"I don't know whether I do or not," Becky said. "I don't even remember it. God in heaven, how can you be raped and not even remember it?"

"It is traumatic amnesia," Bob said. "It's not that uncommon. I've experienced it myself."

"But you won't tell? Promise that you won't tell."

"I won't tell," Bob promised.

When Bob and Becky returned, James was back with Sarah safely in tow.

"She was all the way down to Ponce de Leon," James said. "She had no idea we were looking for her."

"How is Becky?" Sarah asked.

"She'll be fine," Bob said. "The nurse doesn't think she has a skull fracture. But she did have a concussion and doesn't remember a thing, so don't be pestering her with questions."

All the women clustered around Becky, anxious to do whatever they could for her. While they were talking, Bob brought up Jake's offer to the two men.

"I don't know," James said. "It's going to be hard to get Cille to leave this house."

"Not as hard as you think," Cille said. "What are you talking about?"

"It's about time we let them in on it as well," Bob said. "We sure aren't going to make this decision without them.

"You got that right," Jerry said. "Go ahead, tell them."

"Ladies," Bob said, "I have a proposition for you."

Bob told them then who was down at the fort. He told them also that he trusted the men and women he had met down there.

"I trust them too," James said. "There are some folks that, as soon as you meet them, you just know what kind of people they are, and these are good people."

"Here's the thing," Bob said. "They have invited us to come down there and live with them."

"What?" Gaye said. "You mean live there, in the

fort? Have you ever been there?" Gaye wrapped her arms around herself and shivered. "Even in the summertime it's cold there. Nothing but brick, stone, and cement."

"Yes," Bob said. "That's because it is a fort, literally, and that's what makes it attractive. There won't be any repeat of what happened here."

"If you ladies decide that you are willing to do this, I'll make you a promise," James said. "I'll build us some place comfortable for us to stay. There is enough building material scattered around here from the hurricane that I don't expect it will be very hard to do."

"I'll say this," Ellen said. "I sure don't want a repeat of what happened to us this morning."

"I'm for it," Cille said.

"If we have a vote in this, I'm for it as well," Sarah said.

"Of course you have a vote," Bob said. "Right now you are one of us."

"Becky? Becky?" Sarah asked. "What do you say?"

"I'm for it," Becky said.

"Gaye, it's up to you," Ellen said.

"No, it isn't up to me," Gaye said. "If we are voting on this thing I have already been outvoted."

"I guess you have been," Bob said. "But I really don't want to force anyone into anything that they don't want to do."

"You aren't forcing me," Gaye said. "Everything you are saying makes sense. If we are down there, inside a fort with a bunch of other people, then it has to be a lot safer there than it would be if we stay here. I'm for going as well."

"Alright, let's load up James's truck with whatever we think we might use."

"Are we going to take any of the lumber, or building material?" Jerry asked.

"What do you think, James?" Bob asked.

"I don't think so, yet," James said. "We'll just take whatever personal items we are going to need on this trip. It's going to take several trips to get what we'll need to start building."

CHAPTER TWENTY-FIVE

After Bob Varney and his group moved down to Fort Morgan they, along with Jake and the Phoenix group, began to build a place to live, using as their scheme a motel-like plan. Jake and James drew up the design of one long, single-story structure divided into individual cabins.

It was decided that each of the three married couples would have their own cabin, Karin and Julie would share a cabin, Becky and Sara would live together, and Jake and Deon would be roommates, while John, Marcus, and Willie would share the final cabin.

They began the structure by using one of the massive stone walls of the fort as their back wall. Next, they built a floor that extended twenty feet out from the wall, and stretched one hundred and five feet long. After they finished the floor, they put in a wall at each end and separated the floor into seven compartments, each protruding fifteen feet out from the stone wall of the fort. This left five feet for a front porch. Next they put on the front wall, with a door and window for each unit, then a roof, with a chimney from each unit. Finally they built a fireplace in each room.

Throughout the entire construction project, James and Jake worked very well together, James, because he was a natural handyman, and Jake, because such work was a product of his youth. He had built many wood-frame structures, even as late as last March when he had gone back home to visit his folks, and helped in a barn raising.

While the men were building their quarters, Bob and the women put in the garden. Ellen was a particularly good gardener, as was Julie, and they took charge of the layout and planting.

Fort Morgan—Wednesday, August 22

So far all of the building material came from the scrap lumber and residue left by Hurricane Ohmshidi hauled down to the fort in James's truck. But midway through the process James announced that he didn't think he had enough gasoline to make another trip.

"We can make our own gas," Bob suggested.

"Ha! How, by eating a lot of beans?" John asked. The others laughed.

"No," Bob said. "During World War II a lot of people converted coal, charcoal, or wood, to a gas that would power their vehicles. John, you are a good mechanic and James, you can do just about anything. You two could build a gas converter."

"I don't have any idea what you are talking about," James said.

"No problem. I'll show you how to do it."

"You?" Ellen said. "Bob, you can barely change a lightbulb."

"That's true," Bob said, "but when I was in the Army, I taught aircraft maintenance. I couldn't do it, you understand, but I could teach it. And I could teach John and James how to make a gas converter. It isn't all that efficient, but it will work.

"Could it work well enough to drive the truck up to Fort Rucker?" Jake asked.

"Yes, I suppose so. But why would you want to go up there?" Bob asked.

"Because I know where there is a thousand gallons of gasoline."

"What?" Marcus asked, surprised by Bob's comment. "Where?"

"Clay hid nineteen barrels of Mogas in a hangar at TAC-X."

"TAC-X? A stagefield?" Bob asked.

"Yes, at Samson. Do you know it?"

"I know where Samson is," Bob said. "Don't know TAC-X. I know TAC-Able."

"TAC-Able? Don't you mean TAC-Alpha?" Willie asked.

"You are dealing with an old soldier here, Sergeant. Before the phonetic alphabet changed in 1956, the letter *A* was Able. Able, Baker, Charley,

Dog, Easy, Fox, George, Haystack, Item, Jig, King, Love, Mike, Nan, Oboe, Papa, Queen, Roger, Sugar, Tare, Uncle, Victor, William, X-ray, Yoke, Zebra."

"Wow," Willie said. He laughed. "And you still remember all that?"

"When you are my age, Willie, you will still remember the current phonetics."

"That's interesting, but let's get back to this thousand gallons of gasoline at TAC-X," John said. "How do you know it is there?"

"Sergeant Major Matthews put it there," Jake said. "Just for something like this."

"Yeah, but what good does it do us up there, if we can't go get it?" Marcus asked.

"We can go get it, if Bob really can tell John and James how to build a machine that will convert wood into gasoline," Jake said

Bob shook his head. "Not gasoline," he said. "Wood gas. When you burn wood, or charcoal, or coal, or any other fuel, if you don't completely consume the fuel, it will emit a gas that is combustible. Sometimes, for example, if the mixture in a gasoline engine is too rich, the exhaust gas can be burned. That's what happens when you see flame coming out of the exhaust pipe."

"Yeah, I've seen that," John said.

"All we need to do is construct a unit that will create this gas, then pipe that gas into the fuel injector on James's truck. The fuel injector will introduce the gas into the cylinders, and that will run your engine."

Using a hot-water tank for the combustion chamber, John and James, following Bob's instructions, built the gasification device in one afternoon. While they were building the device, Jake, Marcus, Willie, and Deon made charcoal, as it would be much easier to handle than wood. By evening they had the truck equipped with the gasification device, charcoal made and loaded aboard, and they were ready to go.

"With this thing taking up so much room back here, I doubt we can get all nineteen barrels loaded onto the truck," James said.

"You won't need this thing anymore," Bob said, patting the side of the gasification machine. "Once you get there, you can dump it, and put regular gas in your car."

"Will the truck still run on gasoline then?" James asked. "Or will this have messed up the engine?"

"It'll still run," Bob promised. "Remember you haven't run anything through your system but gas."

"Yeah, I can see that," John said.

It had grown dark by the time they finished building, and testing the device. So they gathered around a cinder-block cooking stove, oven, and grill for a supper of grilled snapper, the fish provided by Jerry Cornett.

Fort Morgan—Thursday, August 23

Jake and John left in James's truck, leaving before dawn the next morning. Jake took John in case they had mechanical problems with the truck on the way. They left James behind because he was too valuable in building their quarters. The others stayed back simply because there wasn't enough room in the truck for them.

A drive that, under normal conditions, would have taken no more than three and a half hours, took seven hours and they arrived at TAC-X at noon. The bad thing was that the power generated by the gasification machine was so inefficient that they could not go over thirty miles per hour. The good thing was, they saw no traffic during the entire one-hundred-and-seventy-five-mile trip. They also encountered no obstacles to their journey.

"You think the gas is still here?" John asked as they approached the locked gate.

"I think so," Jake said. "Otherwise I think the lock would be broken."

"Unless somebody changed the lock," John suggested.

"Yes, I hadn't thought of that. This is the key Clay gave me. If this key fits the lock, then yes, I think the gasoline will still be here."

Jake slipped the key into the lock, then was gratified when it opened easily. "Alright," he said.

Jake pushed the gate open as John drove the truck through. Then he shut the gate behind them and relocked it. That way if someone happened by, they wouldn't notice anything different.

When they reached hangar three, Jake unlocked it and opened the door, then closed it once John drove inside. The closed door made the hangar darker, but there was enough light, filtered through the dirty panes of the high-mounted windows to allow them to see what they were doing.

John and Jake moved the empty drums out of the way, removed the trash from the tarp, then peeled back the tarp to disclose nineteen barrels. The top of each barrel bore the broken lettered stenciling, in yellow.

GASOLINE, AUTOMOTIVE COMBAT MIL-G-3056

FOR USE IN ALL MOBILE AND STATIONARY SPARK-IGNITION ENGINES

"John, we have just struck gold!" Jake said, happily. "Let's get them loaded.

The first thing they did was get rid of the gas generator that had brought them up here; then they put gasoline into the truck. They did that by rolling one of the barrels up into the bed of the truck, then using a hose to siphon gas from the barrel and let it flow into the gas tank. It worked well, though it was much slower than it would have been at a normal gas pump.

When the truck was fueled, they rolled the remaining drums onto the back of the truck. There was only room to get fifteen barrels loaded so, reluctantly, they left four barrels behind, including the one they had drawn the fuel from for the truck. John started to put the tarp back over the remaining barrels, but Jake stopped him.

"We might be better off spreading that tarp over our load," he said. "If somebody sees us driving a truck with all these barrels, that would be like having a big sign that says, 'We have gas, please take it from us.'"

"Yeah," John said. "I see what you mean."

"The problem is going to be holding the tarp down," Jake said.

"Not a problem," John insisted. "We'll tie it down with safety wire."

"Where are we going to get safety wire?"

"I'll show you," John said. He walked over to the hangar wall, then stuck his hand down behind the cross brace, and pulled out a spool of safety wire.

"Damn, how did you know it would be there?" Jake asked.

John laughed. "Before they closed this stagefield I came out here to do some first-echelon maintenance. I hid the safety wire there so that if I came out to do any more maintenance I would have it. But they closed this field and I never came back."

"That was against regs, wasn't it? Wasn't the safety wire supposed to be returned?" Jake asked.

"So, take a stripe from me," John said, and both men laughed.

With the safety wire it was easy to secure the tarpaulin, so within twenty minutes they left, locking both the hangar and the gate behind them.

They made it all the way back to Fort Morgan Road before they ran into trouble. John was driving, and he stopped when they saw that the road in front of them was blocked off by a pile of old refrigerators. There were at least ten men sitting on top or standing on the ground around the blockade. All were armed.

"Oh, oh," John said. "That doesn't look good."

"No, it doesn't," Jake replied.

"What do we do?"

"Nothing for the moment. They aren't mobile—we are."

"A lot of good that does us. This is the only road. We're blocked here."

"I wonder how far we are from Fort Morgan," Jake said.

"That mileage marker says seven," John said.

"Let's see if we can raise Deon and Willie. It'll be a long hike for them, but if they come up behind the blockade, we might be able to force our way through."

Jake cranked in some power to the radio, then picked up the mic.

"Phoenix Base, this is Phoenix One, do you copy?"

"Phoenix One, this is Phoenix Base, over."

Jake recognized Karin's voice.

"Phoenix, we've run into a little trouble here. We are at the seven-mile marker on Fort Morgan Road. There is a barrier across the road in front of us, as well as several armed men."

"Are you in danger?" Karin asked, and Jake could hear the concern in her voice.

"Not immediate danger," Jake replied. "We are mobile and they aren't. The problem is, we can't get through. We may need a little backup."

"Phoenix One, what do you propose?" This was Deon's voice.

"It'll be a long hike for you, but maybe if you

came up from behind, put pressure on them, we could get through here."

"Will do. Out."

Jake put the microphone down and continued to stare through the windshield at the barrier in front of them.

"What do we do now?" John asked.

"We wait."

Fort Morgan

"Marcus, Willie, grab a weapon. We have a long hike in front of us," Deon said. Deon picked up the M-240 machine gun.

"You don't have to hike," James said. "We have plenty of bicycles down here."

"Yeah, that's right, you do, don't you?" Deon said.

"You can ride a bike if you want to," Bob said. He was looking at the Huey. "Or, we could bring some heavy firepower down on them."

"What do you mean?" Deon asked.

Bob pointed to the helicopter. "Marcus, when you left Hanchey Field, did you have a full load of fuel?"

"Yes, sir," Marcus replied.

"You flew straight here, didn't you?"

"Yes, sir."

Bob smiled. "Then you've got at least a hundred and fifty miles' operating range remaining," he said.

"What are you thinking, Mr. Varney?" Deon asked.

"Didn't you tell me your dad was a door gunner in Vietnam?" Bob replied.

"Yes, sir, he was. He was with the sixty-eighth."

Bob nodded. "Sixty-eighth? Ahh, Top Tiger," he said. "Good outfit. How would you like to be a door gunner?"

"Wait a minute, are you saying you are going to try and fly that thing?" Marcus asked.

"I'm not going to try, I'm going to do it," Bob said.

"Oh, Bob, no!" Ellen said. "You haven't flown in almost forty years!"

"I hadn't ridden a bike in a longer time than that, but first time I got on one down here, I was able to ride, wasn't I?"

"That's not the same thing and you know it," Ellen said.

"Sure it is. The only difference is, I have a hell of a lot more time in one of these than I ever did on a bicycle. What about it, guys? You want to try it?" Bob asked.

A huge smile spread across Deon's face. "Hell yes," he said. "Let's go!"

Deon and Willie began putting their weapons in the helicopter while Marcus untied the blade. Bob did a walk-around pre-flight inspection, and as he climbed up onto the deck to examine the rotor head, it was as if he had done this just yesterday. He took another look at the jury-rigged drag brace; then he jumped down and started to get in.

"Wait a minute," Jerry said. "I'm going too." Jerry was carrying a bow and a quiver of arrows.

Willie laughed. "Do you plan to scalp them too?"

Marcus laughed as well, but Deon held out his

hand. "No, wait," he said. "I've got an idea. Wait here for a moment."

Deon jumped out of the helicopter and ran into the nearby casement. When he came back he was carrying something.

"I'll be damned," Marcus said. "That's a good idea."

"What's a good idea?" Willie asked. "What are you talking about?"

"That's C-four," Marcus said.

Deon got back into the helicopter. "Hand me a few of your arrows," he said.

Jerry complied, and Deon wrapped the C-4 plastic explosive material around the arrows, then, using a knife to cut off the arrow heads, replaced them with blasting caps. He did four arrows that way.

"Now," he said. "When we go in, we are going to go in heavy."

"Clear!" Bob shouted as he pulled the starter trigger.

Chapter Twenty-six

"Is that a helicopter I hear?" John asked.

"It is, yes," Jake said. "I hear it, but I don't see it."

"It's close," John said. "Look, they hear it too." John pointed to the men who were standing by the barricade. They could be seen searching the sky and talking to each other, obviously looking for the helicopter.

Suddenly a Huey popped up just over the roof of the houses along the beach. "Damn! That's our Huey!" John said. "Who the hell is flying it?"

Jake laughed. "It has to be Bob," he said.

The helicopter did a quick pass by the barricade, and Jake saw an arrow streaming down.

"What the hell? He's shooting arrows at them?"

There was a loud explosion where the arrow hit, the blast big enough to throw several of the refrigerators around.

Jake laughed out loud. "C-4!" he said. "They've put C-4 on the arrows!"

The helicopter made another pass. This time Jake and John could see tracer bullets coming from the cargo door. There was also a second arrow fired, and another explosion.

Some of the men at the refrigerator barricade started shooting back at the helicopter, but the M-240 in the cargo door of the Huey was too much for them and those who weren't killed began running. The Huey chased down the runners and fired again, until the area was completely cleared of any would-be bandits.

"That old man can handle it, can't he?" John said.

"Phoenix One, this is Goodnature, do you copy?"

"Goodnature?" Jake replied.

"It was my call sign in Vietnam. I figured I may as well use it again," Bob said.

"Roger, Goodnature," Jake answered.

"If you can negotiate the barricade, I'll fly cover for you back to base," Bob said.

"We're on our way," Jake said.

"If you can't get through, get out and move one or two aside," Bob said. "Do not get off the road—if you do you'll get stuck axle deep in the sand."

Starting the truck, John drove up to the barricades, then stopped. "We're going to have to go around," he said.

"No," Jake replied. "Bob lives down here, so I'm sure he knows what he is talking about. We're going to have to push a couple of the refrigerators out of the way."

John put the truck in neutral, and he and Jake got out and started pushing refrigerators aside until they had opened a path big enough for the truck to get through.

"I think we can do it now," Jake said.

"Yeah, we've got it made in the shade," John said with a happy laugh.

Jake heard the solid thunk of the bullet hitting John. Blood and brain detritus erupted from the wound on the side of John's head and he fell toward Jake.

Jake caught him, and held him up.

"John! John!" he called.

John didn't reply, and as Jake made a closer examination of him, he realized that he was dead.

Another bullet whistled by Jake's head, coming so close that he could hear the pop of as it snapped by his ear. The only weapon Jake had with him was the pistol he was wearing on his belt. He jumped behind the refrigerator then tried to look for the shooter. The only thing he knew was that the shot had come from the row of houses nearest the beach.

Jake could hear the radio in his truck, but he couldn't get to it.

"Phoenix, this is Goodnature. Keep your head down."

A moment later the Huey passed low overhead with the machine gun firing from one cargo door and an M-16 from the other. It zoomed up over the beach houses, then made a circle back. This time there was no fire coming from the helicopter.

"Phoenix, target neutralized. You are clear to proceed," Bob's voice said.

Jake waved at the helicopter; then he picked John's body up and put it in the cab of the truck. Starting the truck, he managed to pick through the rubble and residue until he was on the other side of the barricade. Now, with an empty highway, and the truck running on gasoline so that the engine was at full efficiency, he opened up. Running at eighty miles an hour, it was all the Huey could do to stay with him, until he pulled in to the fort.

The Huey landed shortly after Jake arrived.

"Jake!" Karin said, running to him as he stepped down from the truck. She threw her arms around him in gratitude over his survival, but her joy over seeing Jake was mollified when she realized that John was dead.

Ellen greeted Bob and Gaye greeted Jerry with equal enthusiasm as they stepped out of the helicopter.

"I was so worried about you," Ellen said.

"Why were you worried? Not one bullet came close."

"I wasn't worried about you getting shot. I was worried that you might not be as good a pilot as you think you are."

"Trust me, Ellen," Jake said. "I've never seen a helicopter handled better. For an old man, he did damn well."

"Poor John," Karin said.

"That's two that we've lost," Jake said. "Clay and John. I don't plan on us losing anyone else."

Fort Morgan—Thursday, November 22,
Thanksgiving Day

In the next three months after John was killed, the men and women who called themselves Phoenix turned the fort into a comfortable and sustainable community. The garden was productive and Jake, harking back to his Amish background, led the others in canning food. They had acquired the jars necessary by raiding the many empty houses up and down the beach.

The motel was complete and comfortable, each unit equipped with a fireplace for warmth in the coming winter. They also had electricity, James having installed solar panels complete with batteries, a charge controller, and inverters. That gave them heat and electricity, and with the desalination device, they had an unlimited supply of water. Bob had even brought his TV down and hooked it up to the same satellite dish he had used back at his house. The others had teased him about it, but he said it comforted him to see it, because it gave the illusion of normalcy.

Jerry and James kept the little community well stocked with fish, fowl, and game, and on this Thanksgiving Day, they were preparing a feast equal to any they had ever enjoyed before.

"Before this, Thanksgiving only really meant two things to me," Bob said. "Food and football."

"You got that right," Deon said.

"But this year I believe it is more meaningful to me than it has ever been in the past. I mean, when you think about it, our Thanksgiving here is not all that different from the first Thanksgiving. We can truly be thankful that we have survived this long and now are at the point where we are not only surviving, we are thriving."

"Yeah, well, there is the food too," Willie said. "Those geese smell so good my stomach is really growling."

"We have a lot to be thankful for," Jake said. "So if nobody minds, I'm going to say a blessing before we eat."

"I think that would be a very good idea," Bob said.

"Jake," Becky said, "maybe you could add an extra blessing."

"Sure, I'd be glad to," he said. "What is it for?"

Becky looked over at Karin. "You can tell them," she said. "I've been thinking about it, and praying about it, and I'm all right with it."

"Are you sure?" Karin asked.

Becky nodded. "I am sure," she said.

Karin smiled. "Folks, we are going to be getting an addition to our little community. Becky is pregnant."

"What?" Sarah asked. "Who is the father?"

"I don't know," Becky replied.

"You don't know?"

"Before anyone asks, I already knew about it, and I'm not the father," Marcus said. He was sitting next to Becky, and he reached out to take her hand in his.

"Do you remember the time when the men came

and robbed you, and you found Becky unconscious on the road?" Karin asked. "She was raped. This pregnancy is the result of that."

"And you are going to have the baby of a rapist?" Sarah asked, incredulously.

"Sarah, you can't be just a little pregnant," Becky said. "I'm three months pregnant—it has only one possible conclusion."

"You can abort," Sarah said.

"I don't want an abortion."

"But the baby's father is a rapist."

"And I am its mother," Becky said. "You cannot hold a child guilty for the sins of its parents. I've thought long and hard about this, and I've kept it secret all these months. The way I look at it, this child, be it boy or girl, is the first link to my future. I will have this child."

"And we will be here for you," Ellen said. She looked at Sarah. "Won't we?"

Sarah broke into a smile, then went over to give her aunt a hug. "Yes," she said. "We will be here for you."

Gaye and Cille brought the two geese out. They were golden brown and aromatic. The table was also set with carrots and peas, mashed potatoes and biscuits, and scuppernong jelly.

"Jake, before you give your blessing, I have something for you," Karin said.

Jake looked at Karin with an expression of surprise and concern. "You do?"

Karin laughed. "Don't get nervous, it's not what

you think," she said, and the others, who by now knew of the depth of commitment between Jake and Karin, laughed as well.

"What is it?"

She went into the little cabin that she shared with Julie, then came out with something wrapped in a sweater. Smiling broadly, she opened up the sweater to show what she was holding.

It was a can of root beer.

"Ahhh!" Jake said. "I haven't had a root beer in three months! I love you! I could kiss you!"

Karin laughed. "James found it in one of the houses," Karin said. "So if you are going to kiss anybody, you need to kiss James."

"Okay, James, I'll kiss you too," Jake said. He held up his finger. "But there will be no tongue."

The others laughed again.

"A handshake will do," James said.

Jake took the root beer from Karin, kissed her, then carried it over to the table and put it down lovingly by his plate.

"I'm sorry there's not enough to go around for all of you," he said.

"That's all right, Jake. I've gotten used to drinking water," Deon said. "It's a lot healthier for you anyway."

Bowing his head, Jake began the blessing.

"*Unser himmlischer Vater*—Our Heavenly Father, I ask that you bless these wonderful people today for their generous hearts, helping hands, and loving souls. And we thank you for the women who prepared the meal that will sustain us through this day. *Segnen Sie dieses Essen zu unserer Verwendung, und wir zu Ihrem Dienst*—bless this food to our use, and ourselves to thy service. Amen."

He had included the German phrases in the blessing because it was an Amish prayer, the same prayer Mr. Yoder had prayed when Jake had gone back home to help build the barn. He wondered for a moment about his parents, and added a silent prayer for them.

"Now, let's eat," he said, popping open the can of root beer.

After a very satisfying meal, Bob went back into his and Ellen's quarters. As he did every day, he turned on the TV, then hit search.

Suddenly the search stopped and a picture filled the screen.

"Hey!" he shouted. He ran to the door and stuck his head out. "Hey! We've got TV!"

"What?"

"We've got TV!" Bob shouted again.

The others came running down to Bob's apartment; then all of them crowded in, finding seats anywhere they could.

At the moment the screen was blue, with the words STAND BY.

The standby card went away to be replaced by a picture. The man in the picture, short blond hair, cherubic face, slightly pudgy, was familiar to them all.

"It's George Gregoire!" Jake said.

Hello, America.

This is a simulcast over shortwave radio, satellite radio, and satellite TV. That's right, I'm back on TV, though the size of my TV audience is probably less than a cable access show of the joys of scrapbooking. Nevertheless, I am extremely proud of our little group of technicians who have managed to put our show up on the bird so that those with electricity and a TV can see us.

First, I will bring you up to date on the latest news we have been able to gather.

It appears that the so-called Islamic Republic of Enlightenment holds only Washington, D.C., and Detroit. The fact that they hold our capital city has given them a great deal of cachet in the rest of the world, but we, here in America, know that they are unable to expand beyond that. Already there have been isolated and uncoordinated raids against the Enlightened ones, none of which, at this point, have been much more than a nuisance. In the meantime the Enlighteneds' atrocities against our people, especially the women and children, continue.

Ohmshidi is alive and well, somewhere, we know not where. From time to time he will make a radio broadcast to rally his base.

Really? Rally his base?

Tell me, friends, does he even have a base any longer? I think not. I think that once we reestablish control, put decent Americans back to work, and reconstitute our government, we will then have time to find Ohmshidi and bring him to justice for all the crimes he has committed.

That means we have much to do, America, and since last I spoke to you much has been done. I have been contacted on 5110LSB by several groups of brave Americans who have banned together to fight this evil that has come into our midst. I will not disclose at this time how many groups I have been in contact with, where they are, or what their strength is. I will only say that for the first time since Ohmshidi was elected president, I am feeling optimistic.

It is my sincere belief that there are many, many more groups than have yet made contact with me, so I feel that, even though Americans made the colossal mistake of sending an arrogant, incompetent fool to the White House, those same Americans are now prepared to rectify that mistake.

During those days when we existed as a democratic republic, we often heard one party or another— whichever party was out of office—adopt the political slogan, "Take back America."

Well, my friends, this is no longer empty political rhetoric. This is a real, and vital, battle cry. And I urge you, with all that is in my being, to hold yourselves in readiness until we can coalesce as a mighty revolutionary army to do that very thing.

Now you may well ask the question, from whom are we to take back our country? Is it from Ohmshidi and his State Protective Service? Or is it from the roving bands of brigands and thugs, people from among us who prey upon the weak and helpless, Americans by birth, but not by any moral code that we all hold dear?

The answer, my friends, is we must be prepared

*to do battle with all of them. I urge those of you
who are watching this program, and those of you
who are within sound of my voice, to establish
contact with the Brotherhood of Liberty, join forces
in this new revolution.*

"What do you think, Jake?" Deon asked. "Should
we contact them?"

"How would we do that?" Jake asked.

"He said he could be contacted on fifty-one ten
LSB," Willie said. "I think we could get through.
We've got a pretty good antenna system here now.
I have it attached to the top of the lighthouse tower.

"Alright, give it a try."

"This is Phoenix, calling on fifty-one ten LSB.
Does anyone read me? Over."

Willie released the switch and listened, but got
no response, so he tried again.

"This is Phoenix, calling on fifty-one ten LSB.
Does anyone read? Over."

"Phoenix, this is Firebase Freedom. Over."

"Hey, we got someone!" Willie said.

Everyone gathered around the radio then to
listen.

"Phoenix, this is Firebase Freedom. Go ahead."

"Tell him we are trying to make contact with the
Brotherhood of Liberty," Jake said.

"Firebase Freedom, we are trying to make contact with the Brotherhood of Liberty. Over."

"For what purpose, Phoenix? Over."

Jake reached for the microphone, and Willie

handed to him. "Firebase Freedom, we want to discuss mutual goals," he said. "Over."

"This is a different voice, over. Identify yourself."

"This is Phoenix." Jake paused for a moment, then looked at the others. "Six," he added. "Do you copy? I am Phoenix Six."

"All right," Deon said. "The six is back." He, Marcus, John, and Willie gave each other high fives.

"What is six?" Cille asked.

"It means the commanding officer," Bob said with a broad grin. "I'm glad to see that some things haven't changed since I retired."

"Roger, Phoenix Six," Firebase Freedom responded. "If you don't mind, I would like to authenticate."

"How are we going to do that without an SOI?"

"I authenticate silent seven."

Jake released the mic button and looked at the others. "Does anyone know what the hell he is talking about?"

"Respond, faithful five," Bob said.

"What?"

"Respond with 'faithful five,'" Bob repeated.

Jake keyed the mic again. "Faithful five. I say again, faithful five."

"Welcome home, brother," Firebase Freedom said.

"Tell him welcome home," Bob said.

"Welcome home," Jake said.

"Maintain contact, Phoenix. As things develop, we will keep you apprised. Over."

"Will do. Out," Jake said.

Jake looked at Bob. "Okay, so tell me what the hell I was talking about."

"He was talking about the eleven general orders for sentry duty," Bob said. "Silent seven is the seventh general order—I will speak to no one except in the line of duty. Faithful five is the fifth general order—I will quit my post only when properly relieved. Of the eleven general orders, they are the only two that have nicknames."

"Eleven general orders? What are you talking about?" Deon asked. "There are only three."

Bob chuckled. "Maybe there are only three now," he said. "But there were eleven when I was in the Army, and evidently when Firebase Freedom was, as well, since he is a Vietnam vet."

"How do you know he is a Vietnam vet?"

"Welcome home," Bob said. "We never got a welcome home, so that is sort of a code we use with each other."

"How come you never got a welcome home?" Willie asked.

"It was the way the war was fought, and the way we deployed," Bob said. "We went to Vietnam as individuals, we came back as individuals. Oh, there would be one hundred fifty to two hundred others on the plane with you, but you didn't know any of them. When you arrived at Oakland, you would be greeted with jeers and curses and thrown objects by the war protestors, so you just sort of kept your head down and kept walking.

"You would be pulled out of the jungle on Saturday, and on Monday you would go down to the local burger joint in your hometown. You would look around at the others and know that, physically, you were here, but in your mind, and in your soul, you were still back in Vietnam.

"Only about thirty percent of those who served in Vietnam are still alive, and today we are all brothers, and we greet each other with the welcome home that we never received."

Deon got up from where he was sitting, and walked over to Bob. He stuck out his hand. "Welcome home, brother," he said. "And I don't mean brother because I was in Vietnam—I mean brother, because I consider us all here to be brothers, and sisters."

Following Deon's comment, Marcus turned to Becky. "Damn, I hadn't really been thinking of you as a sister."

Others in the group, well aware of the growing relationship between Marcus and Becky, laughed.

"I think Deon meant it figuratively," Bob said.

"I wonder what the future holds for us," Karen mused.

"What future?" Julie asked. "We don't have a future."

Jake looked over at Becky, who was sitting in a chair Willie had pulled up for her.

"Sure we do," he said. "The child Becky is carrying is part of our future. And when you think about it, Adam and Eve started with a lot less than we have."

"Whoa! I hope you aren't planning on any of us adding anything to the population," Jerry said, taking in himself and the other two older couples with a wave of his hand.

Jake laughed. "Well, we aren't exactly alone," he said. "We've already established radio contact with some others just like us. I've no doubt that we will join them soon."

"Then what?" Willie asked.

"Then?" Jake replied. He raised his arm over his head and made a fist. "We take back America."

The others, as one, repeated his words.

"Take back America!"